A NEW BREED OF WOMAN.
A NEW BRAND OF TERROR.

You've seen them. Maybe they live in the apartment next door or above. They work in offices in the day, swarm to singles bars and discos at night. They make it with whomever they want whenever it clicks. Marriage and kids are for the distant future, if ever. The highs of the present are what count, and they don't care if they never come down.

This is a novel about two of them. One who made the scene and loved it and one who tried but was terrified by it. Each too close to the other for comfort—or safety. . . .

ROOMMATE

A lot can happen to two young girls living alone in the big city. Especially when they're single. And beautiful.

Big Bestsellers from SIGNET

ROOMMATE

JACQUELINE WEIN

A SIGNET BOOK
NEW AMERICAN LIBRARY
TIMES MIRROR

This is an authorized reprint of a hardcover edition published by
Crown Publishers, Inc. The hardcover edition was published
simultaneously in Canada by General Publishing Company Limited.

SIGNET, SIGNET CLASSICS, MENTOR, PLUME, MERIDIAN and NAL BOOKS
are published by The New American Library, Inc.,
1633 Broadway, New York, New York 10019

FIRST SIGNET PRINTING, APRIL, 1980

1 2 3 4 5 6 7 8 9

PRINTED IN THE UNITED STATES OF AMERICA

for Aaron Sussman,
with admiration and affection

CHAPTER 1

□ 1 □

As soon as she put her key in the door, she knew something was wrong. The key twisted inside the Segal, but there was no resistance, no bolt unsnapping. Stephanie fumbled for the other key and stuck it in the doorknob lock. It turned easily, and she pushed the door open with her shoulder.

She put her Gimbels shopping bag down. Pressed against the wall to balance herself, Stephanie unzipped her boots, pulled them off, and dropped them on the Sunday *Times* still stacked on the floor.

"You home?" she yelled down the dark hallway. "Marilyn? How come you didn't double-lock the door?" The sounds of trucks shifting gears on Second Avenue and tires swishing on the wet street outside only magnified the silence in the apartment.

"Marilyn?" she called again. Probably just ran down for a pack of cigarettes, Stephanie reassured herself as she walked toward the bedroom. The linoleum was cold under her stockinged feet, and a real chill started at her toes and slid up to her shoulders. She shivered. The bedroom door was closed. It never was, unless Marilyn was "busy." "Not at this hour—she better *not* be," Stephanie mumbled.

She raised her fist, hesitated, then knocked hard. There was no answer. Stephanie stooped a little to put her ear against the crack. "Marilyn, if you don't answer, I'm coming in." She waited a minute. Just in case. Then she turned the knob very slowly, picturing a movie screen showing a close-up of her hand clutching the brass. Her scalp tingled.

It takes an almost imperceptible fraction of a second for

1

the brain to receive the eye's image and send an impulse back to the body. Which is exactly how long it took for Stephanie to open her mouth and scream.

□ 2 □

"Where's the roommate?" Detective Nick Lascano asked, billowing the sheet back over the body.

"She's in the uh . . ." the uniformed policeman gulped, "uh . . . downstairs neighbor's apartment." Embarrassed by the nausea he thought was scribbled on his face, he picked up his pad and pretended to check his notes, as if they revealed the whereabouts of the other girl.

"Well, as soon as they've finished," Nick waved his arm toward the men busily powdering surfaces, snapping pictures, "I'll talk to her." He walked out of the bedroom and pulled the cord on the venetian blinds in the living room. Clean slats.

"Hey, Lascano, hands off, we're not finished in there!" someone yelled through the open doorway.

Nick looked out the window and studied the identical brownstones across the street. So he would get the body out of his mind for a second. Unlittered steps. Nice block. When he was a kid, they used to play stoop ball on blocks like this. But kids didn't do that anymore. Stoop ball. Stick ball. Marbles. Today, they just stood in doorways, sucking on pot. Shit.

This was disgusting. You'd think you'd be immune after all these years. Not so much to death. But to the sickening lack of privacy of murder. Being exposed to all those people. It was bad enough, but this one. . . . A wave rolled over in his stomach.

Another two minutes and he would've been on his way home. Well, he would only have had to come back uptown anyway. But at least they'd have taken her away by then. What luck. He and Mal had left together, what was it, about an hour ago. If he hadn't stopped to b.s. with the friendly neighborhood saloonkeeper, if he hadn't run back to the precinct because he left his keys on his desk, if he hadn't come in five minutes after they got the call . . . *IF*. Where the hell did Malcolm say he was going? Yeah, the movies. Well, old buddy, hope you saw a good comedy cause you're not going to be laughing tonight!

Grisly. What kind of nut would do something like *that*? You could almost understand how people killed one another. Maybe not understand, but you could *see*—a woman takes a lot of crap from the husband or he knocks her around a lot. A man comes home and finds his wife's been cheating on him. A fifth of the murders committed in the city were by people with some kind of close relationship to the victim. Not talking about criminals or drug abusers, who got killed more than anyone. Deserved to. Okay, so you shoot somebody. That was the most popular way to do it anyway. You don't have a gun, you use a knife. You could almost see a person having it up to *here* and just exploding. But how could a person do a thing like *this*? He wasn't just out to kill her, this one, he wanted to . . . what? Torture her? Get back at her?

He patted his breast pocket. Flat. He forgot for a minute that he left his cigarettes in the car. Another trick so he wouldn't be tempted.

They were packing up their things now. The cameras, the fingerprint kits, the technological doodads and thingamajigs that measured death—or tried to make some sense out of the *how* of it. The *why* and the *who* were up to him and Malcolm. Finally they left, and Nick Lascano walked to the doorway of the bedroom.

The Medical Examiner's men had moved the sheet. Her head was covered but the sheet was crooked, and its weight hung off the bed. Her legs were spread, and that thing . . . Thank God her face was covered. Nick didn't want her to know that he was looking.

"Je-sus." Jim Hastings' head was behind his neck.

"Je-sus," Hastings repeated, unable to take his eyes away.

3

□ 3 □

Malcolm Hodges and his wife got out of the movies at five to eight. The ticket-holders' line from the entrance of Cinema I went all the way to the corner and turned down 60th Street. The people on the shorter line, waiting to buy their tickets, studied the faces of the people coming out, trying to tell from their expressions if it was worth the wait.

"Hey, was it good?" a dungareed teen-ager yelled to Malcolm as they walked by. Without breaking his stride, he answered, "If you like cops-and-robbers," and gently squeezed his wife's hand.

"Let's go for a sandwich at the El." He steered her across the street. This was their usual Friday night out, ever since Marcy moved out. When he could manage it, that is.

"I'm glad we didn't have to wait to get in," Lydia said, taking off her gloves and straightening the placemat in front of her.

"We never do at this hour. For the six o'clock. Everyone else is eating. Wonder why nobody but us ever thinks of going early and eating late? Anyway, what did you think?"

"It was all right. Not terrific. I'm surprised Burt Lancaster agreed to do it. I mean the script wasn't that good. Did you like it?"

"So-so," Malcolm muttered, looking at the menu.

"Why do you bother studying it, when you know what you're going to have?"

Malcolm shrugged. "I just might surprise you and have something else. Always keep 'em guessing is my motto. Thing is," he closed the menu, "it's so unrealistic. I mean, I could just see myself going off half-cocked like that, breaking all the rules, not letting anyone know what I was up to, just so I could solve a case on my own."

4

The waiter came and Lydia laughed when Mal said, "Lox and cream cheese on a bagel—well toasted—raw onion ring.

"Just for spite, I should've ordered something else! And lying to your partner, Jesus, that's really smart. If I did that, even if I solved the crime, Nick would never speak to me again. He'd be right of course. That is, if I didn't get myself killed first."

"How *is* Nick, by the way?"

"I don't know."

"What does that mean?"

"I don't know. He's kind of edgy lately."

"I've been meaning to call Cynthia the last couple of weeks, maybe get together. But Mal, I really don't feel like talking to her. Not that I blame her, but she's, I don't know, it's not that she complains or anything, it's just that I always end up feeling sorry for her. Because, without actually saying anything, she sort of makes it obvious that she's not very happy. And then I feel guilty."

"Why should *you* feel guilty?"

"Because *I* am. Happy. I just seem to have so much going for me, mainly you," she blew him a kiss, "and it makes me feel funny to talk to her."

"That's ridiculous. Nick hasn't said a word, but I've had the feeling things aren't so terrific between them either. It's too bad. I really thought it was what he needed."

"Me too. Well, look, maybe they'll get straightened out yet. You going to call in?"

"Naw, I'll wait till we get home. Don't want to spoil our date."

"Burt Lancaster wouldn't do that," Lydia winked. "The thing about those detectives is . . . well, they don't seem real somehow."

"That's because they're not like the detectives *you* know."

"They never are. I mean either he's old and on his last case before retiring, or he's young and this is his first case; or his job is on the line and he has to prove himself; and, besides, he's always divorced, widowed, or his wife is on the verge of leaving him because of his job."

"Just like me, huh?"

"Well, do *you* know anybody like that? In the whole Department?"

"No, I guess not. Maybe New York cops are different."

The food came, and they didn't talk much. They didn't have to. After twenty-four good years, they knew how to be quiet with each other. They dawdled over the coffee. Malcolm paid the cashier and came back to the table to leave the tip. Then, his hand on her shoulder, they walked out.

Malcolm looked back up the block and said, "Can you believe they're gonna wait a whole hour till the next show? Look at that line!" Shaking his head in disbelief, he bent his arm and stuck it out so Lydia could put hers through it. Slowly they walked down to 53rd Street and took the subway to Queens.

The minute they got up to the porch, he could hear the phone ringing.

□ 4 □

Nick Lascano squinted at the name under the peephole. All that he could make out on the original plate was "R. Bas . . ." He took out his notebook and checked the name. Rosa Bassetti. Had heard the screaming, gone up there. She was the one who called it in. Said she was taking the roommate down to her apartment with her. Nine-one-one had told her they both had to wait where they were until the police came. According to Hastings, who heard the playback of the conversation, she said "Up yours," before slamming the receiver down. Maybe that's why they recorded the incoming calls— to trap unsuspecting citizens. Nick shrugged and rang the bell.

"Whossere?"

"Detective Lascano. I'd like to . . ."

"Come in, come in," she was saying before the door was even open.

"Is the girl here?" he asked, putting his shield away.

"Come in." The woman tugged his arm, pulling him into the living room. Or dining room. Or whatever it was. She slammed the door, muttering "terrible thing, terrible." Double-locked it, put the chain on.

Typical, Lascano thought. Didn't look out the peephole, didn't look at my i.d., lets me in believing I'm a detective, and *then* she double-locks the door with me inside.

"I'd like to ask her a few questions."

"You can't *wait?*" she slapped her cheek in indignation, ". . . maybe a little?"

"I'm sorry. But we have to notify the dead girl's parents, and we don't even know where they live. And she probably knows *some*thing to help us get started."

"She just fall asleep. I give her a pill. You not gonna make her go back up there?" The black eyes and pointing finger dared him to say yes.

"No, I can talk to her here. By the way, this yours?"

"Ah, *si.*" She took the key with the paper tag, which was dangling from his finger. "In the excitement, I forget."

"Wondered why it was there. Since the door was wide open."

"Who can think? Poor girl, screaming in there, you think I'm gonna close the door? Not knowing what happen? I never been so scared in my life. I go wake her up," she said, and walked through the doorway.

She looked like . . . a schoolmarm. That was it. On the short side, stocky; thick black hair pulled into a big bun. It was kind of comical to think that this sweet, aging lady with the broken English would say "up yours." To the *police.* Well, she did have a loud voice. Naw, she wouldn't have . . .

"Stephanie, Stephanie, you wake up dear." Nick could hear her through the open doorway. "Police wanna talk to you."

Then a mumbled "Oh, no."

"They not take long. He. There's only one. They need your help. Come on now, sit up. I go make some hot tea. You feel better. Lieuten, she's up."

Nick went into the bedroom, smiling at his promotion. There was no room to walk around between the bed and the

7

dresser. The old lady must have to stand on the mattress to get the drawers open. He didn't know what else to do, so he sat down on the edge of the bed. That's when he noticed the dog. Curled up, fast asleep, on the other pillow. Scroungy little thing. Had bald spots all over.

"Stephanie?" She was lying on her side, one arm a shelf for her head, the other bent over it, hiding her face. Her legs were tucked up under her chest, pulling her thighs out of her hem. They were very white against the brown skirt. Lascano wanted to tug it down, but he was embarrassed. Instead, his finger drew squares around the tufts in the worn chenille bedspread. He cleared his throat and looked at the dog for help. It never woke up. Even with the strange voice.

The girl moved her arm and slowly turned onto her back. A few strands of hair were matted to her temples. Had probably done a lot of crying. No wonder. Nick smiled, even though her eyes were closed. "That your name—Stephanie?" He could barely hear the "Yes." "I'm sorry, but you understand, we need your help and we can't wait."

"It's okay." She opened her eyes and the mascara smudges, like Indian kohl, exaggerated the green of her eyes. Red now. She pulled herself up so her shoulders were against the old-fashioned headboard. Nick was going to move, but she folded her legs to the side and spread her skirt over them. "Did they . . . take her away yet?" As soon as she asked, her chest was caught in a spasm of gasps, like hoarse hiccups.

"They're doing it now. But it's all right, you won't have to go back upstairs." Nick doodled, waiting for her to gulp her breath in. He couldn't cope with crying. But this was the end of a good sob session, not the beginning of a new one. He hoped.

"Now, what was her full name?"

"Marilyn Wechsler."

". . . c-h-s-l . . ." Nick spelled out loud as he was writing. She didn't make any corrections. "Do you know her parents' address?"

"They live in Florida now." Stephanie examined the stitching in her hem.

"Do you know *where* in Florida?"

8

"Hallandale, I think. I have their address in my book. Oh, I don't have to go get it, do I?" Another gasp.

"No, just tell me where it is."

"In the drawer of the night table . . . the one by the window."

"Okay. Now, can you answer just a few questions for me?"

"I guess so." She shifted, straightened up, and wiped her nose with a shredded tissue. Her light yellow blouse looked faded against her ashy hair. The stains on her cheeks and the artificial black bags above them made her pathetically appealing.

Nick looked out of the corner of his eye, feeling funny that the dog might be listening. But it hadn't moved. "What's your full name?"

"*My* name? Stephanie Hillman."

"Where do your folks live?"

"You're not going to call them, are you? Oh, God, they'll die!" She slunk down again. Her face screwed up, and tears slid sideways off her cheeks onto the pillow. Nick cleared his throat and said softly, "They'll have to know sooner or later."

"Out on the Island. Cedarhurst."

"Maybe it would be a good idea for you to go there . . . for a few days. You know, so you don't have to go back to your apartment alone. It's better for you to be with someone for a while, don't you think?"

"No, I don't want to go!" she wailed.

"You crazy? *Scusa.*" Miss Bassetti came back inside holding two cups. "I hear. Can't help it," she said, putting a cup on the tiny night table next to the girl's head. "Now, Stephanie, you gotta go stay with your mama and papa. You gotta. You crazy, wanna stay here alone?" She held the other cup out to Nick.

"That's all right, thanks." He waved it away.

"C'mon, you need it too. I go back outside. Don't worry, I don't listen." With that she leaned over to squeeze the dog, then left. Nick tried to keep the tea from spilling while he pressed his pad on his other knee. She was considerate anyway. Nice woman. Even though her ear was probably stretching into the bedroom.

"Maybe it would be easier if I call them for you, explain what happened. Don't worry, I'll do it easy."

"Okay."

"What's the number?"

"Nine-nine-eight, oh-two-four-one. That's five-one-six." Her eyes started to close.

"Okay, now can you tell me anything about all this? When did you come home?"

Stephanie Hillman shook her head to clear the sleepiness, and took a sip before answering. "It was about five-thirty I think."

"Did you notice anything when you got home?"

"You mean besides . . . her body?"

"I mean, was there anything really strange that you noticed before you went into the bedroom?"

"I don't think so. I wasn't looking. Oh, the double lock wasn't locked."

"Did uh . . . ." Nick glanced ·at his notebook, ". . . Marilyn have a boyfriend?"

"Yes. Pete."

"Pete what?"

"I don't know."

"Do you know where he lives?"

"Uh-uh, on the West Side somewhere." Stephanie's lids came down in slow motion, and stayed there.

"Oh boy."

"But I know where he works. In the Pan Am Building—I met him once near my office—he's a copywriter. Something like that."

Nick tried to finish the tea so he could concentrate on writing. It was still too hot. He put the cup and saucer on the floor, reminding himself to be careful not to knock it over. "Did she see him a lot?"

"Once or twice a week. Sometimes more. But," Stephanie stared at Nick for a second, "she saw other guys too."

"Who?"

"I dunno." She seemed to doze off.

"Stephanie, open your eyes," Nick said as he watched her head slide down. "Try to stay awake for a few minutes and then I'll let you sleep. Stephanie . . ."

10

"I'm awake." But her eyes were still closed.

"How long you been living together?"

"About a year and a half."

"Where did you live before that?"

"At home. I mean in Cedarhurst."

"So this was your first apartment?"

"Yes."

"What about Marilyn? Did she live at home before, too?"

"No, when she came to New York, she lived in the East End Hotel for a while."

"How long did she live there?"

It was a minute before she answered, in a dreamy tone. "I don't know. A few months. Just when she first came to the city."

"Where did she work?"

"Bloomingdale's. She's an assistant buyer. Children's shoes." The voice trailed off.

"Where did you meet her? Stephanie . . ." She was fast asleep now, her forehead still pleated from crying. "Okay, you sleep now, we'll talk again."

□ 5 □

Corrugated steel shades cut off the familiar passageway from Grand Central to the Pan Am Building. Malcolm Hodges came out to the street on Vanderbilt and walked to the entrance of 200 Park Avenue. He tried the door next to the revolving one. It was locked. He bent his hand in a salute, pressed it against the glare of light, and peered inside. Nobody.

He stepped back to the curb and looked up at the fifty-eight floors that seemed to be squatting over the terminal, as if he could yell up, "Anyone home?" to a lighted window twenty or thirty stories high. He went back to the door. This time he saw a stooped figure, scrubbing something. He took a quarter and banged it against the glass. The man waved his hand, motioning to the right.

Malcolm walked to the corner, looking through the windows of the ticket office, its wall-to-wall relief map blinking Pan Am's routes around the world. He turned into 45th Street, and felt a little foolish when he tried the door and it opened.

He took the escalator up to the lobby. A uniformed guard sat inside a huge arc of buttons and flashing signals. Malcolm showed his credentials, then stuck out his right hand.

"Harold Lewis." The guard stood halfway to shake his hand.

"You have a list of tenants I could see?"

"Yeah. Why, what're you looking for?"

"A guy who works in the building. Official business."

"Jesus, do you know how many people work in this building?"

"I'd guess . . ." Malcolm's eyes measured the lobby, "mmm, anywhere from twenty-five to thirty-five-thousand. Am I close?"

"Can't say, but it's a fucking city. Know the name of the company?"

"No. Just that it's an advertising agency. Or public relations firm."

"Lotsa luck," Harold Lewis said. He swivelled around so his back was to Hodges, lifted a receiver, and pressed some buttons in the board. When he hung up, he unlocked a drawer underneath the electric panel and took out a loose-leaf binder. He handed it over.

Malcolm thumbed through it, glancing at the corporate names listed by floor. "What about the *type* of business?"

"It's in there. Next to the names; the parentheses have it. Law. Architect. Import. Like that."

Hodges weighed the book in his hand. "How many tenants you have here?"

"Who knows?" Harold Lewis stared at him.

"Bet it must be around seven, eight hundred."

"Give or take."

"How many square feet you got?" A squint. "And you're in charge?" Malcolm tried humoring him.

"Yup. Right now, anyways."

"How many men you got working for you?"

"A lot."

A walking encyclopedia, Hodges smirked to himself. "I bet it's a tough job. Being in charge of the security here."

"It's not easy, I'll tell you."

Lewis had obviously been warned against giving out any confidential information. Such as how many offices there were, how many stories there were. That would really be a threat to security.

"Know where I could find a men's room?" he finally asked. "Never mind." The humor was obviously lost on Harold Lewis, who took his responsibilities very seriously.

Malcolm leaned against the marble counter of the security desk and copied names. A half hour later, he had his list of companies. "Now, what I need is the home phone number of someone to contact from each."

"Shit," Harold grumbled about the difficulties of watching over the nighttime domain of the Pan Am Building.

Impatient to get on with it, Hodges interrupted. "But you must have emergency numbers. Suppose there's a fire or break-in? Look, I could get a court order." He was tired of a.k.-ing Harold Lewis.

"Yeah, we got 'em." He again checked through the receiver. Then he took another book out of the locked drawer. "You really think you're going to get anybody tonight, anyways? Three-day weekend. You know, for Washington's Birthday. Most everybody's away."

Malcolm kept shifting the weight on his aching feet. He ignored Harold Lewis, who took turns watching him and his computerized buttons. Another twenty-five minutes, and Hodges was ready to go back to the station house, his memo book tucked in his breast pocket. Better buy a refill pad tomorrow. He hoped there'd be enough men back at the office to help make calls. Ask if anyone had a writer named Pete.

Before he got on the down escalator, he turned to look back at the security guard, perched in front of his flashing panel. Malcolm was sure that as soon as he was out of sight, Harold Lewis would pick up the receiver and whisper, "Control tower to spaceship, control tower to spaceship: come in."

13

CHAPTER 2

□ 1 □

"Come, *bambina*. Mama take you for a walk now. Wanna go wee-wee?" Rosa bent down and clasped the rhinestone-studded collar around Princess's tiny neck. "Too tight? We move it one hole." She gently tugged the little black poodle out the front door, then scooped her up and carried her down the eleven stone steps to the street. Princess had arthritis. Among other things.

They stood for a minute in front of the building. "Which way we go?" Rosa asked, looking toward the nearest corner, which was Second Avenue. "Maybe we go this way and stop for a hello to Mr. Hahn," she said, more to herself than to Princess. She glanced toward the other corner and saw Hector, from Number 566, sweeping. He waved. Rosa pulled the leash, but Princess didn't move.

Rosa Bassetti was as much a part of 82nd Street as the fire hydrant, the lamppost in the middle of the block, the mailbox on the corner. Her roots were imbedded in the cement like the scrawny trees stretching under the sidewalk.

The dog was her excuse. Poor thing, it could hardly walk anymore, had to be carried up and down the stairs. Practically blind. At one time, Rosa used to brag about what a good watchdog she was. And when someone would say, "That little thing, what good would she do if someone broke in?" Rosa would remind them that "the robber can't tell she's little, he just hear the loud bark." But now Princess was stone deaf and didn't bark at all.

Some of the neighbors, the ones with their own dogs, would *tsk, tsk* and say she should put her to sleep. But they

15

knew better than to say it to Rosa, whose eyes would fill. Everybody remembered Rosa as always having been here. Always being a part of the neighborhood. But, funny, nobody could remember what she was like before Princess.

Rosa tried not to think about it. About losing her. Sure, she got up every day and had to pull up her girdle and get into some clothes to take her out. Well, she didn't *have to* take her out. She could always let her piddle or poo-poo on paper. This way, she talked to people, stood in front of the building, or walked up the block. How could a person just stand around with nothing to do? If the leash wasn't attached to her arm, she'd feel foolish. Like just another old woman. Half of them didn't even bother getting dressed anymore. Just hung around the house all day in a bathrobe. Only time they went out was to go to the store. That was the event of the week.

But, more than that, her whole life revolved around Princess. For the last sixteen years. The little dog really was her baby—the only one she ever had. She talked to her, rocked her, cooked for her. Loved her.

Sometimes she worried about being selfish—keeping her baby alive just for her own sake. No, Princess was happy, she was sure of it. She'd never be able to do . . . *it*. She prayed God would let Princess die in her sleep—when it was time— so she wouldn't have to face making the decision. Like now, when she was feeling guilty. Princess lying down on the sidewalk, too tired to get up.

Of course, lately it was different. Taking care of Vilma. Gave her something to do all day. But how long would that last? Doctor said, the kind of stroke she had, it would come back to her soon. The speech. Movement. Even without the therapy, although that helped. A lot of it started to. She could even use her right hand to move the wheelchair now. Couldn't do—she forgot what the doctor called it—*refined* things yet, but some things. Soon she'd be okay and Rosa wouldn't have to go in there anymore. Wouldn't be needed. Except by Princess.

Rosa picked the dog up, cradling her, and walked over to 566. "Morning, Hector."

"Hi, Rosa, how're you?"

16

"Ah, how good an old lady can be? I get up in the morning, I pinch myself to see if I'm still here. Then I thank God I wake up to see another day. Me and Princess, we're falling apart. I wait for us to die and that poor young girl . . ."

"C'mon, I should have your energy. My back is killing me." He proved it by holding his waist with his palm and stretching backward. "What's the scoop?"

Rosa pulled her hand out of her pocket, and poked the sandwich Baggie and paper napkin at him. "I always clean it up," she said indignantly. "Even before they make a law, I pick it up."

Hector leaned on the broom handle and roared. "Such a little bag! What would you do if you had to clean up after a Great Dane—carry one of those huge green plastic garbage bags? Anyways, I didn't say *where's* the scoop; I said *what's* the scoop. Didn't you ever hear that before?"

Rosa stuffed the paper and the plastic bag back in her pocket without answering.

"I mean, anything new about that?" Hector swivelled his eyes over the rooftops, in the general direction of Rosa's building.

"Naw, I don't know. The other one, she go home to her mama for a few days. Terrible, terrible. She's a good girl. Keep me company a lot, you know that?"

"Which one, the dead one?"

"Yeah, yeah. We was friends. Honest. She likes me, useta come down all the time. For spaghetti. Oh, don't look like that, I don't mean friends like *that*, but we . . . we could *talk*. You know?"

"I know." Hector squeezed Rosa's arm. "Well, I gotta go get the garbage. Before the truck comes. See ya later," he said, disappearing under the stairs.

"*Ciao*," Rosa replied. "We go soon, baby. Mama gonna take you home in a minute."

She waited until the dim figure near the corner materialized and she could see the bluish-gray shape out of the opaque mist that seemed to halo everything these days.

"*Bon giorno*," she called up the street.

"Hey, Rosie," he shifted the mail sack to wave, "I heard on the radio . . ."

□ 2 □

No, Lydia, you wouldn't catch Burt Lancaster doing this, Malcolm Hodges thought, dialling again. They never show you that most of it is stupid, detailed, boring routine.

"I have some good news and some bad news," the young detective interrupted his thoughts. "First, the good news. I found him. Pete. The office manager knows him very well and gave me his address. And it was only the eighth call!"

"Great. So what's the bad news?"

"Went skiing for the weekend. Won't be back till Monday night."

"You ask him anything else?"

"Uh-uh." He wasn't sure from Malcolm's expression if he had done the right thing or the wrong thing.

Hodges called the office manager back. When he hung up, he jotted down some notes. Mr. Blanford Peterson looks good, he thought. The only reason the office manager knew Pete's real name, even before they had gotten chummy, was that he made out the payroll checks every week. Peterson hated his first name and never used it unless it was absolutely necessary. Had moved around after college, not exactly drifting, but looking for his niche. Tried business administration. Twice. Wanted to get into something creative; worked for an advertising agency, then came here. Doing all right. They like him.

According to the roommate, they'd been going out for about four months. Casual, she thought. But often. Slept together of course. Who didn't, these days? Wonder if Marcy ever did it. Had a fight, one neighbor says. And he conveniently goes off to Vermont. "Yup," Malcolm said aloud, "looks good."

But they still had three days before they could talk to

18

him—*if* he came back. Might as well check out the other stuff.

The Manhattan phone book lay open next to the phone. It weighs four pounds, two ounces. Just the white pages, of which there are 1,520. A "font of trivia," he laughingly told Lydia when he came out with these facts, some of his little gems of useless information. He was looking for a Martin or Marvin Friedman. Lots of luck. The roommate thought that was his name—the guy Marilyn had picked up at Wednesday's two weeks ago.

While Malcolm was waiting for someone to answer, he counted. There were twelve columns of Friedman. Three and a half of Freedman. And if he struck out, he'd have to check the Freemans and Friedmanns. Hopefully, the phone would be listed under Martin (nine) or Marvin (only four). Or else he'd have to start on the *M*'s (thirty-four). But what if he lived with his parents and it was under his father's name? Naw, nobody lived at home anymore. Not even Marcy.

There was always the chance, of course, the guy didn't live in Manhattan. God forbid. Then he'd have to start on the other boroughs, and then the Island and Westchester.

After seven rings, Malcolm hung up and tried the next number. "I hope Nick's having better luck," he said to Benowski as his finger turned the dial. "Oughtta put in a requisition for a touch-tone phone. In quadruplicate."

☐ 3 ☐

The heavy canvas sack was turned over and dumped into the tray with the first load. The clerk grabbed his coffee container with the soggy rim and gulped down the cold remains, before it spilled on the mail. His hands dealt the envelopes faster than a croupier's. He tossed them into slots, according to the forty-six routes handled by the Gracie Station, United States Post Office, zip code 10028.

His eyes mechanically scanned the felt-tip scrawl, and the smudged red ink that the mark-up section in Cincinnati had used to stamp "Return to sender. No such number." He glanced at the upper-left-hand corner to "M. Wechsler, 558 East 82nd Street." Periodically, his eyes doubled-checked the addresses and route numbers on the large wall chart over his head. As he threw the yellow envelope into Route 34's slot, he smiled at his accuracy. Even knew, without looking, that it was Frank Layton's.

He was getting bleary. Even though he liked the midnight shift, he always seemed to get more tired in the morning than he would in the afternoon if he was working days.

He turned around to see what all the noise was. The rest of them were drinking their coffee and laughing. Carriers would be in at six to sort out their own piles by address for delivery. And they're standing around kibitzing, he thought disgustedly.

The reports showed that the total volume of first-class mail in Manhattan was 29,122,014. Daily. The clerk grimaced, sure that, even with 25,496 guys in sixty-five Manhattan post offices, he was sorting at least fifteen million pieces by himself.

□ 4 □

Nick Lascano walked through the door under the two green lights of the station house on West 84th Street. He passed the desk and nodded to the sergeant on duty. But he had nothing to do with the Eleventh Precinct, or its crime problems. He ran up the stairs and pushed open the door of "Homicide, 2nd Division." Which took in, and hopefully solved, all murders committed between 59th and 110th Streets, East to West, river to river. Didn't sound like much—fifty-one blocks—but in New York, that was a handful. Last year alone, there were 1,557 homicides in the city, 575 in Manhattan.

Detective third grade Murray Klinger spread the index cards on the desk. He slid them into groupings with his thumb. "These here are the neighbors."

"Anything?" Nick Lascano asked hopefully.

"Don't think so. Up here, we've got the victim and her roommate. In the front apartment, there's a single girl. Nurse. Works at Bellevue Emergency. Usually works nights. We verified she was at the hospital on Friday night. Didn't see one another very much, because of her hours. Although the dead girl sometimes had a cup of coffee with her.

"Next, third floor rear, vacant. Until the first anyway. Old man died in there about a month ago. Couple signed a lease on it. Would you believe, they're getting four and a quarter for it, a walkup?" Klinger shook his head.

"Front, two guys. Look queer. Moved in a few weeks ago. They didn't know either of the girls. Keep weird hours, never heard anything. If you ask me, they're probably out cruising or dancing together in one of the new gay couples' places," he spoke out of the side of his mouth. "But I don't think there's anything there.

"Next, second floor. There's a Mr. and Mrs. Webster. He's a drunk. She says he works at home, writing. But, according to the rest of them, he works at home sleeping it off. When she comes home, they have terrible fights. Whatdya expect, she's out working, he's home drinking. Checked. Used to write a lot for *Life* magazine. When they folded, he sort of did too. Occasional articles now and then. Nothing too recent. Understand he went on a real bender when *Life* came back—without him. Gone for a couple of weeks. Never does anything. Neighbors don't think he's normal. Mainly because they hardly ever see him, don't even know what he looks like, some of them. She's a little hifalutin . . . thinks Eighty-second Street is Skid Row. Well, to her it probably is. Used to live—"

"Webster?"

"Yeah, they say they sometimes get packages for the dead girl. Or vice versa. Once or twice somebody rang the bell, looking for Wechsler.

21

"The other apartment on the second floor, a women's-libber type. Pushing fifty. Real bitch. Snooty. Been trying to organize the building, the block, the whole neighborhood, to save Yorkville. Restore its old character. That kind of crap. Probably wrote to the Commissioner, the Mayor, and her Congressmen already because we didn't get the murderer yet. You know the type.

"First floor." Klinger moved the last two cards on the right in line with the others. "On the left of the staircase is Rosa Bassetti. Neighborhood ornament. Italian." He looked meaningfully at Lascano.

"Yeah, I met her."

"Been there for years. Since they broke it up into apartments. Is she nuts?"

"What?"

"You said you met her. She was the one who told Communications to stuff it."

"Naw. A little . . . forceful, maybe. I didn't really talk to her much. Just spoke to the Hillman girl in her apartment."

"Oh. Well, she's always walking her dog, standing on the street, talking to everybody. Knows everything that's going on."

"Alone?"

"Yeah, husband died before she moved in here. Long time ago. They never had children. She knew the dead girl better'n anybody else around here—except the roommate."

"Who's in the other one?" Nick Lascano pointed to the last card with his cigarette.

"A partially paralyzed old lady. Owns the building. Had a stroke a while back. She can get around a little, but not much. Doesn't go out. Speech is defective, can't use her right side. Seems this Bassetti woman sort of takes care of her. Shops, cooks extra, and brings it in. Collects the rent for her. They have a visiting nurse come in a coupla times a week. And a therapist."

"Does she pay her—the neighbor?"

"Not in money. About three months ago, Karlmeier—the owner—well, her son realized how much the woman was doing for her. He doesn't want to put his mother in a home. So he tells Bassetti she doesn't have to pay rent anymore, if she'll keep on doing things for her. He had a buzzer installed. The old lady wants help, she presses a button, it rings in the other apartment."

"Can she afford that—what with the taxes—having a non-paying tennant?"

"Brother, *can* she? Everybody thinks of her as a poor old lady, having a hard time making ends meet. After her husband died, back in the thirties or something, she had to turn the building into apartments. Typical German type. Frugal. Saved as much as she could and bought up some other property on the block. She owns five of those brownstones, although nobody seems to know it. Does *all* right."

CHAPTER 3

□ 1 □

She wanted to sit. The back of her neck tickled. Everyone must be staring at her. The congregation sat. She studied the prayer book in her lap, pretending to follow the words. Instead, she traced imaginary patterns in the colors reflected in the rich wood of the bench. She mumbled "Amen" when everyone else did.

Marilyn's mother was in the first row, wedged between Mr. Wechsler and their other daughter. She didn't know who the rest of them were.

"We are here today to say good-bye, to bestow our love . . ."

Mrs. Wechsler screamed, and her body folded over. The service continued, all the faces intent on the rabbi's mouth. Nobody wanted to look at Mrs. Wechsler or acknowledge that they had heard her utter a sound.

A steel rod inside Stephanie's spine held her upright and perfectly straight. But she could feel the muscles and bones crumbling around it. Oh God . . .

She was motionless, except for the ripple of her cheeks over her gnashing teeth.

The glossy black-and-white photo glinted under the fluorescent light as Nick Lascano held it up for the men to see. "Okay. For those of you who weren't at the scene, take a good look. Study it." He handed the picture to Benowski, who glanced at it silently and passed it on. When all of them had seen it, Lascano indicated they should sit.

"Let's go over it. For openers, we have a dead Caucasian female, age twenty-four, long brown hair, brown eyes, pretty face, five-six, one hundred eighteen pounds. Here's what she looked like last year on the beach," he added, holding up another photo, this one in color.

"She was built, all right," Benowski muttered.

"As you can see," Nick spoke loudly, giving Benowski a look, "there are multiple wounds in the chest, abdomen, and groin areas, made with a sharp instrument. This here," he pointed to the picture, "is a pair of nude lace panties, folded neatly and shoved in her mouth—maybe when she opened it to scream. The brassiere—also nude color—is knotted around her neck. Doesn't look like it killed her, but . . . we'll know that soon enough."

"At least we're dealing with a *neat* psycho—the pants I mean."

"You might think that's funny, Brown, but it *might* mean something. Bear it in mind, all of you."

"That takes care of the upper torso." Lascano paused before going on. He inhaled deeply. "As you can see, a ski pole, the long end of it, was jammed so hard up her vagina that you can make out the end under the skin of her stomach. Looks like it's going to break out." Lascano paused. Not for effect, but to swallow. "The wounds *could* have been made by the aluminum tip. Okay, let's hear it."

"Well, obviously, we got a pervert. I mean, first he rapes

her, then he shoves a pole up her pussy. And stuffs her with her own underwear." Gallahan shook his head in disgust.

"Maybe he just doesn't like skiing." That was Greenspan.

The men didn't laugh. Some things you really couldn't find any humor in.

"We don't know for sure it was rape yet. Anybody else?"

"He probably has a thing for his mother."

"What? How d'ya figure that?"

"They *all* have a thing for their mother. He thought sex was dirty. I mean why the ski pole, for chrissake, if he didn't think there was something ugly about her body? And most of these weirdos who think it's dirty have some hangup for their mother."

Shit, Nick thought, watching them all nod in agreement, they sound like a bunch of *psychiatrists*. What the hell was going on? If they weren't already college graduates, they were taking night courses in psychology or criminology or sociology or public relations for crying out loud. What the hell did they go to the Academy for? To learn how to sit on their asses and try to *guess* who they were after? "Murray?"

"Something doesn't fit. Like the room is messy all right. Bloody clothes on the floor. Sheets all full of blood. A real mess. But not a shambles. So, if this nut attacks her and goes through a whole scene, maybe raping her, didn't she try to get away? Wouldn't she have tried to run, hit him with something? In that case, the furniture would be moved, something knocked over."

"Yeah, but what if he had a knife against her throat and she couldn't run?"

"Well," Brown stretched back in the chair, sticking his legs straight out, "as I said before, we're dealing with a neat nut."

"Maybe he thought *she* was dirty. Instead of *it*. I mean," Benowski spat out quickly so he wouldn't lose his idea, "if he thought she was fooling around a lot, or having a lot of sex, then in his mind she was dirty. Maybe sex was beautiful to him, but because she was loose she made it dirty and he was trying to punish her."

"Vell," Nick stroked an imaginary beard, "if you loin-ed gentlemen vould care to adjoin da Viennese conference . . ."

27

he stopped, smiling at his appreciative audience ". . . then get the fuck out of here and do some investigative work!" he shouted.

□ 3 □

"*You're shaking.*"

"*I can't help it.*"

"*Why are you so nervous?*"

"*What kind of doctor are you? She's lying there—my best friend—and you ask me why?*"

"*I realize it's a shock. But I think it's a very personal reaction.*"

"*Whatdyamean?*"

"*Don't you think there are other feelings involved? I mean, besides fear, repulsion . . . the horror of it all?*"

"*Like what?*"

"*Like maybe you're feeling guilty?*"

□ 4 □

"Report come in yet?" Malcolm asked, tossing his hat on the tree in the corner.

"Just got it. I'll give it to you in a nutshell. Death between four and five, can't narrow it any more, chest punctures cause, instrument three-quarters of an inch wide, same as ski pole—it fit the wounds. Semen in vagina, a few bruises on thighs. Looks like rape."

"What about the lab?"

Lascano shrugged. "Just what we expected. By the way, if

it's any consolation, she was dead before the ski pole was rammed up . . . and before the job on her neck. No prints on the tip. Just a smear left on the handle. Doorknob probably wiped clean—just the roommate's, outside and inside. Bassetti's on the phone, a couple of unidentified ones to check."

"Anything else?"

"Sent Klinger back with some men to check the garbage pails again, alley in back of the buildings, see if they could find a weapon . . . before I got the report . . . before I found out it was in her *poop* for chrissake."

Malcolm took the folder out of Nick's hand, sat down, and put one leg up on the desk. He read the medical examiner's report, the lab report. He turned them over and stared at the picture again.

"Pretty, huh? How'd you make out?"

"Well, we located Friedman. A real kook. Thinks he's a ladies' man. Have somebody on him. I'm gonna pick up the car and drive out to the Five Towns to talk to the Hillman girl. Hope they didn't have her doped up . . . for the funeral. Coming?"

"Okay," Nick said, "might as well get it over with. I know where it is, since I ended up driving her out there Friday night. Father wasn't home, mother was hysterical. To put it mildly."

"What's she like, anyway?"

"The mother?"

"No, the roommate."

"Seems like a nice girl." Nick shrugged. "I mean, you can tell she comes from a nice family. Very pretty. Reminds you of traveling salesmen jokes, you know, the farmer's daughter. That's what she looks like. Fresh from the country."

"You mean like a hick?"

"No way. You wouldn't taker *her* into the barn. Uh-uh. More cuddle-in-front-of-the-fireplace type. Put your arms around her to protect her from the cold, cruel world."

"Oh, it's like that, is it?"

"C'mon. You asked me. I'm telling you. She can take care of herself. At least she puts on a great act of being independent. She's one self-sufficient young lady."

"What's she look like?"

"Pretty . . . but nothing distinguishing. Kind of tall. You wouldn't call her stacked, but everything's in the right place. Tries to underplay it, even the way she walks. Sexy. Yeah, I guess you could call her sexy."

"What?"

"You get the feeling, to look at her, that she's just . . . well, not terrific or great but, you know, *right*. It's not so much what she *has*, but what you *think* she has. Like somewhere beneath that cold exterior there's a wild woman ready to explode."

"You mean for the right man?" Malcolm punched Nick's shoulder. "C'mon, let's get outta here."

□ 5 □

"*You mean, the old thing about wishing someone dead, and they really die, and you feel responsible? No, I don't think that's it.*"

"*That wasn't exactly what I was thinking.*"

"*What then?*"

"*I'd like you to try to figure it out.*"

"*I don't know what you're talking about, Doctor Fredericks.*"

"*I know you don't. You've turned me off. Maybe you just don't want to look inside.*"

"*It's not that. I just don't know what you're talking about. And I'm not in the mood to think about it, is all.*"

"*What are you thinking about?*"

"*Nothing.*"

"*See how you're acting? You're getting annoyed with me. Irritable.*"

"*So?*"

"So nothing. But why are you doing it? Why are you angry?"

"I'm not. I don't know. Maybe I'm just tired."

"Maybe you're trying to hide something from yourself. Maybe my talking about it brings it just to the edge of your awareness. When you get close to it, maybe you get scared at what you'll find. So you shy away."

"That's your opinion."

"Of course."

"I don't know what you think I should be thinking about."

"Don't you?"

CHAPTER 4

□ 1 □

"I thank God a hundred times a day it wasn't you." Her mother was moving back and forth, opening the refrigerator, checking the fish sizzling on the stove, twisting her nose to keep it from running. "Put the ketchup on for Daddy." Stephanie methodically folded the paper napkins in half and smoothed out the triangles.

"We never said anything about your moving into the city. We understood it was something you had to do. Don't forget the salt and pepper. It broke our hearts, but we didn't say anything. We know times have changed. In my day, if a single girl were to take a place of her own . . ." Her eyes were scrunched up now, trying to hold back the tears.

Here it comes, Stephanie thought, intent on placing the glasses exactly one inch above the knives.

"It was one thing, Annette engaged. That was different. We didn't worry because Fred would be moving in as soon as they got married. And it was a doorman building. Do you think this is enough salad?" Stephanie looked into the bowl and nodded. Their eyes stumbled on one another. Her mother stood there, fingers clutching the sides of the wood. Suddenly she just let go. The bowl clattered onto the Formica, spilling lettuce and tomato. It bounced, then dropped on the floor. Mrs. Hillman put her hands in front of her face and bawled.

Stephanie winced. She wanted to put her arms around her mother and comfort her. But she didn't know how. She stepped closer and awkwardly put her hand on her shoulder. "Mom . . ." She froze with humiliation—at her mother's emotion, and her incapacity to show her own. "Mom . . . please."

Her mother put her arms around Stephanie's back, both of them swaying with her sobs. "I can't help it, Steffie. I don't want you to go back. I don't want to be like Marilyn's mother someday, standing in the cemetery, watching a casket with her daughter in it going into the ground. Steffie, you don't know what it's like to bring a child into the world and then lose it. God, it's the worst thing, to lose a child. I can't help thinking of the Wechslers. What they're going through."

Mrs. Hillman broke away. She took a clean bowl out, held it under the cabinet, and swept the salad into it with her hands.

"Ma, I understand how you feel. But it was just something that *happened*. It could've been anywhere. I could get hit by a car. Or a building could fall on my head."

"Your father and I were talking about it. Why couldn't you move back?"

"Ma . . ."

"No, listen. You had the experience. Fine. So why does it have to be forever? Think how much money you'd save. No rent, no gas and electric, no phone. We could move the TV and the chairs out of your room and get the bed out of the garage and . . ."

"Ma, *please* . . ."

"Listen. If you felt bad, all right, you could pay fifteen dollars a week. We could have the room painted. I mean, it's a good deal. We'd never say anything. You could go and come as you please. No questions."

"Mom, you don't understand. It has nothing to do with the money." Stephanie wanted to cry. She wanted to go back to her apartment and crawl into her bed and beat her fists on the mattress and wail at the top of her lungs. Her throat constricted. "When a woman is . . . well, a woman, she's too old to live with her father and mother."

"Why? Where is it written? You're embarrassed maybe to say you live with your parents? There's something wrong with having a good home, Miss?"

"For one thing, I need privacy."

34

"Privacy? Did I ever snoop or pry? You haven't got privacy here?"

"Maybe I don't mean privacy. Maybe I mean . . . freedom. You know. If I'm not hungry, I don't have to eat. If I want to stay up till three watching TV, I'm not disturbing anybody."

"But you can *do* all that." He mother's lips twisted into a smile. "A beautiful room—when it's painted—a good meal every night when you come home tired, laundry, phone. I could never understand why you gave it up in the first place for that . . . that shithole."

"Mom, it might look awful to you, but don't you understand, it's *mine*? It's not *your* house, *your* kitchen, *your* bathroom I'm using. It's *mine*."

"So it was unbearable here this week? We *did* something to you?"

"No it wasn't unbearable." Stephanie strained to say something nice to her mother. Just once. "As a matter of fact, it was kinda . . . well, nice. It made me feel like a little girl again. But," she added quickly, "it was only temporary. I *have* to go back."

"Supper ready?" her father yelled on his way to the bathroom.

"Five minutes," Mrs. Hillman talked toward the sound of water slapping against his hands, her eyes staring at Stephanie in a final plea.

She knew her mother would make light, cheerful conversation as soon as her father came in, pretending they hadn't been talking about anything in particular. Why, she didn't know, because her mother would repeat everything they had both said, word for word, as soon as they were alone.

□ 2 □

"How you *think* I feel," Rosa spattered at the group, "a woman alone, knowing some looney's running around with a hard-on and a knife?"

"*Rosa!*"

"It's true. You never hear such words before? And in *my* building, too? I tell you, I don't sleep at night anymore."

"Who's not sleeping?" Mrs. Webber from across the street asked as she joined the five people and three dogs having a conference outside 570 East 82nd Street.

"You didn't hear?"

"Hear what?"

"Where you been?" Hector asked incredulously. "Police cars all over the neighborhood, detectives walking up and down every apartment asking questions."

"What happened? I just come back. I was by my son."

"Helen," Rosa put her hand on her arm, "there's been a murder."

"Someone get killed?"

"In my building, too. You know those girls from fourth floor? The roommates?"

"Yes, the one with the long skirts and the other one the blond?"

"Them two. It was the one with the skirts. They find her Friday night. The roommate. And me. It was awful."

"Oh my God, what's going on in this city? Don't nobody care? Did they get him?"

"Who?"

"Who? The milkman who? The one that did it, who else?"

"Not yet."

"I'm telling you, it's not safe, nowhere in this city," Mrs. Kaufmann, who owned the deli on Third, piped in. "It's got-

36

ten so I take my life in my hands just walking to the corner to open up."

"I told you it wouldn't be long," Peter Hahn waved his cane in their faces, "before *this* neighborhood would go too. That girl, the one from your building," he looked at Rosa, "is right. We all ought to sign her petition."

"What petition?"

"The one saying they got to get rid of the junk places on Eighty-sixth Street, clean up the prostitutes and everything, have more police around."

"Did you *know* her?" the deliveryman, wire hangers dangling from his index finger, directed his question at Rosa.

"Like this." She showed her crossed fingers. "We speak to her the same morning, don't we, Princess?"

"Did she tell you anything?"

"Like what? Like somebody gonna kill her?"

"I mean, was she afraid of anything?"

"Naw. Such a nice girl. Always smiling. Always in a hurry. For a date, for shopping."

"Well, I heard from Mrs. Freulich . . ."

"Who's Mrs. Freulich?"

"The one from six-oh-seven . . . the one who limps."

"Ah." They all nodded their recognition.

"Well, she told me the other day that Freddy . . . the one who picks up the garbage for the yellow buildings . . . on the next block . . . Freddy told her they were robbed a few times. Just recently."

"Sounds to me like someone was deliberately after them. Or her."

"Shit. You got it all wrong," Rosa said, bending to pet the dog. "I got it from the horse's lips . . . from herself. It wasn't no robbery. It was more like somebody was trying to . . . I don't know. How you call it when you go outta your way to bother someone?"

"Harrass?"

"That's it. Someone was tring to get her ass all right."

"*Ro*sa!"

"It wasn't like somebody breaks in. Or shoves a gun up at her. Nothing like that. They don't take nothing big, like the

37

TV and the hi-fi or stereo or whatever they call it nowadays. Silly things."

"Like what?" Mrs. Webber wanted to know.

"First it's an earring she wants to wear. Not a pair. Just one. You know, so you think you lose one or put it in the wrong place. She don't even think about it till later. Then it's a glove. So she goes down to Alexander's, gets another pair. On sale. Then one of them disappears too. First, she's real upset. Then, suddenly, only the other day, she don't wanna talk about it no more."

"Maybe she was just absentminded. Why should somebody go to the trouble to steal one glove? Or one anything?"

"That's it. No reason. Just to annoy her maybe."

"Well, Mrs. Freulich said . . ."

"Mrs. Freulich don't know. See how a story gets started? Mrs. Freulich gets it from Freddy and he gets it from someone who gets it from someone. I tell you. I get it from *her. I* know."

□ 3 □

"Let's try it this way. What was your first reaction when you saw her?"

"I was . . . I don't know. I guess . . . horrified, shocked. I mean the way she looked."

"Okay. What else?"

"Well, it was pretty gruesome you know, all the blood and everything. And . . . well maybe I was scared too."

"Why would you be scared? Did you think the murderer was still there?"

"No. But to think it could happen at all makes you think it could happen to you. Is that what you were getting at?"

"In a way. But there's more. Didn't you feel something else?"

"No."

"Stephanie, please think about it. Your very first reaction. Before you became shocked. Before you got scared."

"I don't know, Doctor Fredericks."

"Let's leave it then. I don't think you want to face this right now."

"I do. It's not that. I just don't know what you mean. It's making me nervous."

"What is?"

"You're looking for something, and I don't know what it is, and you keep asking me all these questions, but you just won't come out and tell me."

"I'll tell you if you want. But my telling you isn't going to help you find the answer. It should come from within yourself. If I tell you, you'll just say, 'No, it's not true,' and dismiss it."

"Maybe I will, maybe I won't. But I wish you would tell me."

"Okay. My thoughts were going in this direction. When you first saw her lying there, no matter how horrible it all looked to you, didn't you probably, for just a fleeting instant, deep down inside, say to yourself—'I'm glad'?"

□ 4 □

Pete backed up till he was beside an old Buick, shifted into neutral, turned the radio up, and opened the window. His fingers tapped a tune on the steering wheel, then made a fist and softly punched the cold plastic. His other hand flicked the directionals up and down. He reached over and unlocked the glove compartment. Old, folded-wrong maps fell into the seat. I oughtta clean that out, he thought, stuffing the maps back inside and turning the key quickly so they wouldn't fall out again.

"Shit," he said out loud, and shifted into drive. He released the emergency brake and stepped on the gas. He just didn't have the patience to wait, double-parked, until someone came out of somewhere and moved a car. He had already driven around the block, actually four blocks, twice, and couldn't find a space. Whenever he did try double-parking, he only lasted about three minutes and, as soon as he drove away, somebody did come and start up a car, close to where he had been waiting. Then one of the other cars doing the same thing he had been doing would zip into reverse, or forward, to get the spot. Well, he'd try again.

When he got to the corner, he checked the rearviw mirror. Somebody was unlocking the driver's side of a car. See, never failed . . .

He went all the way up Riverside to 102nd on the service road, turned into the street and, lo and behold, there was almost enough room to squeeze in near a pump. "Wish I still had the VW," he mumbled, pushing the car in front of him a few inches. Well, it wasn't exactly legal, but who was going to come with a ruler to notice that he was too close to the hydrant? The towaway truck, probably, that's who.

He reached over and grabbed the handles of his duffle bag on the back seat, swung it over the front, and got out, locking all the doors. He unclamped the skis from the roof. Ah, the beauty of having a car in New York! Now he only had to walk seven blocks back to his apartment, holding the skis high enough so they wouldn't scrape against the sidewalk, and lugging the heavy bag. He should have taken the books out and left them in the trunk.

Leaving for anywhere, it was always so gratifying to know the car was there, at least within walking distance; coming home was another story. And besides, he'd have to move it before eight in the morning.

Pete leaned the skis against the outside door while he got out his keys. He kept his foot against the door and spread his legs so he could reach inside to unlock the other door without having to let go. He got the skis inside and propped them on the radiator cover. A man was sitting in the plain kitchen chair that the doorman-guard used. When Pete went to the mailbox, the man got up.

"Peterson?" he asked, flipping open a leather case. He snapped it closed before Pete had a chance to see what was on the gold shield.

"Wanna come with me?"

CHAPTER 5

□ 1 □

Rosa studied the brown envelope with its scalloped *Italiana* stamp. She took out the letter, unfolded it, and ironed out the wrinkled paper with her hands. It was over seven months old, yet she relished each word as if she were reading it for the first time.

"Ah, Princess. I wish, I wish. Maybe someday." She put the letter, some of the ink smudged with old tears, back in the drawer, under her stockings.

To see Josie. She was a great-grandmother. That would make *her* a great-aunt, wouldn't it? No, a great-great-aunt. She pictured Josefina the last time she saw her, young and pretty, the wind wrapping her thick black hair across her face. Waving, while her other hand clutched their mother's arm. "Rosalinda!" she had shouted over the blast of the fog horn. "Don't forget to write to us!" She didn't forget—for those first lonely years, living with her aunt and uncle, being quiet in school so nobody would laugh at her English.

"Josie, Josie. Ah, she was so pretty. Everybody used to talk about those beautiful Donato girls. Now Mama's gonna fix some stew for Princess. With lamb in it."

Rosa bustled around the tiny kitchen, thinking of how she and Josie had had such different lives. How Josie's crying prediction that day at the pier had come true—they'd never seen each other again.

Rosa plopped in her chair, blowing into the bowl on her lap. "Come, *bambina*, we eat." She put each piece of meat in Princess's mouth, pushing it behind her teeth. Princess couldn't see her food very well. Rosa rocked herself and,

43

while the noise of the traffic drifted in the open window, she dreamed of the hills, chickens waddling around on the cracked earth, the fire in the hearth. And Josie.

□ 2 □

The silver crept out of the tunnel as the lights hit the rail. Seconds later, the local roared into Grand Central. Stephanie was shoved along the platform to the open door. She tried to get near the center pole to hold on, but the train was so crowded it didn't matter. The rush hour crowd, body pressing body, held each other up.

At 59th Street, a lot of people pushed their way off—to change trains or go to Bloomingdale's—and made a little breathing room. At the next stop, two girls carrying books for Hunter night classes left seats empty. It didn't pay to sit now. Stephanie edged toward the opposite side, where the door would open at 77th Street. She should have let them drive her back. But, no, then she'd have to wait for her father to get home from work, and eat, and her mother was driving her bananas.

After less than a week, the station she had walked through twice a day for so long felt familiar and strange at the same time. Like a date on last year's calendar.

When she got up to the street, Stephanie was suddenly overwhelmed. She wanted to get back to the apartment, but she was hesitant. Funny, she never called it "home." When she was going to visit her parents, she always said she was "going home." But her apartment was always just her apartment.

As she started walking, the cool air chilled the perspiration under her clothes, turning her skin clammy.

□ 3 □

He was exhausted. From the shock, from the ordeal of being brought here, even though he wasn't under arrest. Yet. And from the strain of talking and trying to find something important in unimportant everyday details. Something that would help him. Anything. But, mostly, from the effort of not allowing himself to think about Marilyn and about the way she had died—of trying to push it back in his mind until he was alone and able to face it in privacy.

"Okay. I got there about three."

"Why didn't you work all day?"

"Because, I told you, they let us off early because it was a three-day weekend."

"What time did you leave the office?"

"About twelve-thirty. And *then*," Pete emphasized the *then* to let them know that he knew they would ask him to repeat what he did, "I went out for a hamburger with Joe Margolin from my office. You can ask him," he said sarcastically, "and he'll tell you I had a well-done burger with a side of french-fried onion rings." Neither detective made any comment, but Pete thought he saw a slight crinkle in the good-looking one's eyes. He continued. "Then I went home to pack my bag for the weekend."

"Why didn't you do it right before you left?"

"Because I wasn't sure how long I would stay at Marilyn's, and I didn't want to waste time doing it at the last minute."

"All right, you packed. How often did you go to Vermont?"

"Every third weekend."

"How many people share the house?"

"Six of us. Two use it every third weekend."

"Why didn't three of you go every weekend?"

"We could've. But there are only two bedrooms and, since

45

we usually each bring someone, it would be crowded, some-body'd have to use the couch, with a date. We worked it out this way and everyone agreed."

"So it was your turn. It's three weeks since you were there last?"

Pete hesitated and was embarrassed, after making such a big deal about the procedure, to admit that they had changed it this time. "No. Actually, I was supposed to go *next* week-end. But Rob Stifer asked me to switch with him. He had this wedding to go to—his sister—and he couldn't go. He thought I'd rather, anyway, since it was a long weekend."

Pete waited for another question, but there weren't any. The two men seemed fascinated by his recital, as if they hadn't heard it before. "So anyway, I packed up my gear and went over to see Marilyn."

"How come she was home?"

"She left early."

"You mean Bloomingdale's also let people off half a day?" the shorter one asked conversationally, lighting a cigarette.

"No, of course not. She said she was sick."

"Why?"

"This might come as a big surprise to you, but she wanted to see me."

"Then why didn't she want to go with you? You said you asked her."

"I don't know. In fact, that's one of the things I wanted to talk to her about."

"Did she go every third weekend with you?"

"Sometimes."

"Did you always ask her?"

"Most of the time."

"If she didn't come, did you ask someone else?"

"We weren't engaged, you know. We both went out. Yes, I brought other girls there."

"Did Marilyn mind when you didn't ask her?"

"No."

"How do you know?" The other detective whirled around, expecting to surprise him.

"Because we talked about it. She didn't want to spend ev-ery weekend with me. Or every third weekend. She hated

46

anything that was scheduled. She didn't want to be committed.

"And you didn't resent that she didn't always want to go with you?"

"Why should I?"

"Well, here we have a handsome bachelor. Probably got lots of girls, right?" Pete didn't answer. "You like this one girl a lot. And she thinks she's too good for you."

"It wasn't like that. She didn't think she was too good for me. She just wanted to be free. And I did too."

"Wasn't it strange that you weren't taking a girl this weekend?"

"No. I didn't decide to go, actually, until only last week."

"How come?"

"Because the skiing hasn't been that great. And it's a long drive. And I like spending weekends in the city."

"How much was your share of the house?"

"Seven sixty."

"You paid seven hundred sixty dollars for—how many weekends?—and you would rather have given up a weekend to stay here?"

"Yes." Pete ground his teeth.

"Let's go back to when you went over. What did you do?"

"I had to wait outside for her to come home. She showed up about twenty minutes after I did."

"What were you doing?"

"Nothing. I sat on the stoop and played with myself."

"Being smart isn't going to get you anywhere."

"I know. I'm sorry. I just sat there. I spoke to the old lady for a few minutes."

"What old lady?"

"I don't know her last name. Everybody calls her Rosa. She lives on the first floor, and she's always hanging out the window."

"So you passed the time of day with her?"

"Yeah. Then Marilyn came home and we went up. We had a drink. Actually, it was some wine. Do you want to know the brand?" As soon as he said it, Pete was sorry. His eyes were burning. Thank God they didn't still grill people with those spotlights on their faces.

"Then what did you do?"

"We made love."

"Did you go over there just to do that?"

"You sound like a girl . . . well, excuse me, you do. 'Is that all you want from me, what kind of girl do you think I am?' Well, what kind of guy do you think *I* am? Besides thinking I'm a murderer, of course. As a matter of fact," Pete's voice was getting louder, "I suppose I did go there for that. Because I care—cared—about her, because I wanted her, because I was going away for three days and wouldn't see her, and, yeah, I guess I did think to myself it would be nice to screw before I left. So what does that make me?"

"Nothing. But what did it make her?"

"Whadya mean?"

"Was she angry? Did you yell because you wanted to make love and she didn't?"

"No."

"Did you fight?"

"No."

"That's funny. One of the neighbors said they heard you fighting."

Pete was silent for a minute, thinking he had goofed this one up.

"Well, I wouldn't call it a fight. We had words maybe."

"About what?"

"About the weekend. I was p.o.'d because she didn't want to go."

"You said you didn't mind."

"Normally I didn't. But she had said she would go. And then at the last minute she changed her mind."

"So she decided she didn't want to see you?"

"No, it wasn't that. In fact, that was what made me mad. She did want to see me, only she didn't want to go to Vermont. She thought we could both stay here and do some things around town. And I told her that for what I paid," Pete conceded a smile, "I wanted to get my money's worth out of my weekend."

□ 4 □

"Th-h-h, th-h-h, th-h-h, that's it, push your tongue against your front teeth. *Very* good." Rosa checked off the sounds they had done on her list. "That's very good. When the therapist lady come tomorrow, she be surprised how good we do."

Vilma Karlmeier shook her head, her eyes trying to talk.

"No? Whattsamatta, you too tired to do the finger exercises? You know you gotta get the strength back. No, not that? What is it, poor dear, can't tell me. Have to go to the bathroom? Hungry? *Mama mia,* you wanna do *more?* That it? God bless, you're trying so hard. Okay, we do the oo-oo-oo sound. No, that's not what you want? You staring over there, let me see." Rosa stood up and tried to follow Vilma's gaze. "Here, you want a candy to suck? This? What . . . the pen? The *pen?* Wanna try that again? Okay. But don't get yourself upset, because you know your fingers not ready yet. Or that little thing in your brain. But we try, okay?"

Rosa pulled her chair next to Vilma's, placed the pen between the fingers of her left hand, and closed her thumb over them. Her hand over Vilma's, she helped her draw a broken black line.

CHAPTER 6

□ 1 □

"I wouldn't say I hated her."

"What then?"

"Maybe it was more . . . resentment."

"Okay, you resented her. Let's talk about that."

"It doesn't seem important now that she's dead."

"But it is important. It bothered you. It still bothers you."

"No it doesn't, Doctor Fredericks."

*The problem didn't get solved. She's not here. But your
feeling remains. Only maybe it's changed a little."*

"How?"

*"Well, you still feel the same, but now that you can't let
your . . . resentment . . . out, it takes another form. And
then there is guilt."*

*"I guess I do feel guilty. I mean I have all these terrible
thoughts about her. But maybe she wasn't that bad really."*

"So why did you resent her?"

"Little things."

"What little things?"

*"Basically, we were so different, you know. I'm extra neat,
and she was . . . well, a slob."*

"Tell me about it."

*"It was awful. I mean, she never put anything away, in ex-
actly the right place. She never closed closet doors or cabinets
or cleaned up after herself. Like she'd take a bath and
wouldn't wash out the tub. Maybe it wouldn't have bothered
me so much if I hadn't just got finished scrubbing the whole
bathroom, and then I'd walk in and there'd be a ring around*

51

the tub, and her towel would be thrown over the side and she'd leave her stuff in there, like a dirty bra or something."

"Go on."

"And the kitchen. That was the worst. I mean, I'd spend all day straightening up, cleaning, polishing, and I'd get it all finished—I mean all finished—everything shining and sparkling and not one single thing lying out. Then I'd walk out for one minute and come back and presto, dirty cup and plate in the sink. Things like that. She infuriated me when she did that. I don't want you to get the wrong idea. It wasn't what she did exactly, but what was behind it."

"What could've been behind it? Do you think she did it on purpose?"

"No. But I tried to understand. I used to think well, I'm a little nuts on the neatness business, and she isn't. Fine. I mean not everybody is the same. I used to tell myself that as crazy as she drove me messing things up, I must've done the same to her. I mean, somebody always around, the minute you smoke a cigarette, coming and washing the ashtray. You know what I mean. But the thing was I tried not to be overbearing about it. I never criticized her, I never complained, I never asked her to clean up."

"You just quietly bit your lip, huh? Then why did you resent it when she didn't do these things you wanted her to? How could she know how you felt if you didn't tell her?"

"Because."

"Because why, Stephanie?"

"Because, damnit, I thought it showed a lack of consideration. And . . ."

"And what?"

"I don't know."

"You were going to say something."

"I forgot. It's just that if she saw that I had just cleaned the bathroom—I mean you wouldn't have to be a genius to notice that the floor was still wet—she'd have to realize that I worked hard to get it looking nice. So what would it take to just put your own things away? Because she didn't, I think she did it out of lack of consideration for me."

"You think she was being spiteful?"

"Well . . . I wouldn't call it exactly that."

52

"Why not? If you think she was aware that you worked hard to clean something and then she deliberately messed it up, it's more than a question of consideration, I would say."

"Well, yes. Even though I tell myself she wouldn't deliberately go out of her way to do those things to me. But maybe she did. I don't like talking about it."

"Why not?"

"I feel uncomfortable."

"Why?"

"Because you didn't know her, Doctor. Maybe it wasn't true. And she's not here anymore and I'll never find out and certainly you won't. It just seems unfair to say these things about her."

"It sounds to me like you had a legitimate gripe. There you go again. Having a reason to be angry at somebody, and then defending the person as an excuse not to be angry."

"That's ridiculous."

"No it's not. It's like you're saying 'I'm not a person; I don't have a right to be angry.'"

"I'm just trying to say she wasn't a wicked person. Or evil. She couldn't help being what she was."

"Yet you feel you have to make excuses for why you are what you are, and nobody else does. Don't you see, you do that all the time."

"I don't want to talk about it anymore."

□ 2 □

Marianne Webster was halfway up the stoop before she saw the nosy old lady smiling at her from the window. Mrs. Bassetti pulled the window up a little more, bent down, and stuck her head out.

"Hello, Mrs. Webster, how you doing?"

"Fine, thanks, Mrs. Bassetti. You?"

"How good an old lady can be? And *Mr.* Webster?"

"Fine, thank you." Mrs. Webster scrambled up the steps. Bitch, she thought. She knew she was smirking when she asked about her husband. *Every*one smirked. Inside. It was humiliating. That's why you could never ask anyone over to the house. Maybe it would be nice to invite a girl from the office for dinner? Hah! You never knew what condition *he* was going to be in. He had his days. Once in a blue moon, when he was sober. See, he could do it occasionally, why couldn't he do it all the time?

She unlocked the mailbox, balancing the bag of groceries on her bent knee. She stuck the envelopes in the bag. "I'm not much better," she said to herself. "I put up with it. Haven't gone anywhere in at least . . . three, four years. Why, why? Cause I'm afraid of what I'll find when I get home, that's why," she said under her breath as she huffed up the two flights.

She pushed the door open and headed right for the bedroom. Standing in the doorway, she checked for signs of life. None. He was out cold. The sheets were all rumpled, one pillow was on the floor. His pajamas looked like they just came out of the machine—soaking. The same blank piece of paper was still rolled in the Olivetti electric she had bought him for Christmas. Her lips folded under, pulling her mouth into a thin twist. It made her look older than forty-six.

Marianne walked to the kitchen, dumped the bag on the table, and took off her coat. The ashtray was filled with butts, the small metal table splotched with ashes. Someday I'm going to come home and find everything's gone, burned out. Not that I have so much to lose. She surveyed the old-fashioned kitchen, the legs on the sink, the ancient stove. Everybody's buying microwave ovens, I got a stove standing on legs!

She unpacked the chicken, sniffing the air for telltale smells. What more evidence did she need than the lump in the bed? Where the hell did he get it from? Somebody must be bringing it to him. She couldn't believe he'd get dressed every morning, soon as she was gone, and walk around to the liquor store on 86th Street. Maybe he was paying someone to get it for him.

With what? How he wangled that last advance out of them

54

she'd never figure out. He still had some time left, maybe he'd write it after all. Suppose he didn't and the magazine asked for it back? Well, that'd be the day. He wanted to piss away whatever he had, his savings, that was his business. But just let him ask her for a cent, one red cent, and that would be it. For sure.

She didn't know how he did it. How he got up at night and got at it. God knows she kept throwing it away. When she found it. Where did he hide it? When did he leave? Sometimes she'd lie there, pretending to be fast asleep, just to see. He would have to get dressed and go outside and then she'd know. The thing that bothered her more than anything was that he couldn't be as drunk as he acted. Does a drunk watch his wife, measure her breathing, waiting for her to be asleep for sure, when she's too tired to play this stupid game anymore?

Marianne emptied the rest of the bag, folded it and stuck it in the slot next to the refrigerator, put the mail on top of the toaster, and started supper. While the chicken was broiling, she set the table. I'm not going to call him in. He can starve for all I care. Unfortunately, he's too smart to let himself die. At least from starvation. Cirrhosis maybe. She cleaned up the day's mess, tore the lettuce into two bowls. Twenty-five minutes later, she shouted out, "It's ready—*if* you want to eat!" and slammed the platter down.

She finished alone, then washed her plate and bowl and the broiler. She went into the bedroom. He was still in a fog. The news was on. She took her nightgown out, slammed the drawers, and went into the bathroom.

After she had showered, she went back into the kitchen, holding her dirty underwear under her arm. She put the kettle on. Chicken bones were littered on the plate. Disgusted she washed it, rinsed out the sink, poured some instant coffee, and went back into the bedroom. She set the cup on the night table, threw her clothes in the laundry bag on the closet door, and got into bed.

"Hi," he turned to her dreamily, his eyes rolled up under his lids.

"Fuck you," she said, settling back to watch the weather.

Stephanie peered over the bannister. She could hear the slow footsteps stop on the second floor, soften in the hall, and start to thud again on the next flight. "Hello-o," she called down. The return hello was shallow, following a breathless gulp.

Mrs. Wechsler started up the last flight, then stopped halfway, her hand on her chest, gasping. "I'm too old for this," she panted at Stephanie before continuing up.

She stumbled into the apartment and collapsed on the couch. Stephanie brought her a glass of water.

"Thank you, dear."

"Where's Mr. Wechsler?"

"Double-parked. Besides, he didn't want to come up." She drank the water and handed the glass back. "Better get this over with," she said as she walked toward the bedroom.

"The stuff's in here." Stephanie pointed to the cartons on the living room floor. "I did what you said—put all the clothes and little things in boxes." She lifted two cartons onto the bridge table.

"Oh," Mrs. Wechsler choked as she started to look inside the top box. "You didn't have to pack the cosmetics and things. And her toothbrush." She held onto the cardboard flaps, and sniffled.

"I wasn't sure."

"It's all right. Look, you keep this stuff. I'm sure you could use some of it. I wouldn't.''

"Okay." Stephanie slid the carton onto the floor.

Mrs. Wechsler lifted out the sweaters and nightgowns, her hands shaking. "I gave her this turtleneck for her birthday. Cashmere. I don't want it, Stephanie. Maybe just the coats. And the jewelry. Like the garnet ring. That was my mother's.

56

And the diamond studs I gave her. That was her sixteenth-birthday present. You know, she felt funny wearing them. But then about two years ago, they became so popular, so fashionable."

Stephanie didn't know what to say. She shrugged helplessly and walked to the bedroom doorway. "She paid for the lamp."

"You can have it."

"I didn't take my things out of the dresser yet. I didn't know when you'd take it."

"Do you have one you can bring here? I'm only asking because I know you didn't have room for two. But, if you don't have one . . ."

"Yes. My Mom said I could have the one from home."

"Good. I guess we'll take the bed back, and the TV and the dresser. My son-in-law is gonna try 'n borrow a station wagon and pick it up this weekend. They could use the stuff in the basement. All the rest, Stephanie, you keep. You were such good friends. I know Marilyn would've wanted you to have it."

"Thank you. When are you going back?"

"Probably Saturday or Sunday. My daughter wants us to stay longer, but. . . well, we just want to be alone. You know. It's hard, anyway, with three kids and the dog. It's such a shame. I haven't seen the children in so long. But I . . . I just can't stop thinking about it. That's the good thing, though. Kids. Whether you want to or not, they do take your mind off things. I mean, they don't shut up, they don't give you a minute's chance to rest. They don't understand at that age. Death. Especially Mr. Wechsler. It's been good for him to be with them. Well, he's probably having a fit in the car . . . I'd better go down. I'll call you before we leave. To say good-bye."

"Okay. Thanks for all the things."

Mrs. Wechsler hesitated at the door, Marilyn's winter coat and raincoat thrown over her arm, and the shopping bag dangling from under them. Then gently, she put her hand on Stephanie's cheek and walked out. Crying on the stairs.

After she locked the door, Stephanie went into the

bathroom. She knelt on the tiles, studying the cracks between the old, chipped hexagons. Then she put her head over the toilet and threw up.

□ 4 □

Malcolm never discussed the details of his cases with Lydia. Oh, sure, he talked about the men in the squad, complained about the Captain, mentioned interesting people he met, fumed about "downtown" . . . but never told her what he was doing about which case. Just in general terms. Until it was over maybe. Besides, he didn't like to inject the dismal, seamy, sordid life he led during working hours into his marriage. He liked Lydia, instead, to bring her own domestic interests, and the completely different business world of her job, into their time together. It made him forget.

But Malcolm was still shaking his head over today's interrogation, and smiling inside. He *had* to share this one with her. No names, of course.

He tore open a package of Sweet 'n Low and sprinkled it into his cup. "I gotta tell you about this, honey; you'll appreciate it as much as I did. Only," he put his finger across his lips, "don't tell anyone."

"Have I ever?"

"No, I know you haven't. But this is an irresistible story. You know, we've been looking for a sex pervert. We picked up all the knowns, of course, and the street types. Dead end. We expect that, of course. Well, the girl sometimes hung out at the singles places, the ones uptown. So we've had some men go check 'em out, talk to the people at the bar, the regulars, you know. Well, we had the name of one guy she picked up. At Wednesday's. You know," Malcolm blew into his cup, "They got a Thursday's and a Friday's too. And I just read there's a Tuesday's. But that's down in the Village I think."

"No kidding? What will they think of next?"

58

"I suppose Monday's. Anyway, we brought this guy in . . ."

"Hey, I just had a great idea." Lydia smiled at him. "Why don't we get that guy—who is it wrote those Rabbi books?"

"Kimmel-, Kemmel- something I think."

"Well, maybe we could write to him and suggest a whole new mystery series. *Wednesday the Rabbi Wended to Wednesday's, Thursday the Rabbi Quenched his Thirst at Thurs . . .*"

"Kemelman. That's his name. Hey, are you going to let me tell you or not?"

"I'm sorry, dear, go ahead."

"Okay. Anyway, we got the name of this guy she picked up at," Malcolm winked, "one of the days of the week. We brought him in and he seemed okay, even had an alibi. But you never know. So we figured we could talk to some other girls he's gone out with and see if . . . well . . ."

"See if he tried to do anything kinky with them?" Lydia finished the sentence.

"Yeah, well, so they bring in this girl," Malcolm grimaced as he took a swallow of coffee, which was still burning hot, "typical East Side swinger, to look at her. Tight jeans, no bra."

"I know the type."

"Don't get me wrong. She was very clean cut looking. Almost naive. Didn't wear any makeup. In fact, she reminded me a little of Marcy at first."

Lydia smiled. "Remind me to tell you something she told me on the phone. Sorry, go on."

"So I sit her down and try to talk to her in a fatherly way, to put her at ease and everything. And I explain that we're trying to find out about this guy's sex life, we can't tell her why, and that we need help and we understand it's very personal, but we know all about these things and she should try not to be embarrassed and it will be confidential and all that crap. And she looks at me with these beautiful blue eyes, like she's putting all her little-girl trust in me . . ."

"Malcolm Hodges, are you trying to tell me you're running off with a younger woman?"

Malcolm reached over and squeezed Lydia's hand. "Come on, listen. I even ask her if she would feel better talking to a woman police officer, and she says no, she's not at all ashamed or inhibited. So she starts to tell me the story. I mean, I thought I'd have to ask her specific questions like . . ." Malcolm curled his index finger through the handle and waved his cup, trying to think of what he would have asked.

"I get the general picture," Lydia said. "So what did she tell you?"

Malcolm considered a minute. He and Lydia didn't talk about sex very often. Didn't have to. He felt, and was sure she did too, that they were very close, spiritually and physically; that the thoughts and feelings of one were transferred through their deep loving to the other. When you came down to it, there was nothing that he would want to say to her in bed that he hadn't already said.

"Well, he takes her back to his apartment. And they start making out, necking and petting and all. Remember how we used to park and watch the 'submarine races' near La-Guardia?—we thought it was the end. Well, to them, it was just the prelude." He shook his head. "Their clothes are off now and they're lying on top of the bed. He ties her hands behind her back."

"And she didn't mind?"

"You ain't heard nothing yet. He ties her hands and rubs his prick all over her chest and neck and stomach. Okay, that's not bad. Then he takes it and tries to shove it in her ear. So, maybe a lot of guys gets kicks like that. He sticks it in her mouth and she sucks him. For a half hour, she says. And every time he's about to come, he pulls it out, waits a minute, and does it again."

"She told you all this, just like that?"

"Ha, I'm cleaning it up for you. You should have heard the way *she* described it. So anyway, he keeps doing that. Okay, he loves writhing. Then, get this, he straddles her face," Malcolm started stirring his empty cup with the spoon, "his ass right over her face. She didn't say this, but I had a feeling, well, she was using her tongue on him. So he sits there for a little while and all of a sudden, guess what, he shits. Right on her mouth."

"Oh, Mal, not while I'm still eating. Ugh."

"Exactly. Did you ever hear anything so disgusting in your

life? And, from what I gathered, her mouth wasn't completely closed at the time." Mal and Lydia sat for a minute, screwing up their faces, having a contest to see who could make the most horrible sounds. Then Mal said, "I'm not finished. I have to tell you the punch line."

"There's more?"

"Get this. I thank her for being so candid, tell her I know it must have been humiliating for her to tell this to a stranger, but that it will help our investigation, blah, blah, blah, blah, and I get finished with my whole speech, walking her toward the door, and she looks up at me with those gorgeous, empty eyes, and says to me: 'But don't you want to hear about the second time?' "

Lydia whooped.

"And all the time I'm thinking why didn't she get up and get out of there, scream, something. Boy, am I square. She went back for more."

Lydia couldn't stop laughing. "It's rotten of you to tell me a story like that and tell me I can't tell anyone. Not that I know anyone but you well enough to repeat it to."

"C'mon," he said, "let's clean up and go to bed."

"Okay, dear, but bring the toilet paper with you!" she roared, carrying the rest of the dishes into the kitchen.

CHAPTER 7

□ 1 □

Soft music filtered into Frank Layton's consciousness. He opened one eye and stared at the digital clock. Four-twenty. In ten minutes the alarm would ring. He'd stay up, so it wouldn't wake Sally. His eyeballs rolled under his lids and he dozed off again. The blast made him jump, and he reached out to shut off the buzzer. "Sorry, honey, go back to sleep," he whispered as his wife turned over.

His toes felt for the slippers on the side of the bed, and he slid into them. He stretched and went down to light the pot his wife had filled the night before. When he finished shaving, the smell of the perking coffee drifted upstairs. He ran down, a towel twisted around his middle, and shut it off. He went back upstairs, put on his shirt and tie and pants, and went back down, carrying his jacket.

He put on the transistor and listened to the WNEW News while he drank his coffee. He put his jacket on, shifted his tie in the hall mirror, poured another half-cup. Not even one more month, one more frigging month. And then I won't have to get up in the middle of the night ever again. Twenty-five years of getting up early. By the time he got home at night, he was too tired to do anything. After dinner, he'd watch a little TV, maybe, have a bath and go to bed, to get up early again.

Funny, he never liked showers. Most men did. But he liked to lie back in the tub and relax. Well, maybe after he retired, he'd have time to bathe in the mornings, and then . . . well, maybe he'd try the shower again. He'd try a lot of things. Maybe even Florida. Who knows?

Frank left the house, double-locked the door, and walked toward Kings Highway. It was still dark. It wasn't so noticeable, unless you were in back of him. Then you'd see he was definitely tilted. Twenty-five years of that heavy bag slung over his right shoulder!

□ 2 □

Rugglemeyer International had spent $130,000 on the 27th-floor ladies' room. Not exactly. $128,736.42. The man in charge of partitioning, sectioning, and decorating when they moved to their new building four years ago had jokingly suggested installing a bidet. It already looked like a brothel and, with all the office sex going on, why not?

If the purpose in spending all that money had been to keep the girls on the executive floor happy, it *had* served its purpose. If it was to increase nine-to-five attendance and productivity, it might just as well have gone down one of the gold-plated drains in the eight lavender sinks.

It was a club room. A gossip center. A beauty parlor. A tranquilizer. The long marble vanity with dressing-room bulbs in the mirror was used constantly. The two chaises (the male bigwigs had assumed the girls would take turns having their period, and each lie in them one day a month) were always taken. The round table was in demand for lunch, for cards, for Scrabble, for elbows, and it had to be reserved for use between twelve and two. The toilets were used occasionally.

Her first day back, Stephanie decided to avoid it, especially during the peak hours. But after catching up on the papers accumulated on her desk, making neat piles of "urgent," "important," and "leisure," she decided to get it over with. Hendricks wasn't in yet, anyway.

When she stepped inside, she stood awkwardly on the thick purple carpet of the lounge area. The ordinary hum of activity and chatter stopped short. Finally Cathy Hopkins, who had been staring at her in the mirror, dropped her brush and walked over to her. "Steffie, we're so glad you're back." She hesitated a second and then put her arm around Stephanie's shoulder. They were waiting for a reaction, she knew, a sign, an indication that she was not on the verge of a nervous breakdown, and that one wrong word would not send her off the deep end.

"Hi, all." Stephanie smiled sheepishly and, the tension dissolved, they all moved closer. " . . . go back to your apartment? . . ." "have any ideas? . . ." "they suspect? . . ." "to stay alone?" "scared to . . ." "what did you . . ." "papers said . . ." "what did he . . ." "read a gruesome . . ."

She only heard snatches. The blood rushed to her feet and she backed up to the counter and leaned against it. "Look, girls, it's been an . . . ordeal, you know. I really can't talk about it yet. Anyway, my desk is a mess and I have to go before Hendricks gets in."

"Sure . . . understand . . . later . . . lunch . . ."

Stephanie went into a cubicle. Without lifting her skirt, she sat down and listened to the abrupt silence. She counted how many times the door whooshed on its hinge. After seven, she yanked the toilet paper. She jumped at the noise the roll made when it spun. Then she flushed and came out. The lounge was empty.

She slapped cold water on her cheeks, careful of her eye makeup, and walked out.

Hendricks still wasn't there. Good. He'd probably swamp her with stuff all day. She'd have to stay in for lunch and do the drawers. She had shuddered when she opened them first thing that morning. Ballpoint pens in the wrong compartment. Clips in with the staples, papers sticking out of folders. That's why she hated to go on vacation, or be out sick.

□ 3 □

Rosa left the bank and crossed Lexington. She walked slowly, nodding at people through store windows. She opened the door of the rathskeller and the owner held his hand up from behind the bar, indicating they were closed.

She ignored him and stepped inside. He squinted in the darkened restaurant. "Rosa!" his voice boomed. "How nice. Come and have a schnapps with me." Rosa squeezed between the stools and hoisted her body up.

"I say to myself, Rosa, you not see Mr. Bruhof in two weeks. Today you stop in and say hello."

Mr. Bruhof finished counting the bills, closed the register, and took two glasses down from the shelf. They motioned a toast to each other and drank.

"How's business?"

"How?" He pulled his nose up to his forehead in disgust.

"Ah, too bad." What did people want with white tablecloths, Wiener schnitzel and a stein of beer today? Thirty years ago, ten years ago—before Gimbels—a person could walk from York Avenue to Lexington and not hear a word of English. Well, you couldn't blame it all on Gimbels. It musta started back in '56, '57, when they tore down the El and, with it, the shabby railroad flats. When the shadow of the gigantic steel structure disappeared, the sun shone down. And new buildings went up. And families moved out, singles in. Now 86th Street was like Times Square.

Poor Mr. Bruhof. His restaurant—at one time it was a mecca for good food, drink, and German song. Now it was surrounded by pizza-slice places, takeout Chinese, deli. When Rosa Bassetti first moved here, she felt out of place. Now a heavy German accent (she always used to think they were going to spit up) was as strange as her Italian one.

"And vat's doing vid you?"

66

"Nothing. You heard about the murder in my building?"

"Ya. They catch the boy. They should lock him up and the key throw away."

"*If* he did it."

"Vat you mean *if?*"

"I ain't so sure. I know that guy. He's nice boy. Always stop to talk to an old lady. No, Mr. Bruhof, I *am* sure. That he not do it."

"You tell police?"

"What? That Rosalinda Bassetti knows in her heart he didn't do it? I could get on the witness stand and say this?"

"If you're right, who you think did do it?"

"I don't know." She shrugged.

"If that boy not do it, and police are busy trying to prove he did, the real person is free. And maybe kills again."

"You make me feel so good, Mr. Bruhof. Suppose he comes back?"

"He's not coming back to get you, Rosa."

"I hope." She tilted her glass and thoughtfully watched the tawny liquid swirl inside. "Maybe he come for roommate?"

"Why?"

Rosa banged the glass down with sudden inspiration. "Because. Suppose he think she know something. Even if she don't, he could *think* she does."

"Mm. Maybe."

It was too scary to think about. Rosa slid off the stool and buttoned her coat. "Well, it's almost time for lunch."

"Nein. Nobody come in before twelve, twelve-thirty. Stay a vhile."

Rosa smiled. "I mean my baby's lunch. I go now. Princess, she's waiting for me."

Rosa hurried home, surreptitiously studying the faces she passed on the street. When she got in, she bolted the door and put the chain on. Then she shoved the dresser along the wall until part of it blocked the door.

□ 4 □

"What else?"

"What else about what?"

"About Marilyn. What else did you resent?"

"Nothing."

"Come on, Stephanie, we've talked about it before. There were other things. Think . . ."

"It all revolved around the cleaning. Even if it wasn't directly, it was just that it seemed that way. As a matter of fact, this is a good example. About a month ago, I went shopping on my way home—I always got home first—and I bought a steak. I came home, I made potatoes and a salad, got the steak ready, set the table. I mean I really wanted to make it a nice dinner . . ."

"Why?"

"Why what?"

"Why did you want to make a nice dinner for her when you resented her?"

"I don't know. I guess I never thought about it. Anyway, the point is I did want to surprise her with dinner. And she comes in, throws her coat and bag on the couch. I bit my lip. I promised I wasn't going to ruin everything by getting upset. Anyway, I yell into her that I'm making a steak dinner. And she says, 'that's nice,' and goes into the bathroom and takes a shower. When she didn't come out in five minutes, I figured she was going to be in there a while.

"I couldn't shut the steak off—it was already in—so I finally took it out, a little well done. Then she comes out, all steamy, sticks her nose in and says, 'that smells good.' Naked. In the kitchen. So I told her to put her robe on, it was ready. And she looks at me blankly and says, 'but I'm going out for dinner, didn't I tell you,' and turns and walks into the bedroom. I mean, she knew damned well that it was for her—

68

why the hell would I have set the table for two and made a whole thing with potatoes and a vegetable and a salad for just myself?

"I was livid. Why couldn't she have told me when she first came in and saw me in the kitchen? Or why couldn't she just mention before that she'd be going out to dinner on Wednesday night? She knew damned well that she never told me. Doctor, that's what I mean by being inconsiderate."

"What did you say to her?"

"Nothing. There was another time. Also about dinner. Only this time she was supposed to be going out. You know, I never invite anybody over. But see, I knew she'd be going out and I invited this really nice guy over. It was the same bit, only in reverse. I set the table—but I opened the bridge table in the living room and put a cloth over it. And I had a bottle of wine that I put on the table. The stuff was cooking and I got dressed nicely.

"Anyway, he rings the bell, and comes in, and we sit down on the couch—it would take about a half hour to get finished—and we talk. He brought a bottle of wine too, so I'm drinking some of that and getting a little, you know, a little silly, and feeling nice and dreamy and everything. And I go into the kitchen and put the meat on the platter and carry it inside, when the door opens. And who walks in but Marilyn. Not the least bit embarrassed that I'm entertaining and she's supposed to be out. She says hi, hangs up her coat—I must say she at least hung it up this time—walks into the kitchen, gets a plate and silverware, comes back, shoves my setting over and squeezes the other one in, pulls a kitchen chair over, says 'mind?' and sits. I mean, can you imagine that? Never asked if I had enough food, if she'd be in the way, just plops down and spoils my whole evening."

"What did you do?"

"What could I do? I made the portions smaller and the three of us sat there and ate."

"How did you act—were you quiet, did you say anything to her?"

"Doctor Fredericks, what could I say?"

"Come on, Stephanie, I thought we got over this part. You could've said something like, 'Oh, I'm sorry, I didn't know

you'd be home, Marilyn, or I would've invited you'—something to let her know that she was not expected."

"How could I? I mean after all, the girl lived there too."

"So you were helpless. The girl has told you she definitely will not be home. You live there too. You will have the apartment to yourself, and you invite a man over. You shop and pay for the food—am I right?—you cook it, you plan an intimate little dinner. And she comes in unexpectedly and you feel helpless to say anything?"

"Well, yes. I mean no. How could I be so rude? How could I just say 'you can't eat here'? I couldn't do that."

"Did you think you had no right to entertain if she wasn't coming home?"

"No."

"Did you think she had the right to interrupt your plans and expect to join you for dinner?"

"No, I didn't think she had the right, but where was she supposed to go if her date was broken?"

"How about out for a hamburger? Didn't you ever do that? Know that she was having company and go out to a coffee shop to get something to eat?"

"Yes."

"Well, why didn't you think she should do that for you?"

"I did. But she didn't, and I guess I sorta felt that maybe I was wrong to expect it of her."

"Maybe you also thought you would be a bad girl if you expressed yourself . . . if you expressed your anger?"

CHAPTER 8

□ 1 □

She didn't know which woke her, but Stephanie climbed up out of a deep unconsciousness to reach for both the radio and the alarm blasting in her ear. The shrill buzz was still echoing in her head, even after her finger found the button in the dark. If she closed her eyes again, she'd never get up. Just for a minute. . . . The radio started again and she jumped up.

She walked barefoot to the bathroom, turned on the top faucet, went to the kitchen and filled the Pyrex kettle with water. Back in the bathroom, she stuck her hand behind the curtain. It was almost hot. She stood back in the tub so the spray hit her feet. She put the washrag under the water, wiped the soap, and quickly washed. The water had gotten very hot, so she moved under it, turning around slowly. She shampooed her hair once, rinsed off the bottle, and put it back on the plastic shelf.

Still sleepy, she spooned the instant coffee into a mug, filled it up, and went into the bedroom. She put a tissue on the vanity and stood the cup on it. She opened her underwear drawer, pulled out bra and pants, and patted the neat piles back in place. She took a pair of panty hose from the bottom, checked to make sure they were ones with a run. Why throw them out when you could wear them under slacks? She sprayed deodorant under her arms, wondering if it was better to have a smelly universe or to protect the ozone. She sat at the vanity and took her first sip of coffee.

Stephanie spread moisturizer over her face, noticing how big her pores were. A thin veil of makeup shrank them. She did her eyes and blew her hair dry, drinking in between. She

71

pulled out a pair of slacks and a top, changed pocketbooks, and put on her boots. She wrapped the cord around the blower and put it back in the drawer. Then she folded a square of paper towel, wiped the mirror, dusted the vanity. She swallowed the rest of her coffee, rinsed the cup, dried it, and put it back in the cabinet.

She bent a tie around the plastic garbage bag, took it down with her when she left. Then Stephanie went to work.

□ 2 □

Lascano stretched his cheeks taut and grimaced in the mirror. "Emptiness can't hurt," he told himself, yet he ached with it. He glanced longingly at the glass ashtray, swiped from a restaurant, on the toilet tank. "Won't be ashes all over anyway," he told his reflection. "And she won't complain about the foggy mirrors and the dust." He finished shaving and jumped under the shower. What's the point of cleaning the outside of your body, when your insides are filthy? He scrubbed vigorously, as if the soap would melt into him, washing away twenty-seven years' accumulation of tar and nicotine that filled his organs.

Still drying himself, he stuck his head into the bedroom and checked the clock. Seven-fifteen. And he'd been up for half an hour. That was pretty good. He started dressing, trying to ignore the contractions in his throat.

"What's wrong?" a small voice said from under the covers.

"Nothing."

"There must be something." Cynthia's voice was starting to whine.

"Uh-uh."

"At least tell me. Talk to me about it."

Lascano, in shorts and a T-shirt, raced into the kitchen and opened the pail. He stuck his hand under the slimy lettuce and half-eaten orange rinds, rummaging around. "Shit," he mumbled, gently pulling away layers of garbage. He saw the tip sticking out of a soggy tissue and, eyes smarting from relief, he got the cigarette out in one piece. He put it between his lips and took a wooden match from the stove and struck it.

The smell of sulphur infiltrated his senses, and he practically swooned. He puffed and held the smoke in his mouth for a minute before he opened it and let his lungs fill with it. It bit into the delicate tissue and cut across his chest with an exquisite sharpness.

He went back to the bedroom. Cynthia was staring at the ceiling, a tear hovering on her eyeball.

"You promised," she said, quivering. He didn't answer. "You're not even trying, are you?"

"I *am*, but this is a bad day. I wouldn't be able to do it today."

"Yeah, when you're down, you need one. When you're feeling good, you need one. When you're depressed, when you're happy. Why don't you just admit you have no will power?"

"Cynthia, lay off, huh. HUH!"

The silence made him feel guilty. Her silence, and his giving in. "Listen, you just don't understand. It's not that easy."

Nick knotted his tie and buckled his holster. Cynthia's bottom lip was inside her mouth. He stormed out of the room, got his coat, turned off the boiling water. Screw it, he'd get a coffee outside. He opened the door, slammed it, and went back. He sat on the edge of the bed. She thought he had left, and was crying softly. He started to put his hand on her trembling shoulder, but changed his mind.

"Look, Cyn. Cyn, stop. Aw, must you? Listen, it's the case, you know. It's getting me down. And I'm trying. Honest. That's why I don't have any patience."

Cynthia sniffled. Her wet cheeks turned into a smile. "Okay," she said, putting her hand on Nick's face.

"I'm sorry, baby. It's just that . . . well, it's frustrating. Here we are looking for a murderer. And we don't even know where to look. Or what we're looking *for*. *A*nd he's roaming around, maybe getting ready to do it again. That's

73

hard on me, it would be on anybody. And trying to quit on top of it. Try to understand. Okay?"

Cynthia gave him an "I'm-still-angry-but-I-can't-help-loving-you" look, and raised her chin. Nick Lascano gave her a peck.

"Gotta go." He went outside and walked to the drugstore to buy a pack of cigarettes.

□ 3 □

"Why did you say 'naked in the kitchen'?"

"When?"

"When you were telling me about the dinner that you made, that Marilyn didn't eat."

"Did I?"

"Yes."

"I don't know."

"Maybe you didn't realize you said it. But it must have bothered you."

"Uh-uh."

"Did she come into the kitchen often without her clothes on?"

"Sometimes. Yes, I guess you could say it bothered me. A little."

"What bothered you? Did she have a nice body?"

"Oh, yes. I mean, that's not why it bothered me. Marilyn had a beautiful body."

"Compared with yours, you mean."

"No, I'm not saying my body isn't good looking and hers was. I think I'm getting better about things like that. I think I have a pretty good body. See, you're smiling. Do I get a gold star?"

"Two of them."

"It's just that she was so . . . sensual about it. I don't mean she wiggled—or did bumps and grinds by the refrigera-

74

tor—or anything. But there was a sexual quality about her. You could sense it. Sometimes you could smell it. Like an animal."

"And that's what bothered you?"

"It didn't bother me exactly. No, it wasn't that. It was that she was . . . I don't know, so sure of herself. Like she knew sex was good for her, and would be good for the guy too. There was no shame in her. No embarrassment."

"She was uninhibited?"

"Completely. Like she expected people to think sex was beautiful, she was beautiful. No, that's not right. I can't explain it."

"Maybe it has to do with your own feelings about sex."

"What feelings?"

"The ones about your inadequacy. We've talked about that a lot. Not that you are, but that you think you are."

"Well, I am. I mean, I think I've gotten to the stage where I think I'm good looking. I believe it now. Although God—and you—know how ugly I used to feel about myself. I don't think I feel ugly anymore. I look in the mirror and I know I'm, well, not beautiful, but attractive. And my body is too. And yes, men find me attractive."

"So what makes you inadequate?"

"You know."

"I want you to talk about it."

"Do I have to?"

"Yes. Try."

"Well, like, when I'm in bed with someone. Sometimes I really feel . . . hot. Sexual. I mean I really want it. And I make love, but it's like somebody else is lying there. I sort of drift away from my body and I watch myself, doing things, touching, being touched, and I can't help but think 'yuck, that's disgusting.' It's not me. But . . . gee, I wish I could explain.

"You're doing all right so far."

"Like, you know, suppose you look at an arm. I do this sometimes. I look at my arm. At first, it looks okay. I mean it's just an arm, right? Then you look closer, and you see long green veins going down, and some pores that are big enough so you can see, and little tiny hairs coming out, and *little defects and bumps in the skin. And then all of a sudden it's not just an arm anymore, it's a mass of muscle, tendon, slimy nerves, and all sorts of things. And it becomes ugly. You think that's crazy?"*

"Do you?"

"Who knows? But it's worse with other parts of your body."

"And when you're in bed with somebody, you think about these things?"

"Yes. Like a guy is kissing me, and it's okay and then I open my eyes and I look at his face. Hair coming out of his nose, and some men have a little clump in their ears, and the bristles of their cheeks and the tiny bumps where hair grows out of your scalp. And nostrils, and veins on your eyeballs, and the sound your breath makes when it goes through your nose. And then I think maybe he's looking at me the way I'm looking at him. Seeing all those things about my body."

"What about besides kissing . . . what about the rest of your body?"

"I can't tell you that."

"Why not?"

"I'd be too ashamed. Even with you, Doctor."

□ 4 □

Frank used his key to pull down the upper half of the brass mailbox panel. He shuffled through the magazines, crisscrossing them into piles on the radiator. He had his system worked out. On the bottom he put 4F, 4R, then 3F, 3R (that was vacant, but mail still came to the last guy), 2F, 2R, 1F, 1R. As he started on the left, which was Bassetti, her pile was on top. He folded each piece in half and put it in the proper slot. He had gotten it down to a science.

Vilma Karlmeier was the only typed name. It had been there for so long. The edges of the paper were worn away, and her name was blurred. He'd better fix it up for the new guy. The other names were all scrawled on masking tape and stuck on the inside of the panel, over the appropriate holes.

He finished the magazines and big junk pieces. Then he took the rubber band off the envelopes and sorted them between his fingers. Suddenly he remembered the sheet inside his jacket pocket. The mail still fanned out in his left hand, his other reached inside his pocket. He peeled a red circle off the waxy paper, leaning against the boxes so he could do it with one hand, and smoothed it above Rosa's name. Then he did the same for Karlmeier.

People were funny. For years he always checked the mail automatically in the older people's slots. Just to make sure there was nothing in the box. Once, when he worked Grand Central on his last route, he noticed an old woman's mail was still there from two days before. When she didn't pick it up the next day, he got in the elevator and went up to her door. Shit, he wasn't going to wait to get anybody's permission to spend a little extra time to do something he thought he should do.

She didn't answer. Frank went to the super and together they unlocked the door. She was on the floor of the bathroom. At first they thought she was dead. But she wasn't. Had a heart attack or a stroke or something. They got her to the hospital, and she was okay after that. Not okay, but not dead either. They all said if it hadn'ta been for him . . . he saved her life. She sent him a present when she came home. And wrote a nice letter to the post office about him. He had it in his album.

He always watched over his people. So now some big shot gets it into his head that all mailmen should watch old people's boxes, to make sure stuff hasn't accumulated. They keep a record of the person's nearest relative or somebody who knows about them, or has a key. If they register, they get a red dot, so you know they're old and you should pay attention. Mail doesn't get picked up, you call a number, they check to see who has a set of keys, get the person or the police to go over there and see if the old lady or old man is alive or lying on the floor in need of help.

Operation Alert they call it. Shit, he had the idea years

ago. So he wasn't smart enough to give it a name, or write an official letter. Now some jerk is getting all the credit.

He told Rosie about it. She had laughed. "Frank, if this old lady ends up with a stroke or a broken hip, it better she just stay there and die." She wouldn't register. Anyway, she had said, she didn't have any relatives here anymore, so who would they call? It didn't matter. He always watched out for them anyway. But, after he was gone, how would the new guy know which ones were old?

Hell, so he put the red stickers up and, so what could she do to him if she saw them?

"I'm listening for you." Rosa's voice as she pulled open the door startled Frank. He turned his back on the mailboxes, to block the red stickers.

"Hi, Rosie, your *TV Guide* came."

"Getting close, eh, Frank? Pretty soon you collect your pension. What is it, three weeks? Two? See, I count."

"Yeah, I can't think of anything else. The wife and me, maybe we'll go down to Florida like everybody else. Just to look around and see what it's like. We can stay a week, a month, who cares?"

"Mrs. Layton, I bet she's happy?"

"Oh, boy, is she? She's talking about taking dancing lessons. The two of us, you know, ballroom. I'd rather keep working than do *that*. Last week it was bridge lessons. She's making all sort of plans. I guess she's entitled."

"We miss you. Me and Princess."

Frank Layton turned and quickly put the rest of the envelopes in the slots. Very quickly, so Rosa wouldn't see the red circles on the panel. Or the mist in his eyes.

"I'll miss you too, Rosie. Maybe I'll come and visit." But he knew he wouldn't.

"That would be nice. And your wife too. Maybe you both come and have a bowl spaghetti with me." She knew he wouldn't.

"Maybe," Frank answered, sticking the yellow envelope from M. Wechsler, marked "Return to Sender" in 2R. "Maybe," he repeated, and locked the panel.

□ 5 □

Stephanie started in the bedroom. As soon as she came home she got undressed. First she dumped the top drawer out on the bed and wiped the inside. She emptied the bag from Woolworth's, the Con-Tact rolling to the edge of the mattress, the plastic hangers clattering. She cut the Con-Tact, pressing it down carefully to smooth out the air bubbles. She used a razor to cut down the corrugated paper, covered it, and placed the new partitions in the drawer. Then she re-folded all her sweaters and stacked them between the dividers. When she was done, she did her lingerie. When all the drawers were finished, she sprayed sachet in them, admiring the precision and organization as she opened each one. Then she did the closet.

She had so much more room now. She could use Marilyn's night table for stationery and clips and things. Tomorrow night she'd do the kitchen cabinets and medicine chest. Then she'd get to the linen and hall closets. She'd have a separate place for each particular thing. She loved looking in house and decorating magazines and planning what she would do with all the cabinets and drawers and closets if she had so many. Well, this might not be so bad, as long as she didn't have to share it. Swinging the rent alone might be a problem. But so would having another roommate.

Dressed in her old sweatshirt and bare legs, Stephanie made a cup of instant coffee. She sat down at the table with a pad, and started figuring her expenses and four payroll checks a month. In June she was due for another raise. They'd give her at least fifteen dollars. After taxes, it wouldn't be very much, but she'd be able to count on another forty dollars a month.

The rent wasn't *that* high. Compared with what some girls she knew were paying. One tenant must have lived in this apartment for a hundred years, rent controlled. Then there was only one other person before they had moved in. So the rent wasn't raised *too* much. Not with that kind of turnover. In fact, it would probably cost more if she looked for a studio somewhere.

The phone wouldn't be as high now. Marilyn was the one who had all the overcalls. And had to have an extension for talking privately. Well, if nothing came up, like problems with her teeth, she could manage. She had always been good at budgeting. Which is why she had a nice little savings account. If she had to, she could always borrow from it for the rent.

Stephanie threw her scribbled arithmetic away and surveyed the little kitchen while she sipped. A cheap piece of wallpaper over the stove would really brighten it up. She could put one coat of enamel on the dish closet and throw away those awful, tacky curtains Marilyn had hung up cock-eyed. Maybe one of those roll-up shades would go nice. She already knew how she was going to fix the bathroom. By the end of the week, the little things would be done and she could start on the major overhauls. They better come this weekend and pick up the bed. Then she'd move hers under the window.

Well, she really wasn't all that tired anyway, and she didn't want to wait. So, at nine-thirty, Stephanie emptied all the kitchen cabinets.

CHAPTER 9

□ 1 □

The next night when she came home from work, Stephanie started making a list of things to clean out, when the phone rang. Her heart fluttered.

"Hello."

"Allo!" the voice boomed in her ear. It was only Rosa. "You wanna come down for supper?"

"That's nice of you, Rosa, but I don't think so."

"Why not? You got a date?"

"Uh-uh, but I don't feel like going out."

"Coming down the stairs ain't going out. You don't have to get dressed. Just wear your bathrobe. You shouldn't be so much alone. Specially now. I got the gravy cooking on the stove."

"All right. What time do you want me?"

"About half hour? Or before, if you want."

When they first moved in, she and Marilyn had gone down there a few times. For a glass of wine or when Rosa cooked a big bowl of her sauce. Stephanie found it boring. Not boring, uncomfortable. Rosa and Marilyn got a little tipsy and laughed while Rosa reminisced. She had some mouth on her, that Rosa. But she *was* funny. After a while, Stephanie always found an excuse. Like washing her hair or finishing a book. It gave her a chance to have the apartment to herself, to straighten up, clean her drawers.

Marilyn used to go there a lot. Rosa didn't have much company. With all the people she knew, she hardly ever invited anybody. Who was there? Most of the women were married. The other ones, Rosa said, she couldn't talk to.

She'd go, but she'd leave right after dinner. Help her put away those ugly white dishes with the navy border and the gold script, which Rosa only took down on special occasions.

Well, it wouldn't be so bad. Rosa was fun. It was just that . . . she was so *easy* or something. Made Stephanie feel weird. If only she didn't mention Marilyn. She just couldn't bear it right now.

□ 2 □

Lydia Hodges struggled to get the key chain out of her bag, Malcolm patiently standing behind her, a brown bag overflowing with groceries in each arm.

"Sorry, honey, just a minute."

"Hurry up—I'm dropping one."

"Here we go," she said, jamming the key in the upper lock. It clicked open and she quickly put the other key in the bottom and shouldered the door open.

"Whew." Malcolm dumped the bags on the hall floor. He took off his coat, hung it up, and handed Lydia a hanger. Then he picked up the bags and brought them into the kitchen, where he left them on the table.

Lydia started unpacking while Malcolm put on the TV and sat down in his chair.

"Which would you rather—the steak or the chops?" she called into the living room.

"Doesn't matter." Malcolm put his feet up on the worn ottoman and closed his eyes. For just a minute. Lydia put the rest of the things away and started dinner. When it was done, she went in to wake her husband. "Nice nap?"

"I wasn't sleeping."

"No? That's funny, what was that strange noise I heard in here? Sounded like snoring."

Malcolm laughed and whacked her on the behind.

They sat down to eat. He was quiet, and Lydia didn't want to interrupt his thoughts.

Finally, over coffee, she asked, "What's the matter?"

He shrugged.

"You haven't said a word since we came home."

"I'm sorry, dear, it's just that . . . I don't know. I suddenly had a feeling I had discovered something and then it slipped away, and I can't for the life of me figure out what it was."

"About the case?"

"I don't know. I think so. It was when we came home. Something lit up in my brain," he smiled, "like a great white light. A second later, the whole thing was lost. It's driving me crazy."

"Well, I'm sure it will come to you. More coffee?"

□ 3 □

"Those are good times, Probition days," Rosa waved her glass. She held it up to her face and stared at the "Chambord" engraved in the crystal, which the ruby-colored liquid made clear and sharp. "Now *that* was a restaurant. Closed. Like all the others."

Stephanie leaned back, her legs curled under her. Her eyes were a little glassy. "I ate there once. After a prom."

"It was the best. Sometimes they call me when the regular hatcheck is sick. Or for vacation, except in summer there's no business. Just cigarettes. I work twelve to two, maybe three, and they pay me real good. The extra money was nice. When they close, they say, 'Rosa, you need some plates, some glasses?' They give me."

"Pretty." Stephanie yawned.

"But Probition. That was something else. I'm working a speakeasy. All the big shots useta come there. Now they call them Mafia. Gangsters, they were. But all gentlemen. And rich. They tip good. Especially if you're pretty. Ah, I was pretty then. I wear my hair loose. Not like now, tied in a bun." Rosa undulated her hands next to her face to show how long her hair had been. "And I have a figure too. I make out real good. I see it all."

"I bet you were something else."

"I was, I was," Rosa said and smiled, happily recollecting. She picked Princess up and put her in her lap, kissing the top of her head with loud smacking noises. "Once this man come in. He has money, you can tell. When he's ready to leave, he say, 'Here's hundred dollars. You come home with me.'"

"What did you do?" Stephanie asked, even though she had heard this story before.

"I push the money back. I smile sweet. I say, 'Tell you what. You give me one dollar, you go home and jerk yourself off, you save ninety-nine dollars.'"

"You didn't?"

"I did."

"What did he do?"

"He laugh. He give me five dollars. In those days, five dollars is like . . . like hundred dollars nowadays."

"You're a riot. I bet you had fun. Did you ever go home with any of them?"

"Naw. Now I wish I did. But I was young. I have a good husband. I run home to him every night." Rosa leaned her head back and closed her eyes, looking at the past on the inside of her lids. She seemed to be dozing.

Stephanie stretched. "I guess I'll be going."

"Don't go yet. I like to talk. An old lady don't have much chance to talk. You young girls understand. You think I tell Mrs. Karlmeier these things? She die. I wish I could be young now. What a world. What fun. Except . . . for Marilyn. Okay, okay, I promise not to talk about it."

"It's not so great." Stephanie got serious.

"You can do anything you want, and nobody say nothing. Nobody care. You can go out with lots of men. Sleep with them. Enjoy them."

"Oh, that's not the end of the world, Rosa, sex. I think, sometimes, maybe it was better in the old days. If a guy wanted you, he had to marry you. Then, well, if the sex wasn't terrific, you were stuck. But at least you were married. Settled. And if the guy fooled around a little on the side, the woman didn't care so much. At least he didn't bother her as much for *that*."

"You crazy. I tell you a secret. A real one." Rosa leaned forward and spoke very softly. "I still want it. Don't look surprised. I gonna be sixty-seven years old and I wanna get laid."

"You're kidding?"

"No. I never tell this to anybody else. But don't believe you don't care when you get old. It's not true. I give anything to have one big, long salami again. Right here." She pointed.

Stephanie was embarrassed and she couldn't think of anything to say. She slipped on her shoes and nonchalantly stretched.

Rosa patted her knee. "You go home now. You get up early." Stephanie turned her head; she couldn't look at her. God, she thought, at her age, thinking about sex. Thinking about a man's ... *thing*. Calling it a salami!

Rosa padded to the door behind her. "Ah, I'm so glad you come, Steph'nie. I have such a good time. I wait till I hear you get in, okay?"

"Rosa, I really enjoyed tonight. Thanks for supper. See you."

"*Ciao.*"

Rosa waited till she heard Stephanie close the door upstairs. Then she locked up, washed her face, and got undressed. The wine was still burning through her veins, and blushing on her neck. She stood in front of the mirror and stared at herself. She lifted up her heavy breasts, remembering when they were not so droopy. They didn't *feel* any different. Her whole body didn't feel any different from the way it did forty years ago. Maybe it was fat and wrinkled, but it felt the same to her. And the ache was still there.

She got into her nightgown and turned out the light. Then she moved Princess from the crook of her leg to her chest and began to stroke her while she stared into the dark, remembering.

☐ 4 ☐

"And the damned skis in the corner of the bedroom. I asked her a million times to move them—she could've kept them in the hall closet—the first thing you saw when you opened the door. Looked beautiful. And she invited girlfriends up and all she ever made was spaghetti and the sauce splattered all over the stove and counter. She never cleaned it up. I had to do it.

"She never changed the toilet paper. Do you know how infuriating it is to go to the bathroom and find one little square left on the cardboard? Oh, sure, she always put one little square back—sometimes I think it was used—just so I couldn't say she used it all up. It was the same thing with stuff in the refrigerator. I mean, if there were some vegetables left in a container, she'd eat the whole thing and leave one string bean or two green peas, would you believe, because if she took the last one, she'd have to wash out the container."

CHAPTER 10

□ 1 □

"Where do we go from here?" Malcolm said, more to himself than to Nick.

"I would've bet even money on Friedman. Just had a feel to it."

"Eh, I knew that was a dead end. You and your hunches."

"Sure you knew. *You* were the one hunting for him. Day and night. Maybe he is the one." Nick's cheeks were tingling. He got up and went to the coat rack. He stuck his hands in the folds of his top coat and patted the twill until he felt the bulge of the pocket, then moved his fingers along the seam till he reached the slit. He pulled out the pack, taking off the horizontal rubber bands, then the vertical. Finally he removed the yellow lined paper. His nails grabbed a filter, and he pulled a cigarette out.

"What the hell're you doing?"

"Wrapping. It's called wrapping, and the theory is if you have to go to all this trouble, you won't bother."

"How's it coming?" Mal asked.

"How does it look?" Lascano lit up, inhaling deeply. The smoke cut into his lungs in delicious agony. He leaned forward and started coughing. His body was trying to tell him about the assault. Destroying the lung tissue.

"Sounds great."

"Yeah, good, isn't it?" Lascano sat back down and smoked, each drag burning less and less as his throat and chest became numb. "C'mon, Mal, you're just fishing. Without bait. All right, he hangs around singles places. Picks up different girls all the time. Does kinky things. Jesus, maybe we're get-

87

ting too old or something, some of the things you learn. . .
So he picks up the Wechsler girl, she goes back to his apartment, they fool around. She says no and leaves. He coulda
been mad. But, Christ, a week later? He would've done something *then*. Raped her. Hurt her. Shit on her." He smiled and
they both chuckled. "He wouldn'ta gone back to the same
place and picked up someone else. Would he?"

"Guess not," Malcolm said. "But you never know how a
sick mind works. Suppose he stewed about it for a week. It
could happen, you know."

"More logical the way he looks at it. They all screw. Why
get hung up on somebody who won't? Just get yourself another. Anyway, what difference does it make—he has an
alibi. Three people substantiate it. I believe 'em. I think you
do too, you just hate to admit it. Let's start again."

"Shit," Hodges said, studying the rope he had just made
out of paper clips, "there's something staring me right in the
eye, and I can't see it."

"Ha, you gonna tell me it's the murderer's face and you'll
open your eyes and know exactly who it is?"

"Don't laugh, Charlie," Malcolm said seriously, "it's happened before. Will you put that thing out? You're killing
yourself!"

□ 2 □

*"I've tried to stop. I read a book on compulsive behavior
and, boy, he was writing about me."*

"I hate labels."

*"Sorry. But it's so spooky to read about yourself like that.
So many things. Like lists. You know, I make a list of things
to do all the time. But I'm not just your average listmaker. I
make lists of the lists I have to make."*

*"At least you never lose your sense of humor. That's im-
portant, you know."*

"If I didn't laugh, I'd cry."

"I know that. But at least you're aware of a lot of the things troubling you. Otherwise you wouldn't have recognized your need for help in the first place. And I know—I'm sure you do too—what an effort it is for you to be funny sometimes. To be able to laugh at yourself. I know you're not really laughing, Stephanie, but it helps to be able to smile about it."

"Doctor Fredericks, that's the first nice thing you've ever said about me."

"No, it's not. You know I like you. I think you're a good person. But I don't think you want compliments. You know you wouldn't believe them anyway. You'd just think I was trying to make you feel good."

"Do you know me!"

"Do you find that spooky too?"

"No, somehow it's a very comforting feeling."

"Isn't it kind of what you mean by being 'close' to someone?"

"I guess."

"Let's get back. To compulsive behavior. What do you do that is compulsive?"

"Everything. My whole life is one big compulsion. Not only the cleaning and the constant moving things so they're just so, but, I don't know, like at the office, I do it too. But I think I understand a little better why I do it now. It's like I'm afraid to make a mistake, afraid to act human, afraid that somebody will say, 'Oh, she did something wrong,' even though I know how stupid that is. But it's like other things too—that I'm afraid people will actually think of me as being human.

"For instance, well, this is kind of embarrassing . . . no, I'm going to tell you anyway. When I go to the ladies' room, in the office, or in a movie, or any public place, or for God's sake even in my own apartment, I always flush the toilet while I'm going—well, not at home, because the sink is there so I can let the water run. Anyway, the other day at work I was, you know, sitting there, flushing away. And then somebody else came in and started going and making all this noise and not in the least bit self-conscious. I had to think about it

and laugh to myself. I mean, what am I trying to hide? Everybody does it. Why does it bother me if people know I do it too? Now that's not normal, I think.

"But there are other things. If I go to somebody's house, you know, for a visit, or just the evening, or especially a weekend, I always clean up so good. I always thought it was part of the compulsive cleaning thing, but now I wonder. Wonder if maybe I try too hard to . . . wipe up any traces of my being there, of my even existing. Does that sound weird?"

"No, it sounds like we're finally getting somewhere."

□ 3 □

Rosa was watching Columbo. She liked him. Not because he was Italian. Maybe because of his scroungy raincoat. And people always thought he was dumb. Until the end. Boy, did he fool them.

She heard a noise. No, it was a not-noise. She turned her head and looked out the band of darkness between the open window and the sill. Somebody was looking back at her window. The only light in her apartment was created by the flickering black-and-white images coming from the screen. But that was across the room, and the curtain hid it from view. She hoped.

He stared. She felt for Princess, never taking her eyes off the figure on the sidewalk. She grabbed the roll of the dog's neck and squeezed. The figure moved. Closer to the stairs. He bent a little to look up through the window and the lamppost lit the side of his face. Oh, God, it was him. The murderer. Rosa could feel her scalp slide back on her head.

"Ro—sa . . ." he called in a loud whisper. Rosa didn't move. *Couldn't* move.

"Ro—sa . . . please, I have to talk to you."

What did he want? If he wanted to kill her, he would've

come to the door and tried to get in. Or crawled through the window. Everyone yelled at her to get bars on the window, like they had next door, and at Number 568. She swore, never. How could she talk through bars? Tomorrow she'd ask someone who to call.

Why would he want to kill her anyway? He looked so pathetic standing there. Gonna put him in jail. Or the lectric chair. No, it wasn't him. She knew it.

She lifted the bottom blinds and stuck her head out.

"Rosa, thank God. They think I . . ."

"Sh-h. You want everybody on the block to hear you? Come up."

Rosa pulled the dresser back into the light spot on the wood floor, took the chain off, turned the bolt, and waited in the doorway for Pete.

□ 4 □

Stephanie lay down on the cold tiles and put one foot on the toilet seat and the other on the sink. She tilted the plastic rim of the makeup mirror on the edge of the tub so she could look inside herself. She did nothing but watch the skin and tissue soften in anticipation. She pretended she was a man about to fuck her. But couldn't imagine the oozing depths of her body being stimulating to him. Her lips, even though stretched apart, were grooved. She didn't have to come in here now that she was alone. Didn't have to lock the door. She could do it in bed. But where would she put the mirror? She'd see if the night table was high enough. Later.

She licked her finger, and then very softly slid it over her clitoris. The saliva was like syrup, and she rotated the cushion of her finger around and around. She could see her vagina making little sucking motions, as if it were looking for a prick to grab. It pulsated. Her legs were spread so wide that

91

her buttocks were lifted off the floor, and her rectum, tight and closed, looked like a rubbery hole.

As her finger moved, her stomach sank against her back, and the hole closed. Then she lifted up, everything tight, her skin stretched across her hipbones, and it closed and disappeared between her cheeks. She lowered herself and it opened. The inside of her cheeks, all around the hole, were dark and brown, and Stephanie wondered if everybody's was like that, or if it was only her. The steady expanding and shrinking of the dark hole hypnotized her, and she moved faster and faster to the rhythm. Until she couldn't lower herself anymore, and her hips were so high in the air, her elbows and shoulders scraping against the floor, that she couldn't see the mirror.

Wings flapping under her ribs, steam burning in her chest. Everything rushed against her breastbone, swirling and pounding. Muscles clenched, bulged under her skin. She couldn't bear it. And her finger couldn't move any faster. She was going to break open. Her whole being was tied into a knot, pulling cords from every direction of her.

Then her spine stretched, and her legs sprang straight out, locking a hinge in place. She stopped. When she put her finger there again, it hurt. She felt drained, without being drained.

She jumped up, her groin still throbbing; got dressed, put the mirror away.

Then she cleaned the linen closet.

CHAPTER 11

□ 1 □

"You saw us go up together. We know that. Fact one." Pete twirled the porcelain Chambord ashtray. "Then you go take the dog for a walk. Right?"

"*Si.* I told you."

"You sure you didn't see anybody on the street—somebody different, somebody who usually isn't there?"

"Ah, I keep thinking and thinking. If I see somebody, I remember. If I remember, I tell you."

"Okay. So you come back—in about twenty minutes—let's say it's about four, no quarter of. You go next door and let the water run for a bath. I'm still upstairs. But while the water is running somebody could come in—you wouldn't have heard—and waited in the hallway or something."

"But how somebody gonna know you upstairs then, and what he gonna do, just stand there and wait?"

"Who knows? I'm just thinking out loud. You give her a bath. How long did it take you, you think?"

"The water runs slow, it dribbles, it takes about twenty minutes to fill the tub, and then I got to get her in—that takes a while—and out again—so all together, half hour, no, forty-five minutes. But I don't let it run right away. We talk for a while right away. We talk for a while first."

"I left about four-thirty. You told the police you didn't hear me leave. So we know why—you were giving Karlmeier a bath when I left. So you were probably still in her bathroom when *he* came in—otherwise you would've heard him. Okay. You finish the bath. You go across the hall to heat up supper—that couldn't take you more than five, ten minutes—and you and the dog come back and ring."

"I don't ring. I have a key."

"All right, you unlock her door. You don't see anybody or hear anybody then either."

"Right. But I wasn't listening. Anyway I telling Princess what we have for supper."

Pete smiled. "But, if somebody or something was there, or if there was a noise, I think you would've heard that."

Rosa considered. "Yes. I know the sounds of my own building. Yes, I would know."

"So, there was nobody there then. So, so . . . so either the murderer was upstairs, or he already left."

Rosa walked into the tiny kitchen. "You need some wine," she called in, taking out the gallon jug. She pulled the little chair over so she could reach up for the glasses. When she came back inside, Pete's hands were over his face. "Here," she nudged the cold glass against her ear, "you drink."

"It's all so frustrating. I don't know any more now than I did before."

"I know, I know." Rosa put her glass down and knelt in front of him. She took his face in her hands and said softly, "Don't worry. Don't worry. The police, they find him."

"But suppose they don't. It really looks bad for me. They know we were together. We had an argument. We had sex. I leave. An hour later Stephanie finds her. Like that. Somebody gets there right after I leave. Within minutes. It doesn't make any sense.

"I know she wasn't going anywhere, and nobody was coming over. I leave her in this," Pete looked away from Rosa in embarrassment, "dreamy, happy state. She wouldn'ta been looking for another guy."

"Maybe somebody come unexpectly."

"Yeah, but she wouldn't open the door stark naked without asking who it was. No, there was no robe in the room. Just her clothes, the way we left them. If somebody came to the door and she asked who it was, she would've gone back inside to get a robe. Unless she thought it was me coming back. That I changed my mind about going to Vermont. Damn. Damn. Why did I go? Why didn't I stay with her? No, she wouldn't open the door like that, even if she thought it was me. Don't you see, something is very strange."

"I see. A nice girl like that. Always happy. Have a nice boyfriend like you. Nothing makes sense anymore. That somebody kill a girl like that. For what reason?"

"Let's forget why. Concentrate on how. Somebody had to get in. But the door was locked. Maybe not. Hey, she didn't walk me to the door, so she didn't double-lock it, so anybody could've gotten in. But the police said there was no evidence of tampering. Suppose the bottom lock was open all along."

"*Ridicolo*," Rosa spat. "You mean somebody knows the apartment on the top floor is unlocked, that a naked girl is lying in bed? So he knows he can walk right up—at zactly the time I'm in with Mrs. Karlmeier—and get her?"

"Shit. Excuse me."

"S'okay. I hear worse than that."

"Bet you have. It's just that, you know, Rosa, I'm scared. There've been cases before—a guy gets arrested for something he didn't do. All the evidence points to him—circumstantial or whatever—and he keeps pleading innocent and nobody believes him and they put him in jail and he rots away year after year after year, still swearing he didn't do it and ten, twelve, fifteen years later, they arrest somebody for something else and he confesses to the other crime. Shit, it could happen."

"Don't worry," Rosa said softly, "I don't let it happen."

□ 2 □

"Don't you think that's unhealthy?"

"Turning off?"

"The way you do, yes."

"No, I think it's the only thing that lets me go on. I mean, if I didn't turn off sometimes, I couldn't face things. I think I'd break down."

"*That's just what I mean. Stephanie, you've told me about incidents when you 'turned off,' as you call it, so completely, that you really and truly couldn't recall something if you tried.*"

"*I know.*"

"*When you first started—your therapy, I mean—you told me about something that happened to you in bed. It was something that was happening to you then. About two weeks later, I asked you about it, and you couldn't remember. You remembered that there was something there, but not what.*"

"*I know. That's what I do.*"

"*But, you see, when you erase something like that, you don't have to face it. But it doesn't go away. It's still there, locked in your unconscious, or subconscious. It's also an excuse you make to yourself so you won't have to take any responsibility for your actions.*"

"*How do you mean?*"

"*If you do something you don't approve of—I don't mean something wrong or something somebody else won't approve, just you—you turn it off thoroughly. That way, you don't have to think about it, you don't have to say 'why did I do that' or 'that was a destructive thing for me to do,' because it's not there anymore. That's what I want you to think about. I know you're aware of doing it. But you've made it such a habit that you do it automatically now. Without thinking. Just wipe it out. Think about that, in terms of what is good for you and what isn't.*"

"*I know you're right. I know I shouldn't. But sometimes I think if I didn't turn off, I'd . . .*"

"*You'd what? What would happen to you? You'd just have face things, wouldn't you?*"

"*No. I think I'd open my mouth and start screaming. And never stop.*"

□ 3 □

Stephanie was sorry she took the bus the minute she dropped the two quarters in. She couldn't move in any further and the people behind her were shoving to get up the steps so the driver could close the door. She thought it would be better than the subway. Boy, was she wrong. The traffic on Third Avenue was at a standstill. She flicked her wrist but couldn't pull her arm out of her sleeve to see what time it was. It must have taken at least fifteen or twenty minutes to go from 42nd to 48th.

The bodies pressing against her weren't as stifling as they would have been underground, but she was still jumping out of her skin. Sometimes it didn't pay to live in the city—it took you as long to get home as going to Brooklyn. One of the girls in the office lived all the way out and she swore, even with getting down to Penn Station, the Long Island Railroad took her forty minutes. But what was the big hurry? What was she going to do, anyway? That wasn't the point, she just wanted to get there.

After 59th Street, it eased up a little—a lot of traffic turned off for the bridge—but it was still bad. She had inched her way to the back of the bus and all her weight was leaning on her arm in the steel stirrup. She was standing in front of a young couple making goo-goo eyes at one another. She couldn't stop staring at them. The girl had a pimple on her nose, and Stephanie wondered if it made her uncomfortable that her boyfriend was close enough to see the pus straining under the skin.

Stephanie always stared at couples, trying to imagine what it would be like to be so close to someone that you just act naturally. Like yourself when you're all alone. Trying to figure out if the other person could tell when your mouth tastes sour or there's a terrible burning inside your behind.

97

She was tired when she got off at 86th Street. She wanted to get straight home, but there wasn't a thing to eat. She just hadn't felt like shopping on Saturday.

She went into the Grand Union. It was mobbed, and she had to wait at the checkout counter for someone to empty a cart. She dumped her bag and gloves in it and hurriedly pushed up the aisles, randomly grabbing cans and boxes here and there. Detergent, toilet paper, napkins, Mr. Clean. She smiled at herself, thinking they would make a great couple—Mr. & Mrs. Clean. She dawdled over the meats, looking for some lamb chops. She found a package of two beautiful loin chops for $3.83, and started to put it in her basket. Then she reached under and checked the other packages. She smoothed over the plastic, as if she could tell the tenderness that way. There was another one for $3.78. She balanced the two packages in both hands, trying to make the decision. Finally, in disgust, she tossed them both back in the case. She didn't feel like dirtying up the stove anyway.

She went back to the frozen food department and picked up a TV dinner, which she hated. Might as well buy the rest of what I need now, she thought, getting instant coffee and eggs and ketchup.

The lines at the checkout counters were so long they wound down the aisles. She had too much now for the express counter. She counted anyway. Thirteen things. She could put back all the paper stuff, which she really didn't need. Oh, what difference did it make . . . another five minutes.

Stephanie flexed her fingers around the cold handlebar of the cart. The snippy redhead was packing two shopping bags for a woman. The woman was talking to her friend, two in back of her in line.

"I don't care, it's a disgrace. They want a raise again, but what are they doing to find the murderer of that girl? Sure, they're always around when you're parked wrong, or some poor idiot is selling belts on the corner, but a vicious murder—right here—and what are they doing?"

"Bothering everyone," her friend yelled back. "Busy writing letters for donations to the Emerald Society or something. When some lunatic is roaming around this neighborhood."

"Poor girl. Looked pretty." Someone else in line joined the conversation. "Like those two a couple of years ago on the Upper West Side. Remember that one?"

Stephanie felt the roots of her hair stinging her scalp. She eased out of the line and pushed her cart straight into the detergent aisle like a bowling ball down the alley.

She stood there, amazed, while a warm wetness trickled down her legs into her boots. Then she ran out.

□ 4 □

Lascano automatically reached into his breast pocket, found a cigarette, and lit it. After he had smoked half of it, and his mouth was burning and numb, he threw it on the floor and ground his heel into it.

It's not impossible, everybody else is doing it, he thought, angry at himself. Okay, next time I get a craving, I'm going to ignore it. Wait for it to go away. He owed it to Cynthia, no—he owed it to himself to stay healthy and live a long life.

Dying wasn't that scary to him, but the way he'd go. Shrivelled up in pain, going from doctor to doctor, looking for hope. Hell, he'd seen enough of it. Especially his father. And *he* never smoked. But he got it anyway. So who could tell? What difference did it make?

Hah, it would be just his luck, he'd go through all the agony of quitting, and get cancer anyway. Cynthia would love that. Of course she wouldn't. But she'd keep sneaking into the sick room, watching him fade away, eaten with pain, and say, "Why didn't you listen to me?" and "Everybody else got smart, why couldn't you?" She'd take it as a deliberate attempt to aggravate her. Then he'd die and she'd keep telling everybody about what she went through, how awful it was to watch him suffer, serve him, give him injections, listen to him beg for mercy. God, she'd be in all her martyred glory.

Nick Lascano lit another cigarette.

□ 5 □

Marianne Webster woke up at four. She could tell he was gone without looking or feeling *his* side. She stared at the ceiling for a while, although she couldn't see it in the dark. Then she put on the light and went to the bathroom. She came back and sat on the edge of the bed. Then, abruptly, she got up and padded into the kitchen and made some instant coffee. God, what a shithouse, she thought. He evidently had something to eat before he left—the bread was out, dishes in the sink, mustard on the table. She couldn't find the cap, and she stuck the jar back in the refrigerator, open. She took the dishrag and started to wipe the crumbs off the table. "What for?" she asked herself and plopped down, her head over her arms.

It didn't matter anymore, anyway. She really didn't care. Whatever feeling she once had for him was long gone. He'd never move out. That was for sure. Well, she had enough saved. She could look for a studio and manage all right. She shivered. Her bare arms, sticking out of her nightgown, had goose pimples. It would be so lonely, though. What would she do every night? But what did she do now? It wasn't as if she had any company, or companionship—Christ, she ate alone every night anyway. She'd look in the Sunday papers, check the ads.

She heard his footsteps on the stairs. She hurriedly got the mustard back out and left it on the table—not that he'd remember. She ran back to the bedroom, jumped into bed, and turned off the light.

CHAPTER 12

□ 1 □

Stephanie shaved her legs. She had already douched. Thank goodness for those cheap disposable ones. She hated the vinyl bag hanging on the shower head, its long hose dancing in the tub. She didn't know why she was bothering. Heaven knows, she wasn't going to sleep with him, and he wasn't going to get close enough to feel her legs. Her mother always used to say, "I don't know why you have to do it. Tiny little blond hairs—you can't even see them." Of course, after so many years, the stubble had gotten darker. She hated that.

Her mother never even did under her arms. Except in the summer. Can you imagine, Stephanie shook her head in disgust, living with a man and not caring. She wondered if they still did it. Naw, too old. But there was that one weekend she stayed over and they closed the door. Probably because she had the TV on.

Marilyn had hardly ever douched. Said it wasn't good for you—washed away natural juices and secretions. Stephanie shuddered and jumped into the shower. Thinking of dried-up semen caked inside. It must smell. Suppose a guy got close and could smell it. Well, of course, Marilyn must have done *that*. You'd think she'd be nervous. About the odor. Stephanie wouldn't do it. She didn't mind the tongue part—that could be very nice probably—but she couldn't stand the thought of a nose so close—in her crotch, for godssake. She knew she didn't have any odor. When she was with someone, she always went to the bathroom first and put her finger inside. Then smelled it. Just to make sure. Of course, she had tasted it too. Sour. How could a guy *do* that?

Well, no sense even thinking about it. She certainly wasn't going to do anything with this guy tonight. One drink and that's it, buster. If he wasn't too bad, maybe a hamburger. She felt a little guilty but, no, it wasn't a *date* date—he just wanted to talk to her. He said on the phone he had gone out with Marilyn the Tuesday before. Strange she hadn't mentioned it, maybe he was too jerky. But they weren't exactly speaking. Oh, of course. She'd gone home that Tuesday. Slept over.

Maybe she ought to call that detective tomorrow and tell him about this. Funny. He said he and Marilyn knew one another in high school. Well, she'd gone to that high school too and she didn't remember him. After all these years, he moves to New York and calls Marilyn? Stephanie wished she could remember if she knew him. When she saw him, she'd find out.

Well, if he wanted to know what was going on, why didn't he just call the police and ask? Why her? They'd probably ask him all sorts of questions. And should. What did he expect her to know? What the police were thinking, where they were looking?

"Yes, Doctor Fredericks," Stephanie said out loud, scrubbing herself, "I knew it sounded silly, but I was curious. All right, not curious. Maybe I was a little bored—you know it's been months since I went out with anybody—and I felt like having a drink and talking to somebody, so I said yes. No, Doctor Fredericks, I was not lying to myself. I knew, deep down, I was kinda hopin' . . ."

□ 2 □

"*Mangia*," Rosa insisted, pulling another glob of spaghetti out of the bowl and dangling it over Pete's plate.

"It's good," he said with his mouth full.

She was in all her glory, feeding a hungry young man. "Now, what we gotta do," Rosa twirled the strands around her fork, "is work on you."

"Whatdya mean?"

"It was this close," she indicated by snapping her fingers, "you probly seen him yourself when you left. You woulda hafta run into him. So . . . so we follow everything you do when you leave."

"I already went over that. Nothing there."

"Well, tell me. We go over it together."

Pete figured he had nothing to lose humoring an old lady who made the best sauce this side of Mulberry Street. "Yessir. Are you going to write this down?"

Rosa glared at him. She was serious. "Now, you leave the apartment. You come down the stairs."

"I come down the stairs."

"You don't see nobody, you don't hear nothing on the stairs."

"Right. I don't see nobody, I don't hear nothing."

"Boy, you talk funny." She laughed. "Okay, you get out the front door. Then what?"

"Nothing."

"Where your car is parked?"

"Are you crazy? I wouldn't use my car during the day. Where would I park it?"

"So how you gonna get home?"

"Bus. I was going to take the crosstown bus."

"On Seventy-ninth Street?"

"No, on Eighty-sixth Street."

"Why? Seventy-ninth Street is closer."

"Yeah, but the Eighty-sixth Street crosstown leaves me off closer to my house."

"Okay, you come out and you walk . . . to the left. You see anybody at all?"

"Just that guy sweeping up outside. In fact, I said hello to him. The skinny Puerto Rican."

"How you say hello—you nod or wave?"

"Neither. I distinctly said hello. I didn't think he knew

who I was, 'cept that I see him all the time and he sees me. I remember thinking he probably thought I lived on the block."

"But, Pete," Rosa put her fork down, "Hector's building is on the right. If you walk left, how you say hello?"

"Let me think. No, you're right, I did walk to the right, not the left."

"Why you do that? Second Avenue closer . . . why you gonna walk half a block more, in the wrong direction from where the bus is gonna stop?"

Both their arms were pressed on the edge of the table, and they stared at one another in silence.

"Think," Rosa finally said. "Why you gonna do that?"

Pete suddenly jumped up, knocking his wine over on the plastic tablecloth. "Jesus Christ."

"What, what?" Rosa frantically stuck their napkins in the little red pool. "What is it, for godssake?"

"Jesus Christ, I saw *her* coming, that's why."

"Who?"

"Stephanie."

□ 3 □

He really wasn't her type, Stephanie thought as she watched him across the table. Kinda fuddy-duddy. Not really. But very intellectual. He couldn't help sounding like a know-it-all. Whatever stupid thing she said in passing, he could give a dissertation on. And did. But he was thoughtful. Sensitive.

"What kind of law do you specialize in?"

"Corporate."

Figures. Certainly wouldn't be a criminal lawyer. She could just imagine him dealing with rapists, robbers. No, he was a good, upright citizen, would never do anything wrong. He probably never masturbated, even as a child. Spit on the sidewalk. Picked his nose. Or shifted his balls in public.

Stephanie smiled, wondering what he would do if the

warm rush of air wooshing through her stomach suddenly burst out of her seat and exploded in her seat. Probably twist his nose, make little sniffing noises, and come out with something like "I say, my dear, have you just passed wind?" In a Rex Harrison voice.

"Something funny?"

"No." Didn't have any sense of humor either. "I was just thinking how odd it is that we should end up meeting." She had to get to the bathroom. She shouldn't have eaten steak, she knew better than that. That, and the wine. A fullness converged in the pit of her stomach, and she was rocking back and forth. She hated to get up and go to the ladies' room in a strange place. The waiter always pointed. If you followed his finger nonchalantly waving in the air, you'd either end up in the kitchen or in somebody's lap. And then you'd have to weave in and out of the tables looking stupid and asking again. Besides, he'd probably watch her walk, and it would make her self-conscious. Mortified.

"Actually, I was just thinking the same thing . . . but that it's a pleasant surprise. Worth waiting for."

Stephanie blushed and said thank you into her glass. His hand grazed her knuckles as she kneaded the crystal stem. She became suddenly aware of an emptiness, not so much a depression as some nameless unhappiness nudging her senses and sending little reminders to her brain. She concentrated on unrolling her plastic stirrer, her face burning from his stare. How did he know? He was awful. A nothing. Yet, when she looked up at him, he sucked all the hunger and loneliness of her being to her eyeballs. Oh, Jesus, don't let me, I hate him. He's a schmuck. Her groin twisted and the pressure on her bladder was becoming unbearable. It's not that I want him, I just have to go, she reassured herself.

"You were telling me . . ." she said.

"Ah, yes. Marilyn was too young for me in those days. I was five years older. At fifteen or seventeen, five years is a lot. But in your twenties, it's just about right. But even then, there was something about her. That first time I met her, at the party I told you about, I thought now why would Chuck—that's the guy whose house it was—invite such young girls. But after I spoke to her, I changed my mind. Not that she was mature, but . . . I can't put my finger on it. She was like a . . . well, frivolous, light, maybe some would even call her flighty. But you couldn't help enjoying her."

"I know. After all, I lived with her. When was the last time you saw her . . . I mean before this time?"

"Oh, let's see, it must have been . . . seventy-three. About six years. I left for college; when I came back, she was away at school. You know how it is. But when I came back to New York last month, I thought about her. When I found her name in the phone book and realized she was still single and lived right here in Manhattan . . ."

"How did it feel? Seeing her again?"

Richard Spencer leaned back and twisted his glass in his hand. See, Stephanie thought, even his name is so right.

"Well, I don't see why I shouldn't tell you," he said after a moment's hesitation. "I guess if I'm honest with myself, I have to admit that for six years I thought about her . . . dreamed about her. When we went out that night, she seemed to be . . . well, everything I remembered . . . and more. You know, I'm a very serious person . . ."

No kidding, Stephanie said to herself.

" . . . and I need a little . . . gaiety in my life. To offset the . . . well, you know what I mean. And I saw her and she made me laugh and she was so fresh and delightful. I decided she was just what I needed. I even thought about marrying her. It was a wonderful evening."

Stephanie wondered if they had done it. Knowing Richard, she doubted it. Knowing Marilyn, she was sure of it.

"But then it changed."

Stephanie straightened up at this new revelation.

"I just . . . assumed . . . well, that she liked me as much as I liked her. She acted that way anyway, that Tuesday night. So I called her the next day and invited her to go out Saturday night. I was in for quite a surprise."

"Why? What did she do?"

Richard Spencer snapped his stirrer in half. "Well, she turned me down, but it was the *way* she did it."

"How?" Stephanie rocked gently in her chair. If she didn't get up this instant, she'd really have an accident. She reached down to the floor and picked up her bag, then neatly folded her napkin next to her plate.

"Doesn't really matter now, does it?" he finally said. "Tell me about *you*."

"Not now."

"Why?"

"Because I have to find the ladies' room. Quick."

Richard stood up and pushed the table out so Stephanie could hurry in the direction the waiter had pointed. She walked with her thighs very close together. It was a great relief to urinate, but the fullness was still there. She stuck her finger inside afterward. "Damn. I'm still wet." But it wasn't the same wetness that had spotted her pants. She willed herself to stop, swearing to go back and act cold toward him.

☐ 4 ☐

"How could you see her? She say she come home about five-thirty—you say you left at four-thirty. What you talking about?"

"I never thought about it. Until you kept asking me why I walked the other way. I mean, it was just something in the back of my head. Jesus, to think I never even remembered."

"Why you didn't tell police?"

"I just told you—it was only an impression—it wasn't even a thought. That's why I didn't remember."

Rosa squinted at him. "You positive, absolute sure it was her?"

"No. What I remember is, I was standing on the top step. I looked both ways, you know how you sometimes do, and I was about to go down and walk left, when I saw somebody turn the corner. No, I couldn't swear it was Stephanie. In fact, all I really saw was a red coat. She has a red coat, you know. so I automatically went down and walked the other way."

"Why you don't want to see her?"

"I don't know. We just didn't get along. I didn't have anything against her, but I always felt she had something against me. Like I could tell she didn't like me coming up to the apartment. And, God, if Marilyn and I used the bedroom, Stephanie was always a bitch after. Not that she did anything or said anything, but you could just feel it. You know, quiet hatred or something. Like she was looking down her nose at us. Or me, anyway."

"Then why you don't use your apartment if she make you feel that way?"

"What are you, a detective, a Miss Marple now?"

"*Si*. Rosalinda Donato Bassetti Marple. Don't you know?"

Pete really adored Rosa. She made him feel so . . . so comfortable. They just didn't make women like that anymore.

"I ask you 'cause cops gonna ask you and I got to know the answer, and I got to know what you gonna tell them."

"It's very simple. My apartment is awful. It's in one of those dinky old buildings on the West Side. Block isn't bad. At one time, those buildings were beautiful. Real luxury. But now . . . now, you know what they're like. Neighborhood is awful. I mean, just to walk from the car to the apartment, you gotta have eyes in back of your head. Watch out for muggers. Anyway, the place is infested, number one; number two, there are four rooms and there's hardly any furniture."

"How come?"

"Because I have no intention of staying there and I didn't want to buy anything until I knew where I was going to live. The way things turned out, I've been there longer than I expected. *I* don't mind, but Marilyn did. She hated coming over there. The only saving grace about it is you can usually find a parking spot somewhere. If I move to the East Side, I have to get rid of my car. That answer your question?"

"Yeah, but what about the other question?"

"What question?"

"What are we gonna do about it?"

"Well, if you think Stephanie did it, that's crazy."

"Course not. But if she come home and see *you* on the stoop, and she goes right up, and you don't do it, how it happen?"

"I don't know."

"If you tell police you see her . . ."

"How can I tell them I think I might've seen a red coat that *might've* been Stephanie's?"

". . . *and* if *she* see *you*, then it makes it worse for you, because there ain't time for anyone else to go up and murder her."

"So what should we do, Sherlock?"

"We have to find out if it's her."

"And how are we going to do that? Say 'Stephanie, by the way, was that you coming down the block at the time of the murder, when you were supposedly shopping at Gimbels?' Come on, we can't do that."

"You, no. Me, maybe."

"How?"

"I don't know. I'm thinking, I'm thinking."

□ 5 □

"No, he didn't actually know her in high school. Just from when he was in high school."

"Why'd you say it sounded fishy?"

"Well, at first it did. I mean it sounded strange that he would call me after learning she was dead. But he did tell me the truth. He wanted to know what the police had found out and all. Sure, he pumped me, but I don't think he's up to anything."

"If that's all he wanted, how come you're going out with him again?"

"I . . . well, I like him."

"Stephanie, I'm glad Really. I hope that you have a good time."

"So do I."

"Tell me about him."

"I did."

"Tell me what it is you find so attractive."

"I don't know. At first, I thought I felt a little sorry for him. He's I guess about twenty-nine, and hasn't had very much social life. I don't think he's dated too much. In fact, I know it, because he told me. He was very shy when he was younger. And then, when he went to school, he was always busy studying because he was on a scholarship. So he didn't have much time for girls."

"And you like that?"

"Kinda."

"Well, that's a nice switch. I truly hope it works out."

CHAPTER 13

□ 1 □

Stephanie stretched luxuriously when the alarm went off, moving her arms through the white dust striping the bed. Sunshine coming through the blinds, and it was only March! She got up reluctantly, singing out loud, washed, straightened up, and left for work. She jumped down the last two steps in the building, feeling . . . well, she could have played potsy on the sidewalk. She walked up to Lexington and joined the pilgrimage to the subway. She was out of tokens and had to wait on the long line at 77th Street. When she stuffed her dollar into the wooden cup and said "Good morning, two please," the man in the booth looked at her like she was crazy.

Actually, Richard Spencer was nice. God, if there were ever a word to describe a loser, it was *nice*. Funny, when you thought about it, he was exactly right, except she was sure she didn't want him. Right this second she did, but not forever. She'd have to go into this with Dr. Fredericks. Here she had had all these bad relationships, bad sexual experiences, and he had helped her to see they were all the same *type*. Shits, actually. She had never looked at it objectively before, she was so busy feeling sorry for herself. But she was attracted to rotten bastards. That had to be it. Screw her and leave her, I'm only interested in my own pleasure, I don't want to get involved. That type. Now, for the first time, she had met a . . . square; that was it . . . and she was attracted to him. God knows. Maybe she was growing up. Well, obviously there was something more to this than she understood right now. She'd have to tell Fredericks about it.

Every time the doors opened and more people shoved their way on to the train, newspapers folded under their arms, Stephanie said, "I'm so sorry, I didn't step on you, did I?" Everyone ignored her, probably thinking "another nut." But she didn't care.

It wouldn't be bad. She'd stay home of course and take care of the house, and just before he came home every night she'd do her hair and her nails so she'd look good for him. And she'd have candlelight every night. They'd go to her mother's, probably every other weekend. He'd sit and talk to her father and she'd help her mother serve. Annette and Fred would come and it wouldn't bother Stephanie anymore when they'd sit and whisper like little children—maybe she'd even whisper in Richard's ear. For spite. And also because she wanted to. And they'd screw every night. And she would have one every time.

She ran up the steps at Grand Central. Her legs didn't even feel tired. When the cool air hit her on 42nd Street, Stephanie inhaled deeply and started walking, skipping every few steps. Oh, it felt like spring was coming soon. She practiced writing *Stephanie Spencer* in her head. And swirling two "S's." For her notepaper.

She turned the corner of Madison Avenue and went through the revolving doors, pleasure ballooning in her chest.

□ 2 □

"Gawhead, try it."

"Okay, give it to me."

"Here, I'm going to move the other chair over, like this, lie across them. Should be about the right height, you think?"

Malcolm waited for Nick to put the two chairs together and lie down, his behind drooping to the floor.

"Okay, ready?" He held the ski pole in his two hands above Lascano's chest.

"See, you got it at an angle. I told you. You have to lift it higher, so it comes down straight." Malcolm lifted it higher, slitting his eyes to measure how straight it was.

"See, I told you, can't do it unless I don't move."

"Shut up, or I'm really going to stab you with it."

Lascano jumped up, pushed the chair back to the desk, and sat down. "You'd either have to be pretty tall, or your victim would have to be asleep. Or perfectly motionless. Not *or*. *And*."

"Okay. So if she's asleep, how did the guy get in without waking her?"

"If it was the boyfriend, he was already there. They had sex, he said that, she coulda been asleep, or just lying there with her eyes closed."

"Suppose it's not him. Who would be there and she would go to sleep in front of them?"

"Has to be something else. Okay, she's lying there, not moving, and he—whoever—picks up the ski pole and jabs it in her chest. After the first thrust, she's probably unconscious, so she wouldn't move *after* that, and he could keep on doing it. Maybe at a little angle. But we *know* the first one was straight."

"Suppose she's standing up, facing him, and he stabs it in—he'd get a better grip on it anyway, at that level, and then she falls down on the bed?"

"Look," Malcolm rubbed his eyes. "I can't think about it any more today. That's what's wrong—we're thinking too hard. Can't see it."

"Maybe you're right. Let's go get a bite."

"Can't. Have to go get Lydia a birthday present. Wanna hop down to Lord & Taylor's."

"Whatdya have to go all the way down there?" Nick asked, blowing smoke rings up to the ceiling.

Malcolm shrugged. "I don't know—it's just something that started a long time ago. I always buy her something at Lord & Taylor."

"Pretty steep prices."

"Well, it's for something special. You know, she even saves the boxes, year after year. She says it always makes her *feel* special getting something from there."

113

"Okay, I'm gonna run down and get something to eat."
Malcolm stood up and stretched. "Well, I guess I'll go with
you. I'm too tired to go down there today. I have time yet.
Two weeks."

"Okay," Lascano said, stubbing out his cigarette, "let's go."

□ 3 □

Rosa stuck her nail under one of the tiny multicolored ici-
cles on the window—fifty years of paint drippings. No use.
She sat down and rocked, rubbing Princess's neck. "Ah, we
could sure use a paint job. It must be, what, eight years?
Maybe we ask Vilma's son. No, he done enough already. Her
too. Maybe a roller would cover that." She studied the
fleurettes of hardened paint on the walls. "Mmm, wouldn't be
too bad. Hector help me. And Pete, I bet if I ask him, he
help too. Eh, baby?" Rosa put her heels on the floor, held the
arms of the chair, and twisted it a little more so she could see
out the window better.

"What we gonna do, sweet Princess?" They just didn't
seem to be getting anywhere. It was a week, more, already,
since she even saw them around. Heard anything. Maybe
she'd call that Lascano. Ah, he was a busy man.

"Let's go next door, baby." She went across the hall. Vilma
was surprised to see her at this hour. Rosa plopped down.
"Restless, Vilma, restless. Something funny I feel—like something should be *happening*. Now, now, don't go getting upset." Rosa walked over to the wheelchair and put her hands
on Mrs. Karlmeier's shoulders to calm her. Vilma's eyes were
staring downward, as if she were watching the grotesque
shape of her lips form vowel sounds as she tried to talk.

"You safe, nobody can get in here." Rosa pointed to the
three locks on the door, trying to reassure her. "Besides," she
said cheerfully, "who wanna murder—or rape—two old
broads like us?"

114

□ 4 □

"Maybe you were jealous of her?"

"That's absurd. Why would I be? Boy, I thought you really knew me! I didn't like the way she lived. I wouldn't have traded places with her for anything. I couldn't stand a lot of the things she did. Like being so lackadaisical about things. She was a real scatterbrain—everybody knew that. Having that guy and supposedly being in love with him and screwing around with other men. And you think I was jealous of her? Marilyn never did things for people, unless she damned well wanted to. Never lifted a finger. I'm always doing things to help out and . . ."

"Wait a minute. We've talked about that before. Why do you?"

"Do what?"

"Do things for people?"

"I guess because . . . I feel obligated to. Even when I don't want to. Deep down, I guess I don't want to, but I feel I have to. The thing is, I know people liked her anyway, sometimes better than me. I mean, they think I'm a good person. I don't mean Marilyn was a bad person. But I think people liked her better. Even if she didn't go out of her way for them."

"Doesn't that tell you something?"

"Like what?"

"Like people like you just as much when you think of yourself, when you do what you want to do, when it's good for you."

"I don't know. But I wasn't jealous. She was always doing physical things. I mean, I envied her a little for that. She was so free and easy with her body. Like in sex. She went skiing with him all the time. And bowling. Things like that."

"Why did you envy her?"

115

"I never do anything like that."

"Why not?"

"Too stiff. My arms and legs are like steel. Don't bend. I know why, too. Because I don't want people looking at me. I feel stupid. Awkward. I can't picture myself running with a big black ball, or swinging a club up in the air on a golf course. Or coming down a hill, feeling free as the wind, not caring what I look like, what other people see. No, I wasn't jealous of her. Well, maybe a few things."

"Look at it this way. Here we have an inhibited, uptight person—think about it—who has to do everything because she thinks it's expected of her, not because she wants to—and she's lonely, unhappy, depressed. Wait a minute. You always ask me to talk and now that I am, you want me to stop.

"On the other hand, there's a girl with the same sort of background, the same kind of environment and education, who's uninhibited, free, confident in herself, and she's always doing things the other one doesn't approve of—and maybe they're not nice things, maybe she doesn't go out of her way to worry what other people think of her—but the big difference is: she enjoys herself. Or tries to. And you don't, Stephanie. Maybe jealous was the wrong word to use. What I mean is you try so hard all the time, and where does it get you? You're not any happier. You only make yourself more unhappy. Marilyn only cared about herself, in your eyes, only worried about Marilyn, only did things that Marilyn wanted to do. And maybe, even though she was all the things you despise and loathe, maybe she was also the things you want to be, and don't know how.

"Stephanie, do you want a tissue?"

CHAPTER 14

□ 1 □

Rosa fed Princess beef stew. Then she wet a washrag and wiped her muzzle off. "My little *bambina,* look how sloppy you are. You like Mama's stew?" She spooned the rest of it from the pot into a bowl, left her door open on a crack, and went in to Mrs. Karlmeier's.

"Sorry, Vilma, we're a little early tonight." She put the bowl on the table, walked into Vilma's kitchen for the silverware, and set it down for her. "Come on, *cara,* supper's ready." She went over to the window, pulled it up, and stuck her head all the way out. She looked both ways. Nobody.

"That's it!" she sang as Mrs. Karlmeier slowly rolled herself over. Rosa pulled up the bridge chair, dipped the spoon in the stew, and put it in Mrs. Karlmeier's mouth. "You looking good, dear. Tomorrow maybe we wash your hair and set it a little. Make you *bella, bella.*" After two more spoons, she got up and went to the window again. "Oh, Vilma, sorry I ain't got much time lately for you, but there are things going on around here. You know that nice boyfriend of Marilyn Wechsler? Well, we been talking. What's that?"

Mrs. Karlmeier made a lot of oohing and aahing sounds. "No, no, he not do it. I try to help him find out who did. Now, easy, you gonna choke. Nothing gonna happen to old Rosalinda." She got up again and went to the window. "Listen, dear, I hafta go for a minute. I just put this over your bowl and keep it hot. Be back in a second. Princess, you stay here and keep Vilma company."

"Hi, Rosa," Stephanie said, coming in through the front door.

"Stephanie, you scare me, I'm just on my way across for supper."

"Where is it?" Stephanie looked at her empty hands.

"What?"

"Supper."

"Oh, I bring it in before. I'm just gonna go back to warm it up and give it to her. Then I come home and eat myself. Going out?"

"No." Stephanie was having trouble turning the mailbox key.

"Here, I hold for you," Rosa offered, taking the tote out of Stephanie's hands.

"Thanks. I'm just gonna wash my hair and do my nails. Relax."

"Why you don't come down? I got some stew."

"No, thanks, I'm really tired."

"I tell you what. Why you don't wash your hair and then come down and we have a glass of wine."

"Rosa, I really appreciate it, but I just want to stay home."

"Sure, nobody want to spend time with an old woman." Rosa's voice cracked.

"It's not that. Come on, Rosa, you know you're good company, it's just that . . ."

"If I'm such good company, why you not keep me company then? We can have some wine and talk a little and . . ."

"Oh, all right. But I'm going to eat first, and then I'm going to wash my hair. And I have to condition it. So it will be a while." Stephanie walked up the stairs.

Rosa closed her door and went back to Mrs. Karlmeier. She took the plate off the bowl and continued feeding her.

"So now I got her. But what I gonna say to her, eh? Oh, don't look scared. It's only Stephanie. See, we think she know something. I'm just gonna try t'find . . . Whassamatta, you're not hungry tonight? Princess eat like a good girl. Okay, we save the rest for lunch maybe. Now, I just help you into the chair. I put it on Channel 11, and then you don't have to change it for 'The Odd Couple.' Here, I leave the thing next to your left hand, right here, so you can push the button to turn it off when you want. I come back later. Come, baby, we go home. And don't be scared. You're safe."

□ 2 □

"*What would happen if something was moved in one of your drawers, out of its place?*"

"*It would drive me crazy. That's why I have to clean them out every week.*"

"*But the way you described it to me, if you keep them so neat, they don't have to be cleaned out every week.*"

"*I know they don't. But it's a part of the thing—I have to take everything out, wash the drawer, refold everything, and put it back.*"

"*Do you see that it's not so much a compulsion to be clean and neat, as it is the need for a ritual? It's ritualistic behavior.*"

"*Right. I just thought of something. When I make my list of things to clean, I have to do them all in precise order. I mean I couldn't clean the kitchen first if the bedroom was number one. I have to follow it exactly. That is a ritual.*"

"*Let me ask you something else. What would you do if you didn't clean your drawers, let's say on Saturday?*"

"*What do you mean?*"

"*Well, it must take—how much time does it take you to do all this?*"

"*Oh, the drawers and the cleaning, about four hours from start to finish.*"

"*Okay, if you didn't have to spend four hours—let's say you had a fairy godmother who came in and did it for you—what would you do with those four hours?*"

"*I never thought about it. I suppose I'd . . . go to a movie or something, or call somebody. I don't know.*"

"*Aha, maybe you'd have to do something with your life.*"

119

□ 3 □

Lydia came out of the bathroom, looked over at the bed, and then tiptoed around to his side to turn out the light and take the book out of his drooping hand. She wished there were something she could do to help him. He was always moody when he was deeply involved in an investigation, but something was really getting him down.

He was completely distracted lately. He nodded his head when she talked, but she knew damned well he didn't hear a thing she'd been saying the last couple of weeks. He was working late and on weekends—they hadn't even been to a movie—and he looked exhausted.

If only he'd sleep better at night. But he constantly tossed and turned. The inconsequential thing he couldn't remember was always on the verge of consciousness, he had told her, but as soon as he got close to seeing it, it melted again.

She kissed his forehead and whispered, "G'night, sweetheart." Then she turned out her own light, threw her leg over his, and went to sleep.

□ 4 □

"Whod'ya think was taking her things?"

Stephanie jerked her hand and spread the polish all over her cuticle. "What things?"

"You know, the earring and the glove and the record . . ."

"Oh, she told you about that. I don't know. I think she was hiding the stuff so she'd have something to talk about."

"C'mon, that's bullshit. I think it really happened."

"Well, don't make a big thing of it, Rosa. Like she did. It wasn't as if it all disappeared at once. I mean, there were only a handful of things over a period of weeks."

"Yeah, but they bug her. Maybe Pete take them."

"Pete? For God's sake, why would he do that?"

"Why he would kill her?"

Stephanie didn't answer, but concentrated on the second coat, her tongue sticking out of the corner of her mouth.

"You think he did it?" Rosa asked, her heart fluttering. Maybe she shouldn't push. Maybe the whole thing was so stupid, an old woman trying to solve a murder. She should just let the police . . .

"If he didn't, who did?"

"He's such a nice boy. And I think he really love Marilyn."

"People do strange things in the name of love."

"But why?"

Stephanie acted smug and wiped the tip of the last nail off. "I just know what I think. Maybe he didn't like her fooling around so much. I mean she was sleeping around, did she tell you that?"

Rosa pretended to be shocked. "Marilyn was?"

"She sure was. And with guys she had just picked up, too."

"I can't believe it. I thought she was a nice girl." Rosa knew about some of Marilyn's dates because she used to tell her things . . . things, she said, she couldn't tell her friends. But Rosa understood. And listened with rapt attention and excitement. And a little pang of envy.

"Let's not talk about her anymore. It depresses me."

"Okay, I get the bottle." Rosa stood and reached over to pour some more wine into Stephanie's glass. Now what? "That's a pretty color."

"Thanks, it's Marilyn's." Stephanie capped the bottle and wrapped cotton around an orange stick. She dipped it into the remover and diligently wiped her cuticles. She looked up and said, "Her mother told me I could keep it. That, and the other cosmetics and things."

"Oh. I always say *you* oughtta wear more makeup. You're so pretty, you look beautiful with a lot of eye stuff on."

"Marilyn wore a lot of makeup. I thought it made her look cheap. I wear it, you know, but I put it on so faint everybody thinks I don't wear any."

"You do such a good job. I think you got nothing on."

"Oh, I don't *now*. But usually. You really think so, that I should do up my eyes more?"

"You got beautiful eyes—makeup only make them more beautiful."

"Thank you. As a matter of fact, I stopped in at Gimbels on my way home tonight and I bought a new shadow. I'm going to try it tomorrow."

"Gimbels? Didn't you say you're at Gimbels same time Marilyn is . . . being murdered?" As she said it, Rose felt her stomach lurch.

"I bought a sweater." Stephanie shook her head back and forth. "Of all nights to stop and go shopping. If I had come right home, maybe . . . maybe nothing would have happened to Marilyn." Stephanie waved her hands in the air, blowing on her nails.

"Why you feel guilty about that? Who knows? Who knows, maybe if you're home, you *both* get killed."

"Why would Pete kill me too?"

"If it ain't him, I mean. If it's some lunatic. Maybe you don't even know you see something important. We gotta help him."

"Why?"

"Why? Because I don't think he did it. Now, just for five minutes, we think hard about it. Please."

"Well, I don't see why . . . oh, all right."

"Now, what time you leave your office?"

"What the hell does that have to do with anything?"

"Nothing," Rosa's back froze, "but, but, but maybe somebody is watching you, you know, so they can get her. If they not expecting you, they musta known where you are and since maybe you come from work a little early, maybe somebody follows you or something to see what you gonna do, and . . ."

"Oh, Rosa, are you serious? That's absurd."

"Maybe." Well, at least she wasn't angry about it. But

don't push too hard. "C'mon, let's just see. You leave work at, what, five?"

"No, I got off at four. They let us go a little early for the weekend."

"Aha, how long it take you to get home?"

"About twenty minutes, half an hour."

"You come right home?"

"How could I? Then I would've come home just at that time. When she was being killed. No, I went to Gimbels."

"You not tired, after work? I mean, maybe you should come home first, relax, change, *then* go shopping."

"Rosa, what the hell is this, you sound like a cop. I think you're drunk, you've had too much wine."

"Maybe, maybe," Rosa leaned back, exaggerating her tipsiness. "So, talk to drunken old lady, okay?"

CHAPTER 15

□ 1 □

Stephanie decided on the black dress. He probably didn't like women in pants. She smiled at herself, aware that she was trying to please someone else again. If Marilyn wanted to wear a bikini to the movies, damn it she would, and she wouldn't give a shit if the whole balcony stood and stared. Why did she have to do what she thought would please him? What the hell, she liked the black dress anyway.

It just went to show you how things could change if you had an open mind. Another gold star. She really hated him at first. But, by the end of the evening, after they stopped into Maxwell's for a drink, he loosened up. And so did she. She was pretty relaxed. A real occasion for her. Who knows, maybe something would work out. God, her mother would die if Stephanie said, "Mom, I've been seeing someone. Well, you couldn't exactly call it that, we've only had two dates, including tonight. But, Mom, I like him." She would faint. And then she'd call her sister and her aunt and half of her friends and say, "Stephanie found someone. I think it's serious." After the third date, she'd start checking her address book for the invitation list. Well, she'd never tell her anyway.

The other night they had sat on bar stools facing one another. The stools were close because it was so crowded, and her heels were hooked onto the rung of his, her knees between his. He leaned over to get the bartender, and their thighs had touched. Jeez, it sounded like a Victorian novel— "They touched." But an exciting shiver traveled up her thighs to her groin to her stomach—all the way up until the roots of her hair tickled. She wanted him to touch her. Was dying for him to put his hand on her.

When they left, he called a cab. She had swung her legs on the other side of the hump in the floor to avoid touching him. He had pulled her arm under his, her gloved hand resting lightly under his fingers. Every time the taxi bounced over a pothole or hit the brake, his elbow dented her breast. Excruciating want twisted in the pit of her stomach. She looked out her window, hypnotized by the blur of neon. She watched the upcoming street signs—72nd Street, 73rd Street, 74th Street—counting between the numbers. The swish of tires on the wet pavement lulled her. The taxi swerved sharply into 81st Street, so the driver could go around the one-way block.

When she unlocked the downstairs door, her heart squeezed in her chest. He said, "G'night, Steffie," kissed her forehead, and ran out. Can you believe that? Didn't even try anything. She wouldn't have, anyway. Oh, who was she kidding? Of course she would've. The urge was like gravity, pulling her insides down to her groin, and the weight was unbearable. She could feel her muscles down there making little sucking motions. Like a fish's mouth.

She had stayed awake half the night, thinking about him, and what it would be like. Of course he would call her again. He knew that she was ready and, even if he was sorta square, he couldn't be *that* square. He'd certainly want to.

Lying in bed, naked—she had never been able to do *that* before—her skin was all tingly, her pores oozing with the warm liquid her body couldn't contain. She imagined what it would be like. It was the same as always, except this time the nameless, faceless phantom of her daydreams was Richard Spencer.

His lips would softly touch her, her face, her neck, her shoulders. They would move down her chest, lightly brushing her skin. In the dark, she could see her nipples tighten up in anticipation of his mouth's slow, maddening descent.

His tongue would lick the skin between her navel and her groin. There was a fine line of golden hair there. She had thought of shaving it off once because she didn't think anybody else had it—at least not the girls on the beach. But, no, she wouldn't mind if he saw it, licked it even. Thinking about it, the pulsing inside became so great, both in the daydream and the dreaming of it, that Stephanie spread her legs.

She glided her finger up her thigh, imagining his tongue, and back down, and then up from the knee, on the outside. Goose pimples popped up all over. She put her finger, hardly touching, on the outside of her lips. Like a feather. Something was contracting, trying to grab it, pull it in. Somehow her burning lips parted by themselves. His tongue would be there, not moving, just teasing her, and the warm breath blowing between her legs made her jerk her hips off the bed, her heels pressing into the mattress. Her clitoris, so big now, would be sticking outside, looking for the tongue. Stephanie could feel her eyes closing with the lids still open. She put her finger inside, very slowly. It was so wet and creamy and thick. Barely touching, she made light circles, and then her finger moved faster in smaller circles. And faster. And smaller. And it started to hurt. She was getting dry. She made a bubble behind her teeth and put three fingers in her mouth; dripping with saliva, she put them back inside and kept rubbing. Harder. Faster.

Her belly was like a yo-yo, wound up into a disk, plunging, springing back. The tension of the string as it dropped and rewound, dropped and rewound, made her think it would snap and her guts would cut loose and surge out of her. It fell shorter and faster, in a dizzying motion. Her blood raced, became rapids swirling in her ears. Her heart hammered against her ribs. Her nerves were electrified, pulling the current from her skin, her muscles, her fingertips, until the fuse was going to explode. Draining her head.

All of a sudden, everything was gone. Stephanie pulled the blanket up to her neck and listened while her heart throbbed in her head. "Bet he could make me do it," she dared the darkness. A tear slid out of the corner of her eye, before she turned over and went to sleep.

Remembering now, Stephanie smiled at the mirror and rolled the mascara brush upward. "*Bet* he can!"

□ 2 □

Lascano was hungry. He looked at his watch. Eight-thirty. He could be home by nine, have some eggs or a sandwich. Hell, she'd come into the kitchen and insist on cooking something, force him to eat a six-course meal. And he'd want a cigarette with his coffee. It he had it, she'd start in again— "Don't you care about me, why are you doing this to me" routine. If he *didn't* have one, he'd do it to her.

He headed toward Lexington Avenue, where he knew the coffee shop would be open twenty-four hours. He was waiting for the light when he saw the old dame strolling along with her dog. All of a sudden, Nick didn't want to eat alone. In fact, he just didn't want to be alone. He didn't have to walk too fast to catch up with her. "Mrs. Bassetti, Mrs. Bassetti."

Rosa stopped and turned. "Lieuten, how you?" Without waiting for an answer, she patted his cheek and made *tch tch* noises with her tongue. "They don't let you go home for sleep? Look at you, pale, bags under eyes." Just like a mother. His mother. Not like Cynthia—"What are you trying to do, Nick, kill yourself? You want to make me a widow?" As if he was deliberately doing it. For spite.

"Hey, Mrs. Bassetti, how about a cup of coffee? I haven't eaten and I'm dying for some eggs. Keep me company?"

"Oh, hey, I like to, but I got Princess with me, can't go into restaurant. Come, you come home with me. I make you eggs. And bacon."

Nick Lascano felt like a schoolkid caught socializing with the teacher. "Thanks, but I couldn't do that."

"Why, you break a law?"

"No, but you know . . ." He smiled sheepishly.

"Aha, you don't come with me, 'cause I'm a *sus*pect."

For the first time in days, Nick laughed. "Tell you what, Mrs. Bassetti. I'm going to take you up on that. Yessir. I'm going to go home with you. Only I hope nobody from the precinct is on the East Side tonight."

"Lieuten, shame. You have unhonorable intentions, eh?"

Lascano strolled the two blocks with Rosa. In between chattering to him, she talked to Princess, including her in the conversation. When they got into her apartment, Rosa bustled around, moving the newspaper off the couch, hitting the cushions. "Just throw it on the bed," she said, meaning his coat. She went into the kitchen. "Now, let's see," she talked into the refrigerator, picking up containers and smelling foil packages. "I have a nice piece Italian salami, I make you a sandwich, or . . ."

"You got eggs?"

"Sure I got eggs. And bacon. You really want eggs, you get eggs. How you like 'em?"

"Scrambled."

Rosa walked back into the living room. Lascano was sitting in her chair. "Now you look," she said, dragging over the ottoman with the fluff hanging out, "you get comf'ble and relax while I fix." She lifted his foot up to slide the ottoman under his legs. "I bring you glass of chianti, you close your eyes five minutes—you look like you don't sleep for days—and then you get your eggs."

Nick leaned back. "Boy, this is relaxing, Miss Bassetti."

"Rosa. Everyone call me Rosa. Unless I'm *suspect*."

"Okay, Rosa. If you're anything, you're a witness, not a suspect."

"Same thing," she called in, banging doors open. He could hear the bacon sizzling on the stove.

"Dear Josie," Rosa composed the letter that had been in her head for months, "I'm like a princess in my own way. Not like you, with the big villa, but sorta queen of my block. Eighty-second Street. Everybody knows Rosalinda, Josie. Tonight, a nice lieuten—from the police—come for supper. And there's this young boy Pete—he come over the other night. See, Josie, in my old age I'm popular. Oh, I like to see you and my nieces and nephew, and the grandnieces and grandnephews and the new baby but, Josefina, I miss it here already."

While the butter was melting in the pan, Rosa pulled the

bridge chair over to the cabinet and stood on it to reach for one of the Chambord plates. She set the table for him, scrambled his eggs, and carried everything inside.

"Perfect," Nick complimented the chef.

Rosa pulled the bridge chair with the wobbly leg over and sat opposite him, glad he was enjoying his supper. *Thank God I blow myself to some bacon. Princess, baby, I'm sorry, I just give away your breakfast, but he's enjoying so much,* she thought to herself.

"So how's it going, the murder?"

"So-so." Nick crunched his toast. "Actually, we don't seem to be getting anywhere. Except dead ends."

"Lieuten . . ."

"I'm not a lieutenant, you know. Call me Nick. Nicky. That's what my mother used to call me. And my wife."

"Okay. Nicky . . ."

"My first wife, that is."

"You divorced?"

"Uh-uh," he said, blowing on the bacon. "Widowed. But now I'm remarried."

"Nice. How long?"

"How long what?"

"How long you're a widow before you get married, and how long you married?"

"Hey, I'm the policeman here. My wife, she died six years ago. We were childhood sweethearts, we were, had a beautiful marriage. Sometimes I'm sorry now. I think about the times—especially when I was young and new on the force—that I left her alone, didn't show up for dinner, couldn't make it to a party . . . you know. But I never expected . . . I guess nobody ever does . . . that she'd get sick and I'd lose her. I wish I could make it up to her."

Rosa walked over and stood behind Nick. She put her hands on either side of his head and rocked it back and forth. "What do you know? She love you, no? You make her happy woman, Lieuten, Nicky, because she love you and she know you love her. Now, you gonna feel guilty and make that poor woman sorry in Heaven?"

Nick grabbed Rosa's wrist and held it for a minute. "You're something else, you know that?" That was it. He really never gave Cynthia a chance. He just realized it. Always thinking about *her,* comparing them. Trouble was, Cynthia didn't know he loved her. He never gave her a chance to find out.

Flushed with pleasure, Rosa bustled about, clearing his dirty dishes. When she cupped her hand under the edge and wiped the rag across the table, Nick thought of his mother. Of their big square kitchen. Of oilcloths—whatever happened to them? Of his small arms outstretched while she wrapped a skein of yarn across them and rolled it into a ball. Of how he used to sit at their yellow enamel table and break string beans into a bowl.

Rosa brought in an old aluminun percolator and two mugs. While she poured, she talked. "You know, Nicky, I got something to say about the murder. Now I ain't in the police station, and you ain't here 'ficial, so what I say is not for police but just, you know, social. Okay?"

Surprised, Lascano nodded his agreement and pulled the ashtray over to him.

"Well, *paesano,*" Rosa leaned back, warming her palm against the mug, "it's like this."

□ 3 □

"She borrowed things. I hated that. I wouldn't have minded if she asked me—God, I would've given her anything at all. But it was the fact that she didn't ask. It was like she'd come home and there she'd be, standing in my coat, or wearing my scarf, or jewelry. And I'd seethe. And in her . . . you know, happy-go-lucky way . . . she'd say, 'I hope you don't mind, I borrowed this, but you had already left and I couldn't ask you.' And she'd give it back, without washing it, whatever it was. I mean how would you like to wear something that had been on somebody else's body?"

"I suppose it depends on what it is. Surely, underwear

would be offensive, but you wouldn't expect her to have your coat cleaned, would you?"

"No. I didn't expect her to do anything. It wasn't so much that she took something, I think, but the fact that she was in my drawer or closet, at least my half of it. Like she was violating my privacy. Sometimes, before she came home, I . . . well, I have this habit of looking in my drawers, you know, just for the sake of looking, and I can tell instantly when something's gone, or moved a drop. That's what kills me."

"Stephanie, do you ever think that maybe there's a relationship between your drawers and your . . . mind?"

"What are you talking about?"

"Think about it. As soon as somebody gets close to you, you say you get turned off, and you don't know why. And it's the same thing with your drawers—if anybody goes near them you get very upset."

"I don't think that means anything. Maybe it's just . . . well, I like things to be in order and I don't want anybody seeing anything, like my drawers, if they're not just right. Oh, I think I'm getting it now. I don't like anybody seeing me unless I feel it's just right."

"Good. But when they—your drawers—are just right, what would happen if somebody opened one?"

"I'd probably go crazy. But what has that got to do with my mind?"

"That's what I'm asking you."

"Maybe I don't like people to see it . . . oh, I don't know what it is, I don't like them to see my drawers, unless I'm watching them do it. Same thing with my emotions. Like, I have to be prepared so I know what they're seeing when they're seeing it."

"So you don't want anybody to look inside you unless you're aware they're doing it, so you can organize everything just so. In other words, you change when you think someone's looking."

"I don't know. I don't want to talk about it."

"Okay. But I want you to think about this. I think we're getting close to something, and you immediately put up this guard. What is it you don't want me to see, or anybody else?"

"I don't know."

132

"Do you understand what I'm saying?"

"Yes."

"If you carry it a little further, think about this. You don't want to look inside. As soon as you think you're getting close to seeing yourself, you turn away. Okay, enough."

"I think you must be right. It's like for the first time something just clicked in my head when you said that. Yes, I think that might be it. I don't want to see."

"What terrible thing do you suppose you're hiding from yourself, what terrible thing that you can't face?"

"I don't know. Do you know what it is?"

"I can only guess."

"Please don't do that, Doctor Fredericks. Please, if you know, tell me."

It's you, Stephanie. You're afraid to look at yourself."

"But why?"

"Why? That's what I'm asking you."

"I haven't the vaguest idea."

"Maybe you think if you really see yourself, you won't like what you see."

☐ 4 ☐

Marianne Webster came back from the laundromat. She opened the door and stopped dead. He was standing in the living room, shaved, washed, and dressed. "Hi," he said, and smiled at her. She nodded and walked inside to dump the pillow case on the bed. The clean wash sprawled out and she picked through the tumble of terry and nylon, folding and smoothing.

"You've been busy."

"Uh huh."

"I thought maybe you'd like to go out later."

She turned around to make sure this was her husband talking to her. "Go out where?"

133

"Maybe to a movie. Or a walk. We could go look in store windows on Fifth Avenue. Whatever you'd like."

"Anything would be nice."

"When will you be ready?"

"I just have to change and comb my hair." She was afraid to look at him, afraid he would disappear into another stupor.

"Want me to help?"

"That's okay, thanks. How about some coffee, and I'll check to see what's playing."

"I'll put it up while you finish," he offered.

She put the laundry away and went into the kitchen. He was spooning the brown gravel into mugs. He set them on the table, poured the boiling water, got out the milk, smiling at her all the while.

"So, you're looking good," she said. Don't screw it up, she warned herself, don't be cute, don't be nasty.

"I feel good. For a change. Mar . . . I'm sorry."

"Let's not talk about it. Let's just enjoy today."

Relieved, he sat down. "What's happening at the office?"

"Oh, nothing too much. Marcia left to have her baby. We all took her out to lunch yesterday, and gave her a little shower. You know, baby presents. And Mr. Coleman is being transferred and . . ." Her words poured out, trying to keep him in touch with her life for the past few weeks.

He sipped his coffee, and listened. While she was gabbing, he got up, took the stack of mail off the toaster, and pulled out the *Cue* magazine from the middle of the pile. "Here, you look, whatever you want to see is okay with me."

She found the page and started reading out loud. "We could go to Eighty-sixth Street, if you don't want to go too far . . . there's a war movie . . . or we could go to the Baronet—and, hey, we could make a real Saturday of it, go to Bloomingdale's first, and then maybe stop in for a bite or, if you want . . ."

"What's this? Another bill from Con Ed? Jeez, did you see the electric this month?"

"No, I haven't opened the mail. For a while. How much is it?"

"Thirty-two bucks. For what? And what's this?" His fingernail ripped under the flap of the phone bill. "Not too bad. Who've you been talking to?"

"Myself, mostly," she said, regretting it the minute the words were out. He didn't hear her anyway. He had all the envelopes upside down for easy slitting. He pulled the yellow sheets out of the square envelope and started to read.

"There's something good down on Thirty-fourth Street—I don't suppose you'd like to take the bus to . . ."

"What the hell. . . ?"

Marianne looked up at the letter. "Who's that from?"

"Damned if I know." Her husband turned the envelope over. "Shit, it's not for us. See, it's M. *Wechs*ler."

"Lemme see."

He handed it over to her. "Ohmygod, it's hers, I mean it's from her and it came back, the one upstairs, the one that got murdered."

"Murdered?"

"The young girl upstairs, I *told* you about it, they found her all cut up and raped, I hear it was horrible, and she wrote this letter a couple of days before and it's the wrong address and it came back and we got it by mistake."

"What does it say?"

"I'm not going to read it. Are you crazy? That's sick. Reading something personal—that a dead girl wrote to her friend."

"Well, how do you know if it's important if you don't know what it says?"

"Doesn't matter."

"Well, you should give it to the police."

"That's dumb. Maybe it just says hello, how are you, I am fine, it is raining here, and what good is that going to do?"

"Well, let them worry about it."

"So they can come around and ask more questions and ask why we opened it in the first place?"

"Well, for God's sake, you could just take a quick look and see if she *said* anything."

"No, I won't. And you're not going to either." Marianne folded the letter and put it back in the envelope.

"Well, Miss Holier-Than-Thou, wouldn't look at anything personal, would you? It's okay you go through all my things

135

all the time—don't look at me like that, I know you do." He was raising his voice now. They'd start a fight, and then he'd storm out and start drinking all over again and come home God knows when and in God knows what condition. And fuck the movie.

This was their last chance. Her last chance. She wasn't going to start up with him now. "Okay, if you really want, if it means that much to you, I'll read it," she said quietly, and took the letter out of the envelope again. When she was through, she handed it to him. As he put it in the envelope he said, "We'll take care of it later. Now, what are we going to see?"

"Aren't you going to read it, now that you made me?"

"No, sweet. Just take it to the police on Monday."

"We shouldn't get involved in something that doesn't concern us."

"Doesn't concern us? Murder concerns everyone. Boy, you're a real good citizen. Look at what happened a few years back when that Kitty Someone was murdered in Queens and she was fighting off the guy and yelling, and everyone looking out their windows and nobody wanted to get involved and call the police."

"What difference does it make? The girl's dead anyway." That's all she needed, having the police come around, when he was out of it. And he would be. How many more people would find out? It was humiliating. "Do you want to sit here and argue about a stupid letter or do you want to go to a movie?" Marianne slammed the *Cue* down and walked out.

"Goddamn," her husband said. Bending down, he stretched his arm all the way back between the refrigerator and the wall. Ignoring the avalanche of brown paper bags that fell on him, he reached for his bottle.

CHAPTER 16

□ 1 □

Stephanie hooked her arm through Richard's when she met him in front of the house. She felt good. Rosa was watching, of course, so Stephanie had to introduce them. It was the only polite thing to do. As they walked to the corner, she leaned toward him, deliberately grazing her breast against his elbow.

"That's what I like, a fast walker," he said.

"Everybody always complains that I'm way ahead of them."

"You're not ahead of me. Not many girls can keep up."

"Well, that's *one* thing we have in common."

"More than that." Richard squeezed her arm, pushing his elbow against her.

At least he took her to nice places, she thought, and smiled as the headwaiter pushed in her chair. Stephanie looked at the menu and said, "Wow."

"Now don't worry about the prices, have anything you want," Richard said.

They had their drinks and talked. Stephanie flushed with the warm joy flooding through her. She knew she was quivering. She decided to have something light, so there wouldn't be any problem with her stomach. And then she wouldn't feel full and bloated. She'd skip the coffee too, maybe have tea, and then suggest they go back to her apartment. She had practically sterilized it, it was that clean.

When the food came, after their second drink, Stephanie pushed the filet of sole around her plate. She hated fish, but it wasn't heavy, and she didn't want to order the most expensive thing on the menu anyway. She had asked for the sauce almondine, or whatever it was. It sounded like it would disguise the fish, but she wished she had something to mask the taste of the sauce. She took dainty little bites, and chewed very thoroughly. Filet of sole wasn't supposed to have bones, but you never could tell. All the time she was eating, the delicious smell of Richard's steak made her mouth water.

She was relieved when the waiter cleared the dishes and brought cups. She poured water from the silver pot, and tried to act sophisticated dunking the bag in it. Why did expensive restaurants serve everything so nicely, except for tea? They had a nerve, charging a dollar for a Lipton tea bag and some boiling water.

"You know, Stephanie," Richard said between sips of his coffee. "I'm glad I found you." Stephanie's cheeks were burning. "I think we're . . . good for each other. That was the thing with Marilyn. I liked her, but I knew she wasn't right for me."

"I know. I've always had that feeling with other men I've known." Or is it, she thought to herself, that you're *right* for me, but I don't really like you?

"Have you known a lot?"

"A fair amount." She tilted her head, hoping she looked coy.

"Have you been intimate with them?"

"Not really." She squirmed in the leather banquette. "Once or twice," she lied.

He seemed disappointed in her.

"You know, I'm twenty-four, and that's not so bad, two men."

"I didn't say anything."

"But I think you were thinking it."

"It's none of my business anyway."

God, she thought, I want it to *be* your business. I want you to take care of me, I want to belong to you, so I never have to do that again. A scene unrolled on the inside of her eyelids and she watched herself crying afterward and telling him how beautiful it was and how awful it had been before. And his stroking her hair and saying, "You're mine now, I'll never let that happen to you again."

Stephanie watched him write in the tip, and was glad it was generous. It was a very fancy place. He stared at her until the waiter came back with his card. She studied the hem of her napkin as she rolled it back and forth to avoid looking at him. So he wouldn't see the desire in her eyes. And her nervousness.

While the hatcheck girl was passing the coats to Richard, Stephanie slipped a little can out of her bag, removed the cap, and covered it with her fingers. He helped her on with her coat. When he put his on, she quickly moved her hand as if to stifle a yawn, and sprayed her mouth.

When they got out of the cab, she didn't actually invite him to come up—it was understood between them. She didn't even mind that he didn't look around the apartment, didn't notice the pretty guest towels she had hung up, or the fresh daisies in the living room. As soon as they got inside, he put his arms around her. She fell against him, her skin on fire. Every part of her was bursting with a givingness she couldn't contain. And couldn't release. He guided her to the bedroom, and pushed her back on the bed.

She sat up, and moved to the edge. "Oh, Richard, we shouldn't."

"Why not?"

"Because."

"Because why?"

"It's not right. I hardly know you."

"C'mon, Stephanie, you want to as much as I do." He started to unbutton his shirt.

"That's not a reason."

"It's all the reason you need."

"Well, anyway, I'm not on the pill."

"Jesus. How come?"

She shrugged in the dark. How come? Then she'd be prepared. As if she *expected* to do it. *Wanted* to.

"It's okay. Trust me." He took off his shirt and stood up, opening the hook of his trousers.

Stephanie wondered if she should wait or take off her clothes. She was embarrassed, but it didn't look like he was going to undress her. Anyway, she was afraid there was a dampness in the crotch of her pants, and she wouldn't want

139

him to see that. She turned out the light and pulled her dress off, wondering if he could see her body in the dark. She hoped not.

He fell on top of her and shoved his tongue in her mouth. In and out, in and out, until she couldn't breathe. She twisted her head to the side and took a deep gulp of air. His head slid down, and she could see the silhouette of her nipples standing straight out. Then he bit the tip of one and she waited. She gently pushed his face away. He touched her. He kneaded her breasts, his nails digging into the skin. "Steffie, Steffie, I need you." His words were coming out in little staccato sobs.

She spread her fingers on his neck, sliding them up through his hair, massaging his scalp, pulling him closer. He lifted himself further up on the bed, so his thing was dangling over her mouth. She closed her eyes. The muscles in her stomach clenched, half with want and half with revulsion. She turned her head to the side, and it rubbed across her face.

"Oh, no don't . . ." she opened her mouth to tell him, but he shoved it in. It was touching her throat. She couldn't swallow, couldn't breathe. Sliding in and out. It kept getting caught behind her teeth. Felt funny. She was gagging. She knew she was going to puke. She dug her head back into the pillow, her eyes wet as they pleaded with him. Finally, he pulled it out and Stephanie's throat closed up, causing a heaving in her chest. She threw her hand over her mouth as the little spasm spread in her throat.

She smiled weakly, not wanting him to think she *wouldn't* do it, it was just too fast, too sudden. He seemed to forgive her, because he raised himself on his hands, his fists over her shoulders. The light from the living room caught him—it—standing straight out from his body. There was a strange bump on the end, which she had never seen before. Oh my God, it dawned on her, it's not circumcised. It had never occurred to her that anyone was not circumcised, and she stared at it in fascinated horror. It looked like a big rubber arrow. Jesus Christ. Of course it didn't matter but, somehow, it did. It seemed dirty—*he* seemed dirty—because of it.

There was a little contraction inside her stomach as the slit in his uncircumcised penis swayed back and forth like a metronome, hypnotizing her. She was still so wet that when he shoved it inside her, he didn't need to use his hands. Although she wished he had.

It was huge. And hard. She could feel it jabbing against her back, the rounded knob she had never known before touching the walls of her insides. She tried to grab him to hold on, but it moved too fast.

"Doctor Fredericks, I felt myself floating away from him, from myself, like I wasn't there and both our bodies were strange to me. I was up on the ceiling watching a foreign movie, with the voices dubbed in like you always have the feeling they're not really talking, but words are coming out of their mouths."

Richard's arms became rigid over her head, the weight of his body supported by his hands. He pushed his head back and a chill touched her chest where his sweat had made her damp. She screamed, "No, you can't!" and punched his shoulders. A force gathered all the strength within him, and he tried to coax it loose with small wailing sounds from his throat. "Stephanie, I'm coming. I'm coming. I'm coming!" he cried, and pulled out of her so quickly her insides stung. Then he crumpled on top of her, squirting millions of sperm onto her stomach.

"I don't even know why I did it. I didn't want to. No, that's not true. I did. But not with him, I guess."

Stephanie lay there in the dark, her heart pounding in her temples. She didn't move. Finally she pushed him, and he rolled over on his side. She slid her palm over her stomach and down. Her hair was all matted. She lifted her hand and slimy strings of semen were hanging off her fingers. She dropped her arm off the bed, fingers spread. Eventually she dozed off.

She woke with a start some time in the middle of the night. Her thumb explored her other fingers. It had dried up. Like snot. She went to the bathroom and washed her hands. Then she took the washrag, rubbed it across the soap, and shoved it inside. She rinsed it and washed her stomach.

Stephanie swirled some mouthwash around, turned out the light in the living room, and went back to bed. She lay close to him so she wouldn't have to touch the cold, wet spot.

She'd change the sheets first thing. She stared at his back in the dark for a while. He had a cluster of blemishes on his behind. Then she fitted her body to his, threw her arm around his shoulders—careful not to let her body touch the pimples—and went to sleep.

□ 2 □

"It could've happened that way," Nick was thinking out loud. "She *could've* changed her mind about coming home."

"Why didn't she mention it in the beginning?"

Nick shrugged. "She could've forgotten, like she said. I mean, she comes home and finds her roommate murdered. Grisly. She's hysterical. Under medication. Being questioned. And maybe it didn't *seem* worth mentioning at the time."

"Well, if she forgot, how come she suddenly remembers when she's talking to your friend downstairs? And then when *we* ask her, for somebody who had a temporary lapse of memory, she sure can describe the sweater she bought, down to the last stitch, knows exactly where the receipt is to prove it."

"So? She's organized, keeps all her bills in one place. There was a Gimbels shopping bag when I got there, come to think of it. I saw it in the hallway, next to her boots. Like she had just put it down when she got home, you know, until she got her boots off."

"That doesn't mean anything." Malcolm studied the sales receipt. "She could've gone there any time. Charge number, clerk number, item number, department number. It was bought on the twentieth. Says so right here. But there's no way to tell what time. Suppose she bought it earlier?"

"You mean so she'd have a receipt? For the same amount? It would have to be for the same thing. She'd still have to stop and buy this same thing. Why would she go twice?"

"I meant earlier the same day. There's just something I don't like."

"Look, she comes home early—terrific, isn't it, everybody gets off early for the holiday, let's complain. She starts to walk down the block, just turns the corner . . . then she decides she has nothing to do anyway, so she might as well go shopping. Store will be empty at that hour. Everybody going away. So she changes her mind about going home, walks up to Lexington, looks around in the store, buys a sweater, walks back home. The call came in, lemme see," Nick checked his notes, "five forty-seven. She got home about five-thirty, walked up the stairs, went into the bedroom, found the body. It takes about two minutes for Rosa Bassetti to hear her screaming, get out her passkey, then, what, three, four minutes for her to walk up there—the flights are steep for her—a couple of minutes to calm her down. Okay, that makes sense. If it bothers you, why don't you go over there? Check it out?"

"Not now. Anyway, a store that size, they probably wouldn't remember." Hodges swung the cover of his memo pad open and thumbed through the pages. "Sweet . . . good natured," he read. Turning another page, he continued, "and according to the office manager, 'Stephanie would give you the shirt off her back.' "

"So, what does that mean?" Lascano asked.

" 'Considerate . . . goes out of her way for everybody' . . . and here's one, from one of the girls she works with: 'Stephanie lets people walk all over her.' "

"So you're just confirming she's pretty, charming, generous, good natured. What does that tell us? Aside from the fact that she's perfect?"

"Maybe too perfect."

"What do you mean?"

"I don't know. Look at Son of Sam."

"A kook. A loner."

"Okay, that's a bad example. How many times do you pick up the *News* and they got some guy who just murdered his whole family, his kids, or his mother and father . . . and all the neighbors say, 'but he was an ideal husband, or father, picture of respectability'?"

143

"In other words, a murderer can act like a murderer, or like a nice person. Good going, Mal, you've narrowed it down to anybody in New York."

"I'm just saying nobody has a bad thing to say about her. She's always going out of her way for people, always doing what's proper. What's *right*. Always. What's eating you anyway?"

"Sorry." Nick unwrapped his cigarettes, lit up, and swallowed the harsh smoke. "It's getting me down, can't help it."

"Okay. Why don't you go to SmokEnders?"

"If I'm going to do it, I'm going to do it myself."

"Yeah, but you're not doing it. You need help."

"I know. Maybe I should just give up. I might die from a heart attack anyway, or who knows what. But I might as well enjoy myself while I'm alive."

"Yeah, but you don't act like you're enjoying it."

"Okay, shut up about it, huh?"

□ 3 □

"I feel so far away, so removed, from everything. You know when you were a kid and you fell asleep in the back seat of the car and when you started to wake up, or maybe it was when you started to fall asleep, the voices in the front sounded so far away and you could hear the words but you couldn't figure out who was saying what? Well, that's the way I feel now. Most of the time. Far away."

"Stephanie, that's a very lonely feeling, isn't it? It's worse than loneliness, it's . . . isolation. It's a terrible thing to go through life, not being a part of it, thinking you're all by yourself."

"The thing is, I used to smile when people wrote in books that they were watching themselves go by. You know how they do?"

"What's funny about that?"

144

"It's not. But I'm worse. I watch myself watching myself. Take, well, anything. Something like sitting down and reading a book. Now, a normal nut would look at it like this: 'She sat down in the easy chair and picked up her book.' But not me. What I do is watch myself thinking I sat down. That's sick, isn't it? Like I pretend I'm writing, or talking to you—I do that a lot you know—and it comes out like I'm narrating this novel, see, 'Stephanie thought about herself thinking about herself.' Oh, I can't explain it. It's very weird. It's like I refer to myself in the third person all the time. More and more. It's driving me crazy."

"What do you think we can do about it?"

"I don't know. Maybe nothing."

"That's no answer. Come on, you can do better than that."

"No. Oh, I know what you mean, and I know what the right answer is, maybe. It's just that, sometimes, I feel maybe it's not worth it."

"What?"

"Thinking about all these things. Trying to figure out why. And how to change."

"If you really thought that, you . . ."

"I know, I know. I guess I don't really. It's just that sometimes, even when I'm talking to you, I wonder if I'm just hopeless . . . like too far gone."

□ 4 □

Richard Spencer pushed the fifty-pound barbell over his head and down. The sweat trickled from his glistening chest onto the bench. Eighteen up, and eighteen down, and nineteen up, and nineteen down. And twenty. He let the iron weight thud onto the carpeted floor. His arms hung loose and he closed his eyes, concentrating on the perspiration crawling along his skin, the blood racing through his limbs, his heart pounding.

Relaxing afterward is just as important, he remembered. So

he relaxed. Boy, he was in good shape. Not that he shouldn't be. He watched his diet, worked out three times a week, sometimes four. As soon as it got a little warmer out, he was going to try jogging. Good for the heart. Maybe he could get Stephanie to go too. She didn't like that kind of stuff, but he wanted to do things together. Maybe for her birthday—he'd have to find out when it was—he'd give her a membership to the gym. Then they could go at the same time. Have dinner afterward.

Too bad she's not more athletic. Well, you couldn't have everything. He'd insist that she learn tennis. That was a must. Socially, as well as physically. That was just about her only failing, as far as he could see. Course he didn't know her all that well. Yet. He couldn't remember ever going into a girl's kitchen and finding the burners soaking in the sink. You could eat off her floor. Like his mother. What luck to find someone like her in this day and age. Marilyn probably never washed a dish unless it was an absolute necessity. He could never live with anybody like that. And to think he might have been willing to try. Slut.

Six fucking years wasted thinking about her. She had grown lovelier and more charming, if that was possible. Beautiful time they had together. He *thought*. He had sent flowers next morning. What girl wouldn't be impressed? Marilyn. When he called to ask her out for Saturday night, and Sunday also—it was going to be a long weekend—he couldn't believe it. Like she was laughing at him. Or being condescending. No chance of someone like her being interested in someone like him. That attitude. And he had the feeling she was actually seeing someone else. After what she did with him, to find out she was involved with someone else. Well, Stephanie had confirmed it. He had the feeling this was going to work out with *her*.

Richard smiled. He had felt himself falling, and jumped up with a start. Dozing is not the same as relaxing, he lectured himself.

He walked into the little alcove, took off his shorts, wrapped a towel around his waist, and went into the sauna. He was relieved no one else was there. Six o'clock was a good time to come. He took the towel off, spread it out on the wooden bench, and lay back. He hated the sauna. Felt like hot honey dripping into your pores. And it was hard to breathe. But it was good for you.

Stephanie would be loyal, of course. She was that type. God, if he ever caught her fooling around, doing *any*thing, he'd. . . . Well, she wouldn't. Once or twice, she said. He didn't like that. He wondered who they were, and if she had gone down on them. But you couldn't expect a virgin anyway, at least not one with a clean stove too. As long as it's over and done with and she belongs to me now, I won't think about it.

But Richard Spencer did think about it. About Stephanie lying on a beach, her soft stomach illuminated in the moonlight, the waves pounding, her silky skin, grainy from the sand, writhing in ecstasy.

Drained from the heat, feeling all the energy pulling out of him, Richard got up and walked out of the sauna. Flushing from the burning coals and his embarrassment, he walked into the shower room, his hand covering his erection.

CHAPTER 17

□ 1 □

Stephanie had to get out of the office. Her nerves had turned into claws, scratching against her insides. They tickled her throat and squeezed her eyeballs and pinched her groin. Pulled her hair. She was going crazy, she was sure. She talked, she typed. Her smile was etched by a stylus of ice, freezing the expression on her face. Thousands of little nails scraping inside her skin . . . she was raw and itchy. She dared not breathe, dared not move, lest tiny hooves slither out of her pores.

At one minute to twelve, she ran. She walked against the wind, hoping the cold would melt the burning sensation inside her head. After three blocks, she felt better. She turned down Fifth and went into Lord & Taylor. She circled the counters on the first floor, fingering scarves and smelling leather pocketbooks.

She touched perfume on the inside of her wrists, the crook of her arms, sucking the scent into her nostrils after each sample. When she ran out of skin, she went on to the makeup. She dabbed lipsticks and eye shadows and blushers on, until the backs of her hands looked like a clown's. She was about to go through jewelry when her eyes stumbled on a reflection in one of the mirrored columns. Her stomach squeezed when she saw him. It looked just like . . . no, it was . . . that detective. Pretending to be looking at necklaces in the glass case. Stephanie couldn't pull her eyes away. As she stood transfixed in front of the Clinique counter, a warm circle spread under the back of her coat.

□ 2 □

"Why don't you go back?" Pete asked her.

Rosa was brushing Princess with her fingers, careful not to stroke the little warts on her back. "Can't."

"But you said she'd send you the ticket."

"I know, I know. It's a dream."

"So why don't you? You don't have to stay. Just because she asked you to come live with her. You could go for a month or two. See how you like it. If you do, you could come back, pack up, and then go for good."

"I wish I could," Rosa said, rocking. She put Princess on the floor and looked at Pete. "But what about my baby?"

"Well, they *said* you could bring her."

"Ah, but she too old to make the trip. Even in my lap. I called, I don't have to put her with baggage. No, trip too long—she ain't gonna make it. Someday." Rosa picked the dog up and rubbed her cheek into the soft belly. "But I don't wanna think about when she go. I know she goes someday, but I not think about losing Princess. Then, maybe, I see. Anyway, this is home now. Eighty-second Street. I miss everybody if I go. Why you so anxious to get rid of me?" She leaned over and playfully slapped Pete's knee.

"I don't want to get rid of you, Rosa. I think you're terrific." He rubbed the cold glass against his cheek. His eyes seemed to reflect the sparkle of the wine.

"Daydreaming?"

"No. I guess so. I was just thinking about her."

"I know, it's hard."

"I miss her a lot, Rosa. I could kick myself that I didn't insist she come with me. Or else I should have stayed in the city with her. Then this wouldn'ta happened. Or else we should've gotten married, and then she wouldn't even have been living here."

150

"Don't blame yourself. It happen anywhere. Even if she lives with you."

"She wanted to wait, be sure of herself."

"Well, ain't that better? Than getting married and finding out a year later it was wrong."

"It wouldn't've been wrong."

"Not for you, but for her maybe."

"I don't think so. She loved me, I know it. Just wanted to get it all out before she settled down. There was a girl who knew herself. In lots of ways. Knew what she liked, what she didn't, knew how to please herself. At first I really didn't like that. But then, I was a little envious, you know, wished I could be more like that."

"Marilyn, she useta say, you only live today, enjoy it."

"She did. That's the one thing, you know. That she enjoyed herself. Never hurt a soul in her life, but she took care of herself first."

"Ah, *Pietro,* if more people like that, it's a better world. Nobody get hurt. If they don't get hurt, they don't do dumb things to other people."

Pete stood up and picked his raincoat off the chair. Rosa got up and put Princess on the couch. "You're something else," Pete said, giving her a hug. Just like Nicky said.

After he left, Rosa checked on Mrs. Karlmeier, and put her to bed. Then she went back to her apartment and locked up. She switched on the TV, flicked the channels, and turned it off again. He was something, he was. And hugging her too.

Rosa sat in her chair, thinking what it would be like—a young man like that, lean and strong and hard. Bet he come six, seven times a night, she thought, and smiled to herself. She tried to imagine being in bed with him—oh, the tricks she had! My God, she knew how to make a man happy. The thought of his horror at seeing her old-woman's body—the wrinkled stomach, the varicose veins. . . . Once, she was going to shave her legs. She bought the razor even, but she couldn't do it. She would've felt naked—even though it was for being naked. It just wasn't natural. Still . . .

Rosa was too restless to go to sleep. She put her coat over her nightgown and carried Princess out. They sat for a while on the stoop. In the dark. Princess slept. Rosa dreamed.

□ 3 □

Richard liked the way Stephanie had set the little bridge table. The flowered cloth, the candle in the glass holder. Very elegant. Not really, but she had fixed it up nice, for what she had. She looked beautiful when the light flickered across her face, softening the color. He couldn't wait to finish and get to bed. As soon as he thought it, he was sorry. Sex wasn't that important. *That* was. The domesticity, the conversation, the being together. But, Christ, he wanted to fuck her.

"It's lovely, just lovely. And everything is delicious."

"Thank you." Her eyes were glowing. She poured the coffee out of a white ceramic serving thing, and put the cup in front of him. Cheap dishes. But he could afford to buy nice china after. A lot of nice things. Then, when he invited clients or friends over for dinner, he'd feel secure and important. She'd be great. Do everything just perfect. In their beautiful little house, or maybe an apartment in the city until they had children, with the crystal and the sterling. "Oh, Stephanie," Richard whispered to himself, "I think I love you."

"Cream?" She tilted the little pitcher over his coffee. Warmth was seeping out of his eyes. He didn't want to finish the coffee. He wanted to feel her body under him, touch her, jab his cock, feel it swallowed up inside her. She belonged to him. He watched the white blend with the black, swirl around the top of his cup, and thought about how wet she'd be. Drowning in her. Being pulled down her throat.

She was so inhibited though. Well, in a way, that was good. He could teach her things. Not like Marilyn. Shocking him—God, he'd never even *heard* of that. Maybe she would be more open if he were more romantic. He knew he wasn't. Girls liked that. His voice got stuck when he tried to blurt it out. "Stephanie, I want you."

"What?"

"Nothing. Just thinking."

"About what?"

"You."

"Me?" She lowered her eyes.

"I like you a lot." There, he said it.

He stood up and walked over to behind her chair. He put his hand on her shoulder, slid it down, and touched her breast. Didn't move. Then she shivered, and the heat shot up his arm. Saliva hung in his mouth. He couldn't swallow. His prick felt like it was going to explode. He pressed it against the back of her head, standing on the balls of his feet, and he could see the little blond hairs stiffen on her neck. He grabbed her under the arms, his hands glancing the sides of her breasts, and stood her upright, Then, consumed with his need, he started to pull her toward the bedroom.

"Hey, not so fast." Stephanie was determined that it would be right. Hoped. "Listen, I want to change into something more comfortable, as they say."

"I want you this way. Just like you are."

"Please . . . don't spoil it. Please." She wanted to be sexy in her own way, when she was ready to be sexy.

He let go. He'd humor her, he thought, as she went into the bathroom.

Stephanie washed, sprayed perfume on her crotch and midriff, and changed her clothes. She leaned back to take a last look in the mirror. The taupe nightgown hung loose from her neck, billowing shapelessly to her ankles. But when she moved, the satin caught on a nipple, or a hip, and froze the sway of the sheen. Her lipstick had been put on and then wiped off, leaving just a tinge of color, which she brought to glistening life with gloss. Her hair had been carefully brushed, then shaken loose to give it a wanton look.

She looked beautiful, she knew. A fist clenched in her stomach when she opened the bathroom door. She went inside. He was waiting on the bed, his bare foot tracing the impressions it had made in the scatter rug. He was in his shorts.

"Now I know what took you so long," he said in a singsong way, emphasizing every other word as if he were reading a poem in meter. She stood in the frame of the doorway. She was annoyed that he was undressed, that he wasn't acting according to the script she had written for tonight. Richard stood up, his thumbs inside the waistband of his jockey shorts.

"Please, just let's take it easy," Stephanie said, thinking It's going to be the same. *"After the wine, I felt warm and cuddly. And giggly. I thought it was going to be okay. But he ruined it."* He put his arms around her, and Stephanie stiffened. Then he threw her on the bed.

He kissed her hard, sucking her tongue into his mouth, straining the muscle underneath it. Stephanie winced as the tip touched enamel, became wet with his saliva. She pulled away and jumped up. After she turned out the light, she took the nightgown off. Better *that* than *this*. Richard's elbows were bent, his head resting on his palms. He watched her, pleased she was in such a hurry. He must really have aroused her.

Stephanie slowly climbed into the bed. Richard squeezed her breasts, bit her nipples. He shoved two fingers into her, and his nails scraped tender skin. Stephanie rolled her bottom lip into her mouth and filed it behind her front teeth. So she wouldn't cry. She tried to think of him doing it, think of it inside her. She was humiliated because she was dry. Another failure.

Maybe he didn't notice, because he was holding himself with one hand and trying to separate her with the other. He finally got it in and, after the first shove, he relaxed on top of her. Stephanie held both edges of the mattress and counted "One and two and" between thrusts. Between the skin of his penis catching on the dry skin of the walls of her body. Like two pieces of rubber trying to slide against one another.

She imagined herself daydreaming. Thinking of her phantom lover touching her, of her touching herself. It became smoother, her muscles softened, it was going in and out real easy, gliding. Richard pulled her ankles up so her heels rested on his shoulders, her knees bent into her chest. Her whole bottom was exposed, her cheeks spread from the strain. His face was right above hers. She kept her eyes closed so he could not see what she was seeing. How ugly it was. Every time he moved, her lips brushed against his chest.

He kept pulling it out farther, sticking it in deeper. So deep it hurt. All of a sudden, as he pushed, a bubble of air broke and shattered her eardrums, the sound repeating over and over in her head. Marilyn had told her about it once, when they first moved in. Had explained, "The cock forces air into your pussy and it always happens." As if it were funny. Stephanie had left the room then, just as she wanted to now. Suppose Richard didn't know what it was. Thought she had done something else. Her face was burning. She mumbled something about a cramp in her shin, and put her legs down, stretched them out.

Richard reached over to the night table. She heard paper ripping. She could see him in the dark, standing on his knees, holding his penis and fumbling with both hands. Putting it on.

"I wanted to be good. For him. For myself too, I guess. Mostly I wanted to like it. I was ashamed that I didn't. I was thinking about cleaning up and doing the dishes. How the food was getting stuck on them, being out so long."

There was a soft slap, then a faint crackling as he unrolled the thing over himself. Richard put it back in and moved rhythmically, as if there had been no interruption, as if she were lying there, just panting. It felt like a balloon rubbing against a face. When his arms stiffened over her and she heard the gurgling in his throat, Stephanie grunted a few times. To be polite. Then she held him tight.

□ 4 □

"I was cleaning out some stuff, rearranging, organizing. You know. Under the lining of my drawer, I found a glove. I don't know what it was doing there. It was hers, I'm sure, because I never had one like that. Short. She lost one, but how did I get it? I asked myself if maybe I took it. I spent all weekend thinking about it, pretending you were asking me questions so I couldn't just shut it out of my mind. Like I usually do."

"And what do you think?"

"I think I must've taken it. Where it was, it was hidden, not just misplaced. Under the lining. So I must've put it there. I guess I stole it."

"Do you guess that, or do you know for a fact?"

"Doctor, I think I know."

CHAPTER 18

□ 1 □

Cynthia wondered what time he came home. She knew he couldn't be asleep, not on his back. She tried to see in the dark if the booklet from the Cancer Society was where she had left it on his night table, or if it had been moved, if he had looked at it, glanced through it.

"Nick . . . ?"

That didn't prove anything. He was probably wide awake and just didn't want to talk. Or fuck. If his first wife was so perfect and loved him so much, how come she didn't try to get him to stop? she asked herself. Well, next time he brought her up in conversation, which would probably be soon the way things were going, she'd come right out and say that. She wouldn't ask. Any man. Even if he was her husband. But, God, they slept together more before they got married. Cynthia turned her back to Nick, and closed her eyes.

Lascano was running the tip of his tongue over his teeth, trying to wipe the film off. His gums felt like sandpaper, and the lining of his cheeks was grainy. Behind his closed eyes, he imagined the nicotine eating away at his cells, eroding his lungs, closing off his blood vessels, weakening his heart. I'm really going to do it, he promised himself. He slid off the bed quietly, took the pack from next to the lamp, and tiptoed out.

He brought it into the kitchen and threw it in the garbage. Aha, that won't fool me if I really want one. He took it back out. One last one. The final. So I can remember it. He lit one and the smoke rushed to his head. He felt lightheaded from

157

the pleasure. Then he took the rest of the pack and held it under the faucet until it was thoroughly doused. Never again, never again, please God, help me.

□ 2 □

"Was it better? What does that mean, a shrug?"

"It was okay."

"Just okay?"

"As a matter of fact, it was . . . the same. I didn't like it."

"Why?"

"I don't want to talk about it."

"Why not?"

"For one thing, I don't feel like it. For another, I don't want to think about it. What upsets me more than . . . than the sex . . . is, well, I guess a kind of privacy. I mean, I spend all my life dreaming about being with someone, sharing, and the minute he came in, I wanted him out of there. I didn't want him to touch my things, or even be there. At first, I did. I mean I cleaned up and everything but, even when I was feeling open and wanting and leading him back there, the minute I opened the door, I felt he was . . . trespassing. And now I don't know what to do."

"What do you have to do?"

"I don't want him around me. He keeps calling and making plans. The first few times, it felt good. Knowing he was thinking about me. That he cared, I guess. But I can't stand his making plans for me, for my life, with himself included."

"Why?"

"I'm suffocating. I don't want anybody doing that."

"I thought you did."

"I thought so too. I mean I always thought the greatest thing in the world was being close to someone. But as soon as someone gets close to me, I cringe. Literally."

"What does it feel like?"

"It's a real physical thing. My skin starts to get hot and my hair stands up. Really. Then my throat feels like it's getting smaller and smaller and I just want to run."

"Where?"

"I don't know. Just get away."

"Where would you . . . ?"

"Listen. This is not just an emotional thing now. It's real. I mean with him. I don't know how to get rid of him."

"Why can't you just say, 'Look, it's been nice, but I'm afraid I don't want to see you anymore'?"

"Because I can't. You know I can't."

"Why not?"

"I just can't say that. Besides, he wouldn't listen."

"Does he own you?"

"Of course not."

"It's your life, why can't you be in charge of it?"

"I'm trying. The other day, I told him I was having dinner with a friend and I couldn't see him. He got angry. Furious. He wanted to know who it was. And he didn't believe it was a girl; he got real nasty about it. When I came home—see, I did make a date so it wouldn't be a lie—he was waiting downstairs. He said he thought he'd drop by to see if I was home yet, but I knew he wanted to see if a guy brought me home. And then he told me what we were going to do this weekend, so I told him I was going to my mother's and he—can you imagine this—he asked if he could come, he wants to meet my parents."

"What did you say?"

"I said that, well, my mother would think we were getting engaged, since I had never brought anybody there before, and I thought it was too soon. Anyway, it doesn't matter. I ended up . . . well, giving in. I told him I'd see him and go home the following weekend. I mean, I just didn't want to argue about it, you know?"

"Why didn't you just tell him the truth—that you don't want to be with him?"

"I couldn't do that. And, I don't know why, I feel sort of afraid."

"What do you think he would do if you told him?"

"Not that he'd do anything. But I'd feel . . . I guess re-

sponsible for hurting him. He's had a rotten social life, I told you, and he thinks he loves me and first he's disappointed in Marilyn and now it would be me, and I just don't know how to do it."

"So you'd rather suffer?"

□ 3 □

She unlocked the door and listened a minute to make sure he wasn't up. When total silence answered her, Marianne Webster walked into the bedroom. It was empty. Sure, it's drinking time, she thought, checking the clock. It was one-thirty in the morning.

She got undressed and walked around the apartment. The kitchen was all straightened up, nothing out. He had even washed out his dishes and put them in the drain.

She went back to the bedroom and lay down in the dark, watching the glare of her cigarette. Maybe it was her. Maybe he was glad to get rid of her. Maybe it was all her fault. Two nights in that crappy fleabag hotel. She should at least have treated herself to a nice place. But there weren't any nice places in Yorkville. Anyway, if she was going to have to start watching her money, she couldn't spend fifty dollars a night to stay out. He hadn't even called her office. Maybe he didn't even notice that she wasn't there.

Marianne turned over and started to cry in her pillow. All the years of frustration and hurt welled up in her throat, and all the same tomorrows, and she sobbed her guts out. It was all her, she knew it. Tomorrow, she'd really pack up and get a place. But she was afraid. To be alone.

She didn't hear the key in the door. He snapped on the light and walked to the edge of the bed.

"Oh, Victor, I love you," she blurted out, wrapping her arm around his neck. She clung to him, crying into his chest. But his stiff, unyielding body made her ashamed. When she

160

had sniffled up the rest of her tears, she moved back. To her astonishment, he was wiping wetness off his own cheeks. He just stood there, a little wobbly, and so helpless.

"Marianne . . ."

"Yes, Vic."

"Baby, when you didn't come home, I swear I stopped. I cleaned up. Look," he ran over to the typewriter and opened the box of bond paper next to it, "see . . ." he took the clip and flipped the typed pages. "I tried. Honest. I promised myself that when you came home I'd be different. But, tonight, when you still didn't come home, I couldn't help it, I had to. I was going crazy."

A great bubble of gratitude and warmth broke in Marianne's chest. He did care, he did love her.

"Oh, Victor, Victor, Victor." She caressed him like a mother who has just found a lost child. Victor got undressed and got into bed. And for the first time in eight months he made love to Marianne.

□ 4 □

Stephanie did her vanity. She washed off the makeup bottles and jars and lined them up evenly. She soaked all the little eyeshadow brushes in soap suds, and then did the nail polish bottles. It didn't take her too long—she had already done it once this week.

She walked around the apartment searching for a picture to tilt or a speck of dirt to press with her thumb. Everything was in order. She looked in *TV Guide*. Nothing much on.

She got undressed and lay down on her side in bed. She put the new *Cosmopolitan* on the pillow and opened it. She stuck her nose into the binding and sniffed. She loved the smell of some of that glossy paper. Or was it the ink? She started turning the pages slowly. She read every ad.

She mentally answered the first two questions of the quiz.

Then she flipped to the answers. There were a lot of questions and it would be hard to remember how many right she had. So she got up and took a ballpoint pen out of her drawer, pushing the others into exact alignment before she closed it again. She circled and checked. Just for kicks. Then she counted. Thirty *always,* twenty *sometimes,* ten *occasionallys,* two *nevers.* Her score was "you're everything a man dreams of." But of course she had fibbed.

She threw the magazine on the floor and turned out the light. She couldn't fall asleep. She stared at the opposite wall, where Marilyn's bed had been.

All of a sudden she started to cry. She didn't know why. If Dr. Fredericks asked her, she wouldn't be able to put her finger on it. Useless passions, unfulfilled dreams. All the dark moods and twisted thoughts she hadn't had time to give in to before consumed her now. Stephanie sobbed and dozed all night, engulfed in sorrow.

□ 5 □

Rosa banged the radiator to stop it from clanging. She was glad Josie couldn't see how dingy it was. That the stuffing was sticking out of her chair. That the slipcovers, which she had made from Woolworth's material, was hiding the terrible couch. The day she saw it, out with the garbage on 84th Street, Hector and that nice boy—what was his name—lugged it back for her. Ah, Josie living in a big house, with a servant, now that her husband was dead. Married forty-two years and Rosa had never laid eyes on him . . .

She hoped Josie would never know. That the $392.50 Social Security check was never enough. Thank God she could still feed Princess good. Up until, what, three years ago, it wasn't too bad. Some of the restaurants she used to work for sometimes called her to fill in. The extra money came in handy. She always put it in the bank.

Well, it wasn't really *so* bad. It was home. And she had a lot of friends. The whole neighborhood. Everybody knew her. Called her by name. That wasn't a bad thing. And the rent helped the last few months. Not paying it at all. What a miracle. Except it was a shame for poor Vilma Karlmeier. Of course she wasn't paying so much to begin with—she was still rent-control. But eighty-four dollars a month extra. At least she didn't have to take any money *out* of the bank lately.

If she got sick, $6,534 wouldn't help much. But it made her feel good to know it was there. Maybe, just maybe, she'd use the thirty-four-dollar part to buy something. She hadn't done that in years. Next month maybe.

CHAPTER 19

□ 1 □

Richard Spencer adjusted the outside mirror, turning his head back and forth to see what was out the back window. Then he fiddled with all the knobs on the dashboard. He turned the key and, while the motor was idling, folded up the rental receipt and stuck it in the visor. "All set?"

Stephanie smiled and rolled down her window. "Looks like it's going to be a beautiful day. I love the beach at this time of the year."

"Okay, then, we're off," he said, releasing the emergency brake. He headed down Second Avenue.

Stephanie looked sideways at him. She couldn't stand the way he drove. Two hands on the wheel, hugging the middle lane. Every time he slowed down for a light, he dropped his hand out the window. Who did that anymore—it was like driving school! By the time they got to 60th Street, she thought he must have a charley horse in his left arm. "Oh, aren't we taking the bridge?"

"Tunnel's faster."

"Oh, but I like the view from the bridge."

"Okay." Richard turned on the signal light, stuck his arm straight out, and made a left turn. "Not much to see."

"I love to look back and watch the skyline. It's so clear, gee, you can even see the Twin Towers."

Richard squeezed her thigh condescendingly. She was such a romantic. It was like pulling teeth getting her to do this. His life was so structured but, jeez, she was worse. If that's possible. If it wasn't planned a week ahead, to the minute, she didn't want to do it. If only she were more . . . spontaneous . . . about things. Well, you can't have it both ways. Like sex. God knows, she was willing. But it always seemed as if she was holding back. Didn't seem, was. Sort of withdrawn, even though you could tell she was boiling inside. If only he could make her come. Damnit, that really annoyed him. He didn't take it personally. Lots of women didn't have orgasms till their thirties, everybody knew that. But *he* knew she was a seething inferno inside, just ready to explode. If only he knew how to make her.

Anyway, it wasn't that important. There were other things. She'd be a perfect hostess, good wife, no doubt terrific mother, when they were ready. He enjoyed screwing her. The little defiance he felt, or whatever it was, he liked that. He liked twisting her wrists over her head, the way she struggled against him. Sometimes he held her down. He liked the way her body moved, trying to get away from him. Gave him a sense of power over her. He liked to feel he was, not raping her, but making her submit to him. Course sometimes it was obvious she didn't want to at all. That excited him. Just thinking about it, he could feel a stirring in his loins.

Maybe he could fuck her on the beach, if it wasn't crowded. And it wouldn't be this time of the year. Then he could see if she writhed on the sand. Like he always imagined she did. "There goes the cable car." Richard pointed to the red car swinging over the river.

"Ooh, who would want to live over there? So far away from civilization?"

"Might be kinda nice. Within the city, but apart. Your own private world."

"But can you imagine being late for work and having to wait for the cable car? No thanks." Stephanie pretended to study the store signs on Queens Boulevard, hoping he wouldn't talk to her. She wished she had stayed home. She could have finished the laundry. Oh, well, it *was* a nice day and she should get away from the city once in a while. Besides going home. And she did love the beach.

But she didn't like the way he had insisted. The way he decided on his own, and then told her they were going. Moving in on her life. Her skin crawled when people did that. Said, "What've you got to do that's better?" Well, it was nobody's business if she wanted to stay home and clean. *"It makes me angry when people tell me what to do. I go along with other people, what they want, all the time. But when I really want to do something, like be alone, I want to do it badly. And then I don't like being forced to do something else. And if I don't want to do something, I can be very stubborn. Yes, I could've just said I'm not going, but I didn't. He was very persuasive. Even nasty. I didn't know what to say. I couldn't not go."*

"Say something?"

"Uh-uh."

"This is my idea of a perfect Saturday," Richard said, not taking his eyes off the road. "A lovely day, sun shining, chill in the air, a drive to the beach with someone . . . you love." He reached over and squeezed Stephanie's hand. She leaned closer to the door.

"Tell you what," he said, "let's just spend the whole day walking on the sand, and then we can go to a nice seafood place on the water for dinner. 'Stead of coming back and getting dressed. How does that sound?"

"Fine." A vise locked Stephanie's jaws open so that her teeth could not touch. Her cheeks were sore from trying to.

"Hey, you know what I'd like to do tomorrow . . . why don't I keep the car and we'll go up to the mountains. We've never walked through the woods together."

"We'll see," she said, little capsules of grief dissolving inside.

□ 2 □

"Hi, Mrs. Bassetti, how's your little dog?"

"Fine, thanks, and you?"

Now what got into her, Rosa thought, watching Marianne Webster run up the stairs with a smile on her face.

Marianne was singing "Beautiful dreamer, wake unto me

167

. . . List while I woo thee, with soft melody," over and over as she climbed up the two flights. She didn't know what came next, but that was all right. "Beautiful dreamer, wake unto me . . ." Her legs felt lighter than they had in years.

The apartment was empty. "List while I woo thee . . ." she crackled softly, her heart pinching her ribs. There was a note on the kitchen table. "6:00—Went out to buy us a bottle of wine. Back in fifteen minutes." Marianne did a little pirouette, dropping her bag on the chair on a turn. She put the mail on the toaster. The yellow envelope caught her eye. Still dancing, she picked it up and put it in her pocket book.

"Okay, my darling, my sweet, I'll do it. But not to the police. They'll only ask why we opened it and what took so long to turn it over. I'll give it to that nosy bitch. She'll know what to do with it. In fact, I'll put it under her door, so she won't know *who* opened it and ask any questions either. Okay, love, will that make you happy?"

Marianne Webster put a steak in the broiler, still singing "Beautiful dreamer, wake unto me . . ."

□ 3 □

"When I see couples together, strangers or people I know, I always wonder the same thing. I know this is sick, but I can't help it. I constantly imagine the guy looking at his wife or girlfriend and, in his mind, he's picturing her the way she comes. And vice versa."

"You mean having an orgasm?"

"Yes."

"I wasn't sure what you meant. And what do you think he thinks about it?"

"I don't know, like say she's talking and she thinks she's saying something important, maybe she is, and he's looking at her and he doesn't see her with her lips moving and words coming out then, but what she was like at the height of pas-

sion, with grotesque noises coming out, and her face pulled together in pain, and then her mouth opening and saying 'ah, ah, ah,' "

"Why do you think he would think about her that way?"

"I don't know. Maybe because I do. Think of guys like that, I mean men I've been with. I can't look at them without looking at them coming. Losing control. Intent on letting go like that."

"Do you mean once you've seen a man do that, you can't see him in any other way?"

"I don't know. Maybe."

"So what does this mean, Stephanie, what are you trying to tell me?"

"I'm trying to say that . . . maybe that's why I can't. Because I don't want to look to somebody like they look to me."

"How exactly do they look, Stephanie?"

"I don't know."

"You must. You just said you remember them like that. Try."

"I guess I think of them as being . . . completely naked. Well, naturally, they are. I mean emotionally. All the pain, all the agony building up, it's on the face. And then, when they come, it's like their whole self is written on the expression. And when they let go of their life—yes, that's what it is, letting go of your life—it comes out, and their expression softens, and there's nothing left inside. I mean they gave it all away."

"Maybe that's why it feels so good."

"Maybe."

"Maybe letting somebody see you like that, surrendering everything inside you, is a matter of trust."

"Trust? Then that must mean I don't trust anybody, is that what you're saying? Anyway, I never thought of it like that before. Do you think that's me?"

"I'm only saying what comes into my mind. I can't say it is or it isn't. That's for you to decide. But if you think it's giving away part of your life, maybe you have to trust the other person enough to let him receive it."

"I'll think about it."

"*Don't you think when a person is having an orgasm, he reveals everything about himself, without holding back?*"

"*Yes, of course.*"

"*Isn't that what you're afraid of?*"

"*I don't know.*"

"*Revealing yourself. Like you won't reveal any of your emotions—you don't want people to know what you're feeling. Having an orgasm would be the ultimate revelation, wouldn't it? That's a little like not being able to look at yourself because you don't want to see who you are. What you are.*"

"*Oh, God, I'm really very sick, aren't I?*"

"*That's what closeness is all about, isn't it, Stephanie? Being able to reveal yourself. Letting somebody see what's inside.*"

"*Exactly. Although I never realized it.*"

"*When you say you want to be close to somebody, isn't that what you mean?*"

"*Yes.*"

"*What did you say?*"

"*I said 'yes.' The more I learn about myself, the worse I feel. I mean, I'm really sick, aren't I?*"

"*The thing is, it takes time. But, slowly, we are getting close. Very close.*"

"*I hope so. Close to the truth.*"

"*What do you think the truth is?*"

"*What I am.*"

□ 4 □

Malcolm bolted up, yelling "I got it!" Lydia floated into wakefulness, thinking he was dreaming. He put on the light and nudged her shoulder. "Honey, wake up, I need you."

She sat up, looking at him as if he was stark raving mad. She yawned and looked over at the clock. "I'm glad you need me, darling. That's every woman's dream. But it's three o'clock in the morning."

"No, listen. I remember what it was in the back of my mind. It was when we came home that night and you opened the door because I was holding the groceries."

"Well?"

"Well, it's such a stupid thing. I mean I always open the door and it's so automatic that I don't pay attention to what I'm doing. But I was impatient, remember, because the bags were heavy, and I was watching you. And then I noticed how *you* opened the door—how most people open doors, actually."

"Malcolm, what *are* you talking about? Get to the point so I can go back to sleep."

"You see, most people keep the bottom lock locked at all times. Right?"

"I suppose."

"So the doorknob doesn't turn."

"What d'ya mean?"

"The knob only turns when the door is open, but everybody I know keeps the bottom locked. So the knob doesn't turn. You use it to pull the door closed."

"So?"

"So, when you're trying to get in, you unlock your top lock, the double lock, and then you put your key in the bottom and, since the knob doesn't turn, you don't use it . . . you usually just push your shoulder or your side against the door, while the key is turned inside it."

"Well, of course, when you think about it, that's true. So what?"

"So what, so if you came home—and discovered a murder inside—and didn't go out again—and all the surfaces had been wiped clean *except* for the ones you supposedly touched in the normal course of things—then how the hell could your fingerprints be on the outside doorknob? *That's* why the Bassetti woman's weren't on there either—she used a key to get inside. And left the door wide open."

CHAPTER 20

□ 1 □

Hendricks called her in. She leaned the steno pad on her knee and wrote little reminders of the things he wanted checked or done. She doodled. Mostly little boxes, because she couldn't really draw.

"And then I think you ought to follow up on that inquiry to . . . Stephanie?"

"Yessir." Stephanie shaded in the square.

"Something wrong?"

"No, why?"

"You don't seem to be paying attention."

"I am, you want me to write . . ."

"Yes, yes, but I mean your mind doesn't seem to be on it."

Stephanie's muscles stretched into long fingers, spreading, bending into a thousand little fists, punching against the walls of her body. She had to get out of there. She could go home and tackle the mess. Or just lie down. "Mr. Hendricks, as a matter of fact I . . . I'm not feeling very well."

"I'm sorry to hear that."

"Mr. Hendricks, I want to go home. I really feel sick."

"Well, sure. I certainly don't want to seem like a monster. Of course, of course. Before you go, will you check downstairs and see if they can get someone up here for the rest of the day?"

"Certainly."

"And listen, Stephanie, if you don't feel better tomorrow, you just stay home."

While Stephanie pressed the receiver in the crevice of her neck, she swooped up all the papers on her desk and stuck

173

them in the IN box. God, she had never left early before. Or been out sick. But she had to go. If Rugglemeyer International didn't like it, screw them.

"Shit," Bill Hendricks said to the original painting on the opposite wall. "By the time I explain to the temporary what I want. . . . What the hell's gotten into her lately? She's been acting very peculiar. Ve-ry peculiar."

He went out to Stephanie's desk and couldn't believe it. Paper clips, broken staples, a half-filled coffee container with a white skin floating in it. Hendricks certainly didn't care—it looked just like all the other secretaries' desks. Point is, *she* cares. Maybe I ought to suggest she go to the company doctor for a good checkup. Wouldn't do any good. What she needs is a good shrink.

He shrugged and went back into his office, closing the door so he wouldn't have to speak to her replacement.

□ 2 □

Malcolm twirled the pencil like a baton. "Just doesn't make sense. Shit, Nick, something smells."

"I think you're off on the wrong track." Lascano swivelled his chair and put his feet up on Hodges' desk.

"Look at the doorknob."

"Mal . . . Mal, we've looked at it, we've thought about it. You talked to her. She never changed her story."

"Well, I think we're going about it in the wrong way. Naturally if you say, 'Miss Hillman, we want to check the details again,' she's going to say the same thing again. Why shouldn't she? She doesn't think we think there's anything wrong."

"Do we?"

"I do. But if we came right out and said, 'Miss Hillman, someone is lying, something doesn't fit . . .' "

"Yeah, then what? She going to confess? Or tell us she saw the murderer and was covering up for him?"

"No. But she'd get nervous."

"IF she has something to be nervous about."

"Let's say she does—if we throw the doorknob at her—that's concrete evidence—she's going to worry."

"Maybe."

"Maybe. Okay, so maybe she doesn't come out and say anything. But she sure as hell is going to be thinking about it. Thinking makes you nervous. Nervous makes you slip."

"I think you're barking up the wrong hydrant, Malcolm. Suppose she *is* covering up. It must be somebody she either cares about, or is afraid of. Just because you ask her again how she opened the front door isn't going to make her give up weeks of silence and blurt it all out."

"Well, you got a better idea?"

"No. Wait a minute. Okay, she's covering up for somebody. So why don't we try to find out who it is? Without her help."

"How?"

"Well, we never really *asked* about her friends, I mean spoke to them, just some of the people she works with and family stuff. Maybe we oughtta go through her address book."

"Maybe you got something. Course, we couldn't ask her for it. She could always say she lost it, and then throw it in the incinerator and poof."

"Well, I blew it. I had it in the beginning."

"Who knew then that it might be important?"

"So whatdya think?"

"I think it's worth a try. Hell, we'll have to sneak in to get it, you know?" Hodges smirked.

"Yeah, I know." Lascano smirked back.

They both sat there, remembering some of the things they had done in their time. And smirking.

◻ 3 ◻

Stephanie moved the dirty dishes to the drainboard, squirted detergent under the running water, and filled the sink. She put the cups and plates in the soap suds. She noticed the crumbs on the counter and the dirt on the linoleum. Well, after the dishes soaked for a while, she'd come back and really give the kitchen a going-over.

She walked to the bedroom doorway and stood there, studying the mess. Then cringed. Yesterday's clothes were on the floor, the blanket thrown into a ball on the bottom of the bed. Her bras and panty hose still hung on the doorknob, and she didn't have to bend to eye level to see the dust on the dresser and vanity.

She took off her blouse and slacks and threw them on the floor. Easier to sort the laundry and then put everything in the machine. She stuck a tissue under the crotch of her underpants, to pat the wetness. Dribble marks had dried into her legs and her behind burned from the growing fissure in her skin. She'd take a bath as soon as she was finished.

She went through the pile, tossing hand and machine washables into two piles, which started to overlap. Her foot tangled in a sweater sleeve and she tripped. Shit.

She sat down on the bed, promising herself to start from scratch. Tomorrow. Stephanie felt a pressure behind her eyes. A soreness in her jaw. Images swam in her brain. As soon as she was able to focus on them, they floated away. Always so close. Like walking down a road cut out of . . . nothing. On either side. As far as you could see, a long white gash. Miles and miles and miles. You could just about make out the end in the sunlight. Almost there. Then the road bends and, as you turn, you see . . . it stretches just as long again.

The heaviness in her stomach spiralled up to her head. Until it was too big to be contained—and burst apart. It shattered through her body, spitting fragments in all directions.

Stephanie shuddered, and a whimpering deep in her throat echoed in her ribs. Tears gushed out of her eyes. Somewhere from the depths of her soul, hopeless despair engulfed her whole being. Her face pulled itself together. Bones folded up. A mass sucked the inside of her skin and grew. Sounds vibrated in her chest before they poured out of her mouth in pitiful sobs.

The relief Stephanie felt in unclenching muscles and letting her grief flood out of her was immense. She cried into the pillow for a long time. When she finally fell asleep, her cheeks were pulled up to her eyes in her suffering.

□ 4 □

"You can't bring a dog up, lady."

"That the law?" Rosa asked, feeling tiny in front of the raised desk.

"I don't know if it's a real ordinance, but it's the law here. Whatdya wanna see Detective Lascano for?"

"None of your business!" Rosa yelled. She might have *looked* like a little old lady from where the officer sat, but he wasn't going to push *her* around.

"Somebody grab your purse?" He was stuffing papers into slots and answering the switchboard. "Eleventh Precinct, Police Officer MacDonald speaking. Right. Right. We'll send a car. Sorry, lady, if you give me a hint, maybe I could tell you . . . Eleventh Precinct, Police Off . . . Yes, sir, we already have a report on that. Be glad to," he stuck his tongue out at the mouthpiece, "give you my shield number . . . I'm only trying to advise you that another citizen has already . . . Shit, so report me," he said, pulling the disconnected line out of its socket.

"Well, you tell him Mrs. Bassetti wanna talk to him."

"I will."

"Well, I gonna wait, so you better do it now." After taking a cab all the way over to the West Side so she could have Princess with her, there was no way she was going to leave without seing Nicky.

This was definitely not Police Officer MacDonald's night. He plugged a cord in and asked, "Lascano there?" A second later, "there's some . . ." he paused before "lady" . . . "looking for you, sir. Says her name's . . ." he looked at Rosa, "whatwassat again . . . *Bass*atty."

The officer gloated when he told Rosa, "He wansa know what you want."

"Tell him *Rosa Bassetti*—from Eighty-second Street."

"She says . . . oh, you heard? . . . I guess they heard on Columbus Avenue too. Well, I can't. She's gotta dog with her. No, sir, I'm sorry. You wanna break the rules, you put it down on paper and . . . He's coming down," he told her, disconnecting.

"Well, thank *you*," Rosa said triumphantly. She sat down on the wooden bench with Princess, the yellow envelope stuck in her pocketbook.

CHAPTER 21

□ 1 □

"I talk. Because my lips move, and sounds come out of my throat. I don't know what I'm saying. Yes, I do, but someone else is saying it. This is a recording. My mind is out. I've left a message at the sound of the beep."

"It sounds to me like you're there, Stephanie, but you're not participating."

"Maybe it's something like that. I'm there, but behind a sheet of glass. Everyone's voice, mine too, is muffled. Sometimes the need to touch, to . . . make contact with life . . . is overwhelming. And I feel myself hold out my hand to do that and . . ."

"And what?"

"It knocks against the glass. I feel like I'm bleeding."

"You are, Stephanie, you are."

□ 2 □

"Read it." Nick Lascano removed the letter from the yellow envelope, unfolded it, and handed it to Stephanie.

Stephanie's muscles froze and the air she had just breathed in hung like a fog in her chest because she could neither inhale nor exhale. She didn't have to turn to the last page to see the signature. She recognized the big, disconnected scrawl

179

before she focused on the first word. All her energy snapped loose and contorted into a fuzzy ball bouncing up and down in his chest. She had to get out of here, before it pulled away and shot up to her throat. She started reading:

Hi,
I can't believe it's February already and I'm just getting around to answering the note in your Christmas card. Well, you know how lazy I am.

I'm glad you finally got the couch. I know how long it takes for furniture deliveries. But now that everything is in, it must look beautiful. Did the drapes ever come? No, I haven't done anything more in the apartment. It's not the money. But more about that later.

Stephanie was rigid. Only her eyes moved. Back and forth across the page. What was in here? Nothing so far, but why did he ask her to come? Why did he want her to read it?

Congratulations to Stan on his promotion. How exciting. But then you knew he was going to be a success before you married him, didn't you? It's just nice that it happened so fast. Speaking of that, can't wait to see the pictures. I'm sure they're great. And if you look half as good in color as you did at the wedding, it will be a lovely remembrance.

Nick watched her. Didn't take his eyes off her. Nothing moved. She didn't blink, twitch, shift in her chair. That in itself was a telltale sign.

About the apartment. I've finally gotten myself straightened out financially. It's really not as hard as it was since I got the raise. I keep promising myself to cut down here and there. Mostly on the phone bills (which is why I didn't call you again). But the thing is, Stephanie is getting to me. I didn't leave my mother and father to get an adopted mother. I swear, she's driving me crazy.

Stephanie's skin prickled, fine hairs bristling on her neck and arms. She swallowed, hoping the loud noise of her throat contracting was not heard by him.

It's not her neatness hangup, which I already told you about. But she's got this disapproving attitude about everything I do. Like when Pete comes over. (Things are going great there. I really care an awful lot, and I think it's mutual. He understands the way I feel about being free. Actually, he's the same way, so there haven't been any conflicts about that. We go out a lot, but if I get another date, I go. So does he. No commitments. For the time being. But I think we both know we're going to end up together.)

But the thing of it is, when he comes over, Stephanie is always slamming things around and I swear to God "pursing her lips," the way they do in romantic novels. In the beginning, I was embarrassed, even feeling guilty. She's a very lonely person, I think. But then I figured, I don't owe her any explanations about what I do. And what am I paying half the rent for if I can't use the apartment when I want to. So I decided the hell with her, I'll do what I want. But now it's gotten very strained between us.

When would it end? She could feel another page, feel his eyes watching her. The roof of her mouth itched, and she curled her tongue backward to try to get at it.

I'd love to move out, but I can't afford to take an apartment myself right now. And I figure if I move in with someone else, it might end up worse. Although I don't know how that's possible. You never know about people till you live with them. (Hope you're not having any regrets there.) After all, Stephanie and I were very good friends in high school. And after. Now, well . . . at least I know what I'm up against. If I roomed with someone else, she could be a different problem.

The lease will be up in seven months and, if I can stick

181

it out that long, I'll decide then. There's no question about our splitting. I couldn't make it for another two years like this.

Nick saw her throat ripple. Like she was having trouble swallowing. Or breathing. Christ, what control. She hadn't budged.

Who knows, maybe Pete and I will work something out. We've talked about living together and I think if I'm still seeing him in September, it will mean we have a pretty strong thing going and maybe we'd both consider it. Actually, I think he wants to, but is afraid to push me. What a gem.

The only thing I'd miss about this apartment is my friend Rosa. She's this Italian lady who lives downstairs. She's a riot. And it's nice, now that my mother's in Florida, to have someone like her around. Old-fashioned type. Cooks real food (ha, ha). Sometimes does my mending for me. You'd love her.

How are your parents? I hope they're both feeling all right.

Stephanie slid out the page on the bottom. Out of the corner of her eye, she could see the *Marilyn*. Thank God it was the last page. But when she finished reading, what would she say? What would he say?

Well, I sure made up for not writing in a long time. I can't believe this letter has turned out to be so long, Elaine, I wish we could talk. I really miss you. I need a good friend to have a real heart-to-heart with. Like we used to in the dorm. I refuse to talk to Stephanie about anything important, unless it concerns the grocery list. And, besides, it's her I have to talk about. Something weird's been happening with my things, and I think it has something to do with her. I can't talk to Rosa about it, 'cause, well, she knows her, I mean we all live in the same building, and it wouldn't be nice to tell her. I think Stephanie's a real sickie.

I thought of calling a few times but you can't pour your heart out long distance. Anyway, it's not the same as sitting on the bed with your legs under you. Maybe one of these days I'll save enough to fly out for a long weekend. I'd love to see your apartment.

Now that I have writer's cramp, I'll sign off. Love to Stan and your parents.

Stephanie carefully replaced the yellow sheets in their old folds, and handed it back without looking up.

"Well, Stephanie?"

"Well, what do you want me to say? When you're far away from friends, you sometimes . . , exaggerate . . . things."

"I know, we all do that." Lascano smiled, trying to put her at ease. "But the thing is, everybody, including you, if I remember, seemed to think that you had a great relationship, that you got along very well." There was no response, so he went on. "Now this comes as sort of a surprise to us . . . to learn that you weren't on good terms, that you weren't even getting along. And we were just wondering why you hadn't mentioned it."

"Sergeant Lascano . . ."

"Just Detective."

"Sorry. Well, are you married?"

"Yes, why?"

"I suppose you occasionally fight with your wife?" Nick didn't answer. "Do you come to work and tell everybody you had a fight? Or that you're angry? Or that you hate her? Sometimes you must feel like that." Stephanie cocked her head and waited for him to say something.

He was annoyed. With her logic. And because she had hit a sore spot. He pulled his chair in closer to the desk, and leaned over, intimidating her, he hoped. "My wife was not murdered, your roommate was. We're not talking about me, Stephanie, we're talking about you. And Marilyn."

"Okay. So we didn't get along that great. There are about

a hundred girls in my office living in the city with roommates. If you asked them, I'd bet ninety-nine of them don't
get along with their roommates. And the things you hear
about girls living together . . ."

"Well, if we ever do a study," Lascano said with an icy
smile, "we'll be sure to interview the girls in your office. But
right now, I'd like to know about you and Marilyn Wechsler,
and I'd like to go over the things she mentioned in the letter.
One by one."

Forty-five minutes later, he opened the door to let her out.
He pointed to the elevator, closed the door, then opened it on
a crack and peeked out at her. Stephanie Hillman, Miss
Calmness herself, was walking back and forth at about
twenty miles an hour, pushing her thumb on the button each
time she passed it. Satisfied, Lascano watched her march into
the elevator. Before he closed the door again, he noticed
somebody had spilled something on the floor in front of the
elevator.

□ 3 □

Claude Fredericks came away from the door stretching. He
went to the bathroom, thinking he almost didn't make it.
How could he say to a patient. "Excuse me, I gotta go"?
Very easily, he supposed, except it would ruin his image. The
whole patient-doctor relationship would be wiped out if one
of them thought he peed like they did. On their time too! He
laughed to himself as he flushed the toilet. He slapped some
water on his face, blinked a few times, and went to get a
coke out of his small refrigerator.

He checked his watch. Eleven minutes till the next one.
Thank God he cut his sessions from fifty minutes to forty-
five. That extra five minutes on his break really helped. Some
therapists he knew gave forty-five minutes and only took a
five-minute break. They'd either get in a whole extra session a

day, or quit earlier. Not him. He needed the time. When someone left, he liked to reflect for five minutes on what had happened during that session. And then spend five minutes reflecting on the next patient. That left him five minutes for a piss and a drink. Usually in that order.

Might as well check my service, he thought. He identified himself as "Doctor Fredericks, one-one-nine," and the operator gave him three messages. He wrote the names and numbers down, thinking Goldenberg is probably trying to change his appointment again, and he'd call Buckley back next break. Now what the hell did this Detective Malcolm Hodges want? If he wanted to come in as a client, he would have left his name only and skipped the "Detective." Claude looked at his watch. He still had five minutes, so he called.

"Eleventh Precinct, Police Officer Cummings speaking."

"Detective Hodges, please."

"Minute," he heard, and Claude found himself on Hold. For a long time. He kept looking at his watch, expecting the buzzer to ring any second.

Finally a voice boomed, "Hodges."

"Detective Hodges, this is Doctor Claude Fredericks. I have a message that you called."

"Yes, Doctor, thank you for calling back. I'd like to see you when it's convenient."

"As a patient, or on a professional matter?"

"Sorry, I should've said. It's business. Actually, I won't need more than fifteen, twenty minutes. I know you have appointments, so—you just tell me what time and I can get there."

"Just a minute, while I check." Claude pulled out the leather pocket diary from his breast pocket. "Well, I'll be free about . . . hell, there's the door, can you hold a minute?" He dropped the phone and went to the brass box in the hall to push the button. He came back, picked up the receiver, and said quickly, "How about tomorrow about one-thirty?"

"That'll be fine. You at five-forty-three East Seventy-second?"

"Right. Sorry, I have to go." Claude Fredericks hung up just as the doorbell rang.

185

She put on her bathrobe as soon as she came home. She left the clothes she had been wearing on the bed to hang up later, and went into the kitchen. She studied the shelves in the refrigerator, trying to decide what to eat. The piece of liver she had bought on Saturday seemed to be breathing in its little plastic tray. The blood had seeped out and dripped onto the glass shelf of the vegetable bin. Stephanie got the dishrag. When she put her hands inside to wipe it up, a wave of nausea broke in her. Just like Marilyn's insides, peeking out of her white skin. Her throat locked for a second before she could swallow again. Stephanie closed the door quickly and went inside.

She sat down on the bed, leaning back against the wall. She opened her book. *"I open a book. The print is smudged and runs off the page. I follow the black curlicues across each line. When I get to the bottom, I go back and start again. It doesn't seem repetitious. Don't you see, Dr. Fredericks, I still don't know what it says. Sometimes I summon up enough strength to propel myself to the TV. I might see something or hear something which will interest me. When I turn it off, I wonder what program was on . . . if I heard anything or, due to circumstances beyond my control, there was still nothing."*

The raw aching would not go away. Nor the throbbing down there. It had been a long time. It still felt like a long time. But he had stirred an urgency in her. She had thought all day about his thing pumping in her. Of course he had been in a hurry. But next time it would be better. Next time it wouldn't have to be so quick. Next time.

She was bored. There was nothing to do. She could hang up her clothes, and there were dishes in the sink. But she could do that later. She took her address book out of the night table drawer and turned each page, starting with A.

Some of the names were old, real old. From junior high. Oh, she had redone the book a hundred times. She always promised herself that she would throw out people she hadn't spoken to in, let's say, five years. But some fear of . . . what, wanting to reach somebody and not knowing their number? . . . whatever it was, she always put them back in her new book. Just in case.

Some of the names brought images to her mind . . . of the boy in seventh grade who kept saying "Kotex" to his friends. All the boys did, when they learned about it. The girl who only got one pimple at a time on her chin when they were fourteen, and used to lord it over the rest of them, who'd break out all over when they had their periods. The kid who used to sneak up behind them—that must have been in eighth grade—and twang their bras. Except Stephanie didn't wear one yet, to her painful humiliation.

So who should she call? Say, "This is Stephanie Hillman, I don't know if you'll remember me, but I was just sitting here wanting to talk to someone and I saw your name and thought I'd call"? Then what? Hear how many kids they had? Meet for a drink? She didn't want to get dressed, she didn't want to go out. She really didn't want to be with anybody, but she didn't want to be with herself either.

She thumbed back to *B* and dialled Rosa's number. "Wanna come up and have a cup of coffee with me?"

"Stephanie, sweetheart, I love to, but you know I can't climb those stairs. Why don't you come down?"

"Naw, no thanks. I don't feel like leaving. Some other time." She hung up fast, before Rosa insisted.

She sat on the bed staring at nothing. It was only six-thirty. The phone rang, and she jumped. She let it ring four times.

"Hi." It was Richard.

"Hi."

"What are you doing?"

"I'm in the tub."

"Sorry, want me to call back later?"

"Yes, would you mind, I'm dripping."

"Sure. Talk to you later."

187

"Thanks, bye."

Stephanie was conscious of a great weariness in her body. Her muscles nagged her with their aching. She lay back, and something seemed to suck all the energy from her limbs. Vacuum her veins. Like a science fiction monster drawing energy from its victim to replenish its own, a presence pulled at her from inside. She was completely exhausted.

CHAPTER 22

☐ 1 ☐

Disgusting. Stephanie pursed her lips and stared at the couple across the aisle. The girl's head was resting on the man's chest and her arms were around him. Even from her back, Stephanie could tell she was much younger.

Did she take the garbage, she tried to remember. Having to get everything done on Friday night was exhausting. But it would've bothered her all weekend—mentally compiling lists of what she'd have to do when she got back. The girl stroked the man's shoulder. Stephanie was riveted to the couple, and a voice kept chanting in her, "tch, tch, public display" in time to the chugging of the LIRR's wheels.

Her mother had been nagging her anyway, so she might as well go and get it over with. Although she had just done it as an excuse for Richard.

The girl sat up and turned her face toward Stephanie. Jesus Christ, it's his daughter, she thought, realizing the girl was only about twelve. She shifted her bottom and cuddled up against the big chest again. Disgusting. Stephanie's eyes narrowed as if her disapproval would shame the girl. I never cuddled up when I was a kid—even a little child. Never hugged. Annette was the affectionate one, at least that's how her mother excused her when cheek-pinching, arm-enveloping relatives were hurt by Stephanie's repulsing look. "Stephanie hates touching," her mother would say, as if she had a child-hood disease.

All the way to Jamaica, where the two of them got off, Stephanie stared. And hated the little girl.

"I'm curious. Did she tell you she was in therapy with me?"

"No. We found your name in her address book and we looked you up and discovered you were a psychologist and, well, we just assumed she was seeing you."

"Well, as I said, I'm sorry you wasted your time coming down here. If you had told me on the phone, I could've saved you a trip."

Hodges leaned forward in the chair, shook out his coat, and rehung it over his arm.

"Doesn't seem like a privileged communication, I mean just saying whether or not she's a patient." Nick made no move to leave.

"You're wrong," Claude Fredericks said without hesitation. "As I told you, aside from the fact that answering your question could jeopardize someone's emotional well-being, it *is* against the Code of Ethics of the American . . ."

"Okay, you've made it very clear," Malcolm smiled and stood up, "and I'm sorry we wasted *your* time. Thanks for seeing us."

Lascano didn't trust Dr. Fredericks. Or any head doctor. Making a fortune just sitting in his deep chair—Christ, you could smell the leather across the desk—listening to a bunch of poor slobs pouring their hearts out. He didn't even *do* anything.

Nick was annoyed because the office wasn't plush—probably doesn't want his clients to know he's ripping them off—and because Dr. Claude Fredericks *seemed* to be an okay person. Well, he wouldn't let him spoil the image in his mind. He got up and walked to the door with Malcom.

"I really am sorry, gentlemen," Dr. Fredericks said as he opened the door for them. When he turned the double lock, he thought he heard one of them say, "Screw him."

□ 3 □

"One time when I was hating her, oh I don't even remember why now, but I kept looking at her, she was just sitting there watching television, and I could see her . . . having an orgasm. I did see her once."

"How did that happen?"

"I was supposed to be home . . . at my mother's . . . and I came back instead and she didn't expect me and they hadn't closed the door all the way. Anyway, I came home, and I was pretty quiet and I went to the bedroom and could sort of hear noises but I didn't know what they were—it could've been the TV or something, or she could've been on the phone—so I opened the door. And you know how you see something only you don't even know what it is you're seeing for a minute? Oh God, it was the most awful thing, they were . . . I don't want to talk about it."

"Stephanie, come on, you're not embarrassed with me anymore, are you? You've been doing so well, telling me so many things. You even told me you weren't ashamed that I knew. We've talked about sex before. It wasn't even you, so why can't you tell me?"

"Because. Because it makes me sick. Just thinking about it now, my stomach is floating around. Well, it was just . . . a surprise that's all, I wasn't expecting it."

"What were they doing?"

"I can't tell you. I turned it off, already. I don't want to think about it."

"I don't know why you can't tell me."

"Tell you what?"

"About the time you saw Marilyn and her boyfriend . . . having sex."

"Why do you keep asking me?"

"Because you turned it off. You should think about it. I want you to tell me."

"Well, every time you ask me, I cringe. I think I will tell you. No, I can't."

"What were they doing?"

"Okay. Marilyn was on her knees, on the floor between the beds. And he was on top of her and he had it in her . . . in her ass, he was on his knees, standing on them, she was bent over, all the way, so her behind was right up in the air, her head on the floor practically. And his one hand was reached around her hips and inside her, in the front, moving back and forth and God, I'm nauseous from this, and he would pull back all the way real slow so his prick was sticking out of her, just the end of it inside, and it was like her ass was spreading open and pushing back for him, and then he'd jab it in real hard. When I realized, I couldn't move. I wanted to run out of there, but I couldn't. They were so intent, I guess they didn't know I was there. It wasn't only that, it was the noises. Like animals. These sounds were coming out of her throat, like they were inhuman, something between a groan and a wail, but in a tone that sounded from another planet, and she was saying awful things, God I'm shuddering to remember, about his cock being so hard, and he was sort of whispering, like he dropped his voice to his balls or something and couldn't talk, saying dirty things, and they just kept doing it. Then, finally, his back stiffened up and his shoulders were up to his ears, he looked headless, and at the same time, Marilyn's chest was slanted off the floor and it slid right down to the floor, but her ass got higher and even with him in it, I could see it open all the way up, I could see the wrinkly muscle around her hole spread and I thought ohmyGod shit's going to come out, but it didn't and he leaned backward and took a deep gulp of air, to give him strength I guess and pushed himself over her with all his weight, I thought his prick would come out the other side, and he was whimpering and they were both saying, 'I'm coming, I'm coming, I'm coming,' over and over again, until well I guess they did be-

cause Marilyn's body just sort of collapsed, and lay out straight on the wood floor and he was on her back and they both looked like they were dead. And I tiptoed out, and closed the front door very quietly, and went down. I stood on the landing below and my heart was pounding. I just waited there about ten minutes, feeling humiliated, for her, and ashamed to be a woman, making a lot of noise with my feet. I spent a lot of time jangling my keys before I unlocked the door. Threw my stuff in the hall, pretended to trip. Then I went straight into the kitchen and got a glass of water."

"Then what?"

"Well of course they heard me, and they came out of the bedroom, and they were both dressed and all. I couldn't look at them."

"When you were watching them, Stephanie, what was going on inside your head, besides thinking it was disgusting?"

"Nothing, I couldn't move, I wanted to, but I couldn't. And I thought, well, now that I think about it, I guess my reaction was that I know this is what people do, but I never saw it with my own eyes and maybe I was—I don't know— horrified to learn that it's all true."

"What else? Come on, I think there's something you're not telling me."

"I thought, God, is that what I look like when I'm with a man? Yes, I think that was the important thing—I was worried that I looked the same way."

"Stephanie, while you were standing there, paralyzed, watching Marilyn and her boyfriend doing something that you've thought of doing but wouldn't, watching them, knowing how deeply they enjoyed their sex, didn't you feel . . . a little excited?"

"Absolutely not."

"There's nothing to be ashamed of, becoming stimulated by some erotic sight, you know."

"Well, maybe. I wasn't thinking about it. I thought it was disgusting, animalistic, dirty and . . . and, goddamn it, at the same time I was real hot."

"Yes . . ."

"And . . . and . . ."

193

"And, what? Come on, now, you're getting so close to this, don't let it fly away. What?"

"I . . . I hated her so much, I wished it could be me, not her, I wished I could like it like that. God, I hated her so much I wanted to kill her."

□ **4** □

"Your daughter, that's who I'm talking about." Mrs. Hillman tasted the soup in the big metal spoon. "She acts like a stranger sometimes. I don't know what to do with her."

Stephanie slid down lower in the chair, twirling her knife between her fingers. She opened and closed her jaw behind her face, without a muscle moving on the outside. Why couldn't they just leave her alone?

Mrs. Hillman ladled the soup into a bowl and placed it in front of her husband. "I ask her what she does, she says nothing; I ask her where she went and she says nowhere; it's like she has absolutely nothing to say. Your own daughter, you'd think she'd be a little communicative. At least try. What did we ever do to her? Annette, she's just the opposite. *She* calls her mother, she talks. Oh," she whirled to Stephanie, "don't say you call me. Sure you do. Sometimes I think the phone is broken, or it's an obscene call. All I hear at the other end is breathing. Annette, she tells me where she went to eat, what she had for dinner, what she bought, what's happening in the office. Not this one." She pointed with the ladle.

"I wanted to. Be nice to my mother. Talk to her. I didn't know what to say. I've thought about that too. I think I don't want her to know what I'm thinking. Feeling. That's what I do with everybody. Try to hide everything, all my emotions. When I'm happy, when I'm miserable—so nobody knows what's inside."

"Harry, you see that? Did you see what she just did? She's mimicking me now. Harry, talk to her."

194

"Ma, I didn't."

"You did, don't tell me, your lips were moving, you were making fun of me."

□ 5 □

Claude Fredericks came out of the bathroom. He had two hours before his first evening patient. He had been waiting all afternoon. It had been driving him crazy, but he knew he wouldn't have enough time on his breaks to think about it. He wondered what she had done. What they *thought* she had done. Well, they wouldn't have come down cold like that if they weren't just fishing. They should know better anyway. Cops. Insensitive bastards!

He opened his bottom desk drawer and took the key out of the humidor. Then he unlocked the heavy closet door in the hallway. He had to squat to get to the "dead" file drawer on the bottom. He stuck his hand between Halleran and Isaacs, and tugged, bending back a fingernail. Some day he'd have to switch to Pendaflex files like his current drawers.

He went to get a coke, the manila folder under his arm. Then he settled down at his desk. There was only one sheet of paper inside. But he didn't really have to look at his notes to remember her. Pretty. Tense. Like pulling teeth to get her to talk. About anything important. Spoke a little about her job, her childhood. But she couldn't express herself. Uncommunicative.

She had come, what was it? three sessions. Seemed like only a few months ago but, Jesus, it was right in front of him—a year and a half ago. He could see her now, squirming in the chair with that frozen look on her face. Could sense the pain inside. Couldn't smile. Or cry. Muscles needed oiling. Then she had quit. Wrote him a polite note. Wasn't ready yet. Maybe in the future she'd be able to open up a little. Then she'd think about coming back.

195

He had heard her crying out for help in her silence. He had just wanted a little time. He knew he'd be able to get through to her. He had called her up and begged her to stick with it for a few months. But she never did come back.

He snapped the aluminum tab off the can, ignoring the fizz going up his nostrils. Then Claude Fredericks took a long sip and leaned back. Completely overwhelmed by a sense of failure.

CHAPTER 23

□ 1 □

Stephanie stared at the ceiling, mentally tracing designs in the cracks of the plaster. She couldn't blink. His hand was inside her, touching, probing. Under the paper gown, her fingers twisted the leather. Her heels dug into the cold steel. She didn't think she had moved, but he said, "Now keep your knees spread, that's a good girl."

It wouldn't be so bad, maybe, if the nurse wasn't standing there gaping between her legs. Expressionless. This had to be the worst humiliation. If he saw ten women a day—no, it had to be closer to fifteen—five days a week, not counting the hospital, that was seventy-five a week. Three hundred a month. Three hundred times twelve. Well, it didn't matter. He saw a lot. It didn't matter to him. But it was the only one *she* had. No wonder it was embarrassing.

Stephanie squirmed as he inserted something. It didn't hurt, but the icy metal against her insides sent a shock through her. How could he go home and look at his wife? Yuck. After he had seen all those women inside out, slimy organs pulsating, how could he touch her? Make love to her?

Suppose hers *was* different. She'd never know. But *he* would. If only she had the nerve to say, "Look, I want to ask you something. I have this sexual problem and I don't seem able to have an orgasm. Is it your professional opinion that all my parts are complete and in the right place?" Sure. She'd really do that. All the articles tell you to consult your doctor.

Nosy bent down a little to look inside and see what the doctor was doing. She's just trying to make it worse. What the hell does she have to see for?

If she ever did ask, she'd also ask if the inside of everybody's cheeks were brown. Once she saw a *Screw* magazine and there was a picture of a girl with her legs up in the air—God, how could she have let the photographer get that close—and Stephanie tried to see, but it was hard, especially since it wasn't in color and the enlargement wasn't that sharp. Just sharp enough to see *it*.

The doctor pulled off his rubber gloves, and slid the bottom of the table back out. Her legs hurt when she stretched them out. He told her to get dressed, and left. Stephanie picked up her clothes and pretended to be having trouble turning her panty hose right side out. She'd be damned if she would get dressed while Nosy was putting the tools in the sterilizer and straightening up. Well, so what if she did see—she saw everything anyway. No, she wouldn't give her the satisfaction of putting on her underwear in front of her.

Finally, the nurse gone, Stephanie dressed quickly and went back to the waiting room. She didn't know if she should walk right to his office, or wait till they called her. The receptionist looked at her as if she were a moron. "Doesn't Doctor want to see you?"

"Oh, yes." Stephanie acted as if it had slipped her mind. She went into his office and sat down. He was filling in her file envelope. She wondered what all the little notations said.

"Well, Stephanie, I can't find anything wrong with you." He smiled. "Your bladder and kidneys and ovaries and everything else seem to be okay. Of course, we have to wait for the lab report—but I think it's safe to say there's nothing wrong. Now, how long have you been having this problem?"

"A few weeks," she mumbled, busily pressing the folds of her skirt.

"Are you under any heavy stress or tension?"

"I guess so. Isn't everybody?"

"Yes, but everybody doesn't go around having accidents."

The blood rushed to her cheeks. "Well, it doesn't happen all the time."

"I know. But it's not as though you can't make it to the bathroom in time. You said that on several occasions you didn't even know you had to urinate until you started doing it." He coughed a few times. "Have you considered seeing another kind of doctor?"

"You mean a specialist?"

"Not exactly. I meant maybe if you could go to somebody to talk about . . ."

"Oh, you mean a psychiatrist?"

"Yes."

"Well," Stephanie played with her hem, "I, uh . . ."

"You really ought to consider it. Well," he stood abruptly, "if there's anything in the lab results, I'll certainly call you. But I suggest, young lady, that you discuss this with an analyst. After you do, if it keeps up, better come back and we'll see about tranquilizers, although I don't approve of them."

CHAPTER 24

□ 1 □

"Let's go over how you left her again. There's gotta be something." Hodges sat down.

Pete made a face. He knew Hodges was only trying to do his job. In fact, he was a nice guy. And, Pete supposed, he should be grateful they were still looking, and hadn't stopped at him.

"She was lying in bed. Her eyes were closed. I remember because I leaned over to kiss her and she opened them to look up at me. I said good-bye, I walked to the door, opened it, slammed it hard, and jiggled the knob to make sure it was locked, and went down. Honest, there's nothing else."

Hodges stretched his legs straight out and started tapping the eraser end of the pencil against the blank legal pad on the table.

"So where do we go from here?" Pete asked.

"Beats me," the detective answered, staring at the wall and playing with the pencil. "Okay, let's go over the room—the way it was when you left. See anything in the picture that wasn't there when you left?"

"No, I don't think so. Can I see it again?"

"Sure." Hodges went over to the desk and took a manila envelope out of the center drawer. "Why don't you think about it first, then look. You might notice something that way."

Pete shrugged. "The lamp by Stephanie's bed was on."

"Why not Marilyn's?"

"I don't know—I guess the other one was further away— seemed more . . . romantic. Does it matter?"

"No, I guess not," Malcolm replied and smiled, thinking how Lydia never wanted to do it with the lights on.

"There was a dress hanging on the back of the door. It was green. I remember it was green. My clothes—that was before I left, obviously—were on Stephanie's bed. Marilyn's skirt was on the bed too—it was brown, or black, I'm not sure, and her blouse . . . her blouse—the pale yellow one—was on the back of the vanity chair. Her underwear was on the floor next to the bed." Pete swallowed, remembering where it was found.

He closed his eyes and moved his hand around, pointing out the layout of the room to himself. "The doll—the one that's sticking out under the bed in the picture—that was on Stephanie's pillow. The blinds were closed."

"They were open. That's the first thing that's come up. But there were no fingerprints on them except the two girls', so it doesn't help."

Pete straightened up. "But if a guy is sneaking in on her, would he come into the room and open the blinds?"

"No," Hodges answered, more alert now. "But maybe she had turned off the light."

"No, sir. Because when I left, I remember thinking it was still light out at that hour—and it must be almost spring. But by the time I got to the corner, it was starting to get dark, so the murderer couldn't have opened the blinds to get light—unless he came in a split second after I left. And it seems a dumb thing wasting time on."

"Let's come back to that later. Where were the skis?"

"In the corner behind the bed. Standing up. She always kept them there. With the poles." His voice caught.

"Now let's look at the picture, and see if anything strikes you. Sorry," Malcolm said as Pete winced, "I know it's unpleasant."

Pete studied the photo, trying to avoid looking at Marilyn's body and that ghastly ski pole. He handed it back. "Looks right."

Malcolm took the picture and started drumming the upper right-hand corner with his pencil. "Mm. Just like you said. Where was the radio? Skip it—I'm just fishing." Discouraged,

Pete leaned forward, his chin in his hands, and dug his elbows into his thighs.

"Wait a minute." Hodges' chair was tipped back. He stopped rocking midway and stared. "Tell me again about the clothes."

"Mine were on the . . ."

"No, not that—what she was wearing."

"A skirt. Brown, black. Dark it was. Oh, I forgot before—there was a sweater too."

"The blouse. What about the blouse?"

"It was hanging on . . ."

"The color, damn it!" Hodges banged the front of the chair onto the floor. Excited, he passed the picture back. "Here, look good. Is it right?"

"Well, it looks like her blouse."

"C'mere." He pulled Pete by the arm to the window and held the picture up to the daylight. "Look," he pointed with the pencil, "it's hard to tell in black and white—but doesn't it look like a faint stripe?"

"Hey, yeah . . ."

A current of excitement raced through Malcolm Hodges. He picked up the phone. "Klinger, see if you can get Wechsler's clothes back from the lab. And find Lascano. Quick!"

□ 3 □

Home. Another day gone. Thank God. Stephanie went into the kitchen, lifted the kettle off the stove. The dishes were so high in the sink that she couldn't get the neck under the faucet. She moved some of the cups and plates onto the drain. She opened the cabinet and dully noted that there were no cups left. She rinsed off a dirty one, spooned some freeze-dried pellets into it, and waited for the water to boil. Saturday I'll have to get busy.

She carried her cup back to the bedroom. Moved her clothes off the bed and threw them on the floor, on top of yesterday's. Then she leaned back, her eyes wandering around the room. I'll take a little snooze and then get up and hang everything in the closet. Maybe I'll even do the wash tonight.

Instantly Stephanie was asleep. No dreams, no nightmares. She didn't wake up till the light hit her eyes.

□ 4 □

Rosa let herself into Vilma's, coaxing Princess, who would rather have stayed curled up in a ball on the couch.

"Ah, you all ready for me," she said, seeing that Vilma was at the table, the pad in front of her. She was hitting it in frustration, trying to swerve the black lines into form. "Now take your time, it comes soon. So, we practice." Vilma kept on, while Rosa pulled up the chair and placed her hand over the knotted fist. After a few minutes, Rosa got up and walked to the window. "Pete come over again last night. We think we got something, but I don't know what we gonna do about it." She turned back. Vilma was stabbing at the paper.

Rosa looked out the window at nothing in particular. "Oh, yoo-hoo!" She banged the glass and waved. "There goes Hector. So anyway, I tell you what Pete remember? After we talk about it? When he leaves here, you know when he suppose to be up there, murdering her or doing something terrible, he comes down and stands on the stoop and he thinks—just thinks—he see Stephanie at the corner. We talk about it and talk about it, but he still not sure. Just maybe, he says." Vilma started grunting to call Rosa.

"What, you make something? Let me see." She walked over to study the pad." Good, good." She squeezed Vilma's arm, but Vilma shrugged her off excitedly and tried to tell her something. Rosa, her forehead wrinkled in realization, said, "Vilma, you trying tell me something? Yes? Something important? What?" Vilma was shaping her mouth into circles and ovals, trying to give the sounds the meaning that was in her head.

"Oh, stop," Rosa whipped the pen out of her fingers, "you can't write."

"Now what you trying to tell me?" They sat facing one another, looking into one another's eyes. Vilma was crying in frustration, the thoughts locked in her brain, unable to communicate them. Rosa's frustration was from her helplessness, from her failure to understand. "Wait, I tell you what we do." She grabbed the pad, wondering why she hadn't thought of it before. "Here's an A. It start with A? Okay, we go all the way down the alphabet, and when we get to first letter, then we start again and get second letter. Okay? Wait, better, I write the whole alphabet. There." She reached over for her knitting needle and put it between Vilma's fingers. "You point to first letter of first word, and I write it on other paper. Till we get a word, a sentence, whole book if you want."

Vilma shakily tapped the needle down the pad, toward the bottom. She jabbed it into the S. Then went back to the top and hit the A. Faster, now, the point of the needle swung down to the W. "Saw, that it, saw? Okay, now tell me what you saw."

CHAPTER 25

□ 1 □

The rattle of dishes woke her up. Her pupils squeezed through the tiny slits of her lids and, without opening her eyes, she could see him putting cups on the little table. She could make out his fuzzy outline, walking back and forth with things in his hand. She turned her face into the pillow. Her eyes stung.

A minute later his weight depressed the mattress, and he touched her shoulder. "Steffie, come on, breakfast." She didn't move. "Stef, I have some fresh rolls, and the coffee's perking." She turned slowly, pretending to be waking up. She opened her eyes and stretched languidly. The stubble was growing out of his cheeks. She closed her eyes again. "Come on, sleepyhead."

She sat up, pressing her weight on one cheek. Just in case anything leaked out. From last night. Then she jumped up and darted into the bathroom. So she wouldn't have to talk to him. And before he could notice her eyes were a little crusty, and there was a film on her teeth. Or maybe a spot on her nightgown. She washed her face, and went through the little makeup kit she had left on the sink. She put on moisturizer, base, a little mascara, a little blusher, no lipstick. It looked natural, she hoped. She didn't care anyway. She brushed her hair, slipped her underwear underneath the nightgown, and came back out.

He was reading the sports section of the *Times*. She doodled on the bottom of her cup with the spoon. It was nine-thirty. She'd wait till ten, then leave. "Wanna go to a movie later?" he asked from behind the paper.

"Not really."

"What do you want to do?"

I want to go home and get away from here, she thought. But she shrugged instead.

"It's supposed to be nice later, we could go down to the park."

"I was suffocating again. My nerves left like tight, thin wires. Every time he spoke, they would boing. Echoes bounced off my insides. I wanted to be alone. Or with someone else. I don't know who. But not with him. I didn't know how to say, 'let me out of here.' "

"I'm sorry, I was rude."

"What?"

"I didn't realize you were talking."

"I wasn't."

"Oh, I thought I saw your lips moving and I wasn't paying attention."

"I didn't say anything."

"What do you feel like doing?"

"Oh, I'd like to go home early, I have things to do."

"What things?"

"Uh, laundry, you know. I have to wash my hair and all, clean up."

"Okay, I'll go with you. First we can take a walk. Sun's out. I'll come back with you and watch the game while you do all your things. Then we can go to dinner."

"I wanted to die. I didn't want him coming with me. I didn't want him in my apartment. That's why I slept there. So I could get away from him when I was ready."

"Well, maybe we could go to an early movie, and then I'll go home alone," Stephanie said hopefully.

"We'll go out for dinner afterward, okay? Here's the movie section—see what's around. Let's figure a two o'clock show," Richard said, going back to the scores.

"It was nine-forty. Four hours and twenty minutes. I'd go stark raving mad. I was trying to think about it, like you said, like why did I do it with him in the first place. It was like the other times. I've been thinking and thinking. It's not that I wanted to really. I mean, I did but I didn't. I tried to remember exactly how I felt when I did it—what I was thinking

when I did it. You know, I think it's the same as the other times too. It was like . . . like all of a sudden I needed human contact. All the detachment and loneliness . . . and all of a sudden feeling like everything, every part of me, is reaching out, opening up. It wasn't the sex. It was just to feel . . . alive, I guess. Like everybody else. It was a physical sensation to be . . . and then I closed up again, even more . . ."

"Stephanie."

"What?"

"You were doing it again."

"Doing what?"

"Moving your lips. What did you say?"

"Nothing. I didn't say anything."

□ 2 □

Malcolm pounded the steering wheel in exasperation. Stupid, stupid, stupid. He shouldn't've taken the car. But if they did go out for dinner in the city tonight, it would be a luxury to be able to drive home, instead of waiting for the train. He made a fist and hammered it over the horn, but didn't blow it. He promised himself he wouldn't. What good would it do? The cars in front of him started to crawl, then stopped. Shit. He could see a flashing light up ahead. The Long Island Expressway, a commuter's joke, sick joke, was bad enough on Monday mornings, but some idiot had to go and get stuck in the right lane. Just what he needed. This time he hit the horn, and started a symphony all around him as other drivers followed his lead. Didn't do a damned thing for the traffic, but it sure made him feel better.

An hour later he pulled up the emergency brake, pulled down the visor so his shield faced the window, and locked the car in a no-parking zone on 87th Street. Well, there *were* compensations.

It took him seven minutes to get around the corner, inside,

and upstairs. He shifted his heels and coughed, waiting for the girl to get off the phone. She looked up, gave him a dirty look, and cupped her mouth over the receiver. Boyfriend, probably. Malcolm cleared his throat for the second time. Without looking at him, the receptionist stuck her hand in a drawer and slapped a piece of paper in his direction. She held her hand over the mouthpiece and said, "Fill this out, then sit over there till you're called."

Malcolm slowly opened his leather case and, with deliberate quietness, said, "Hang up."

"Call you right back," she whispered, and looked at Hodges.

"I want to see the Personnel Director. Now." Malcolm turned to the six hopeful applicants sitting in the multicolored plastic chairs. He smiled. He hoped he *had* intimidated her, bitch. It's degrading enough to be looking for a job without having to be at the mercy of people like that!

Three minutes later Malcolm was seated across from a Mrs. Lafine. He handed her the charge slip. "This is what I want to know. Can you tell from this what *time* this was bought and who the saleslady was?"

"God, no. The clerk number is easy enough. We have almost five hundred people and they have a number, so that won't be hard. But no way we can tell the time. Sorry."

It didn't take long for Mrs. Lafine to check her list and find out that the department and class number meant Boulevard Sportswear, the last three numbers indicating that it was a sweater, and that 698224 was Sylvia Katz. He followed her into the elevator to four. Whatever happened to "Second floor, lingerie, dresses, ladies' coats; third floor, housewares, furniture, linens?" Automatic elevators must take the fun out of shopping, he thought, not having been in a department store for years. Except Lord & Taylor. And they still had white-gloved elevator operators.

Mrs. Lafine found Mrs. Katz in the dressing room and brought her out. At this hour it wasn't very crowded, and the three of them walked into a corner, Malcolm leaning his arm on a sale rack.

"Sort of," Mrs. Katz said when he asked if she remembered the sale. "Well, not for sure, if she's the one I'm thinking of, the one in the picture. I've seen her in here. Lots of times. Unless I'm thinking of someone else."

"Do you remember what she bought?"

"It says right there, that number means it's a sweater, but I don't remember exactly—oh, now that I see the number, I think I know what sweater it is, but I can't say I remember *her* buying it."

"Okay, thanks. You sure you have no idea what time of the day it was?" Malcolm asked, already turned and halfway out of the department.

"How could I remember that? I get twenty, maybe thirty customers a day, you think I know a couple of weeks later when they were in here? You tell me it was Friday of Washington's Birthday, the sales slip says it was the sixteenth, but you think I remember that, off the top of my head?"

"Okay, just trying. So long."

"What'd she do, anyway? Why do you want to know?"

"Nothing, probably nothing. We're just investigating another matter and she came into it. Probably has nothing to do with her. Just wondered where she was about four-thirty, that's all. Nothing important, don't worry about it. Thanks again." Malcolm and Mrs. Lafine were headed for the escalator.

"Wait, come back!" Mrs. Katz was running after them, waving her arm. Malcolm had already gotten on. He about-faced, holding onto the rubber rails with both hands, and tried to walk up so he could hear what she was saying.

"Couldn'ta been four-thirty, that I know," Mrs. Katz yelled down the moving stairs. "I have my supper break on Friday four to five. Hear? It was either before four or after five. I was having my supper."

Malcolm went down to the third floor, walked around the skirts and blouses, and got back on the up escalator.

□ 3 □

"You don't know how to deal with your anger."

"I'm not angry."

"Ever?"

"Well, of course, sometimes. But not often."

"But you see, the anger is there, inside you, you just don't know how to let it come out."

"Like all the other things I don't let come out."

"What things?"

"Happiness, sadness."

"Why do you suppose you do that?"

"I've been thinking that it's because, this sounds strange, I don't want anybody to know what I'm feeling. Ever. Sometimes I think to myself how happy I would make a person if I showed they did something to make me happy. Even, I don't know, a present. If I'm really pleased, truly, I don't let my face move. I don't even smile."

"Why wouldn't you want someone to know he had pleased you?"

"I don't know. It bothers me. I mean, I know if I go out of my way to get something really nice for somebody, I get very excited. I want them to like it. If they didn't act pleased, I'd be crushed. Yet I do that all the time. To everybody. I don't want to. But I don't know how not to."

"It doesn't take much training to smile."

"Don't tease me, Doctor. It's hard. I do the same thing with sex. That bothers me the most. If somebody touches me, or does something to me, and it feels good. I feel good. But I keep my face perfectly still. Sometimes a guy will say, 'does that feel good,' or 'do you like that.' I might nod. But it annoys me because I think he must know that I like it. But I don't want him . . . well, maybe I don't want him to see that I like it. Once, I was with someone, and I was touching him.

212

Nicely. I liked doing it. Most men make a lot of noises, you know, say things. Groan. He didn't do anything. It upset me. I thought maybe he didn't like it, but I wanted him to. I wanted to die because I couldn't get up enough nerve to ask him. Then I think I understood what I do all the time, and I didn't like it. Knowing what it's like to be on the other end, you'd think I'd change, wouldn't you, but I haven't. I just can't."

"There's no 'can't,' Stephanie. What do you think people would see, or know, if you let your emotions become visible?

"I don't know. You know how I think of myself sometimes?"

"No."

"It's dumb."

"That's okay, tell me anyway."

"I don't know . . ."

"Do you want to?"

"Yes. Okay, I will. I feel like my body is a hollow crystal statue that has been splintered and glued back together. But all the fragments are cockeyed. Like the lip is stuck on a little crooked, the cheekbones contorted in an agonizing smile. One eye slanted down in indelible grief."

"Go on."

"Well, my nerves tinkle against the bones, echoing in my skull. I get dizzy from my insides swaying against the fragile glass skin, and I gag on a heavy tongue. It's like if one feature relaxed, the movement would release it from the chiseled expression, and it would fall. Then, slowly, one by one, slivers would break away and the whole thing would shatter into a thousand pieces."

"That's rather tragic, Stephanie, so tragic. To constantly have to make an effort not to be you."

Stephanie unlocked the door, double-locked it, chained it, threw her bag on the couch, and started peeling off her clothes. A heavy hand pressed the back of her neck down, and the effort to lift it was a terrible strain on her whole body. Her bra straps dug into her shoulders, and the sleeves were tight, twisting her flesh around. Too impatient to get the buttons open, she grabbed the two halves of her blouse and yanked them apart.

By the time she got to the bedroom she was naked. She dove onto the bed and put the pillow over her head. Her throat was gurgling and she was sweating underneath goose pimples. Her skin felt like clammy sandpaper.

Screams echoed in her head and, unknowingly, the sound was coming from her own mouth. No matter how tightly she squeezed her eyes, blood and cut skin and red sheets flicked across her brain, like a broken film reel. Her body convulsed in gulping sobs. She felt herself sinking into some thick depravity—quicksands slowly bubbling from the depths and holding her neck with muddy gloves. Paralyzed, unable to thrash or drown or escape, doomed to live in a suspended death, dangling in eternal perversity.

Her body froze in a tormented cry, and she lay motionless for a minute. Then she jumped up and went into the bathroom. She couldn't believe what she looked like. Her hair was matted, her eyes were slits, her face was swollen. She cupped her hands under the faucet and slapped them against her face. *"Doctor, I woke up in someone else's nightmare."* She walked through the kitchen, looked at the mess, and went back into the bedroom.

She closed her eyes and was orbiting in a vast blackness. A universe of emptiness. A feather drifting in a dark and endless galaxy. So alone, with nothing to touch or step down to or reach out for. Suspended in an eerie dimension between living and death. A black stillness.

Suddenly bright lights made stripes across the dark, and in their dust she saw spiralling fires. Violent seas and swirling winds. And explosions tearing the stillness and illuminating the darkness.

Although she could not perceive what it was she saw, Stephanie knew.

CHAPTER 26

□ 1 □

Nick was still a little bleary. Cynthia must have gone out shopping. Thank goodness he didn't call her to say he was on his way home. It wasn't really her fault, he *was* very moody lately. The Wechsler murder for one thing. Smoking, for another. It was really getting him down.

He peeled down to his shorts and went into the bedroom. Jesus, you can't even take a nap around here without going through a whole thing, he muttered to himself, taking all the needlepoint pillows and throwing them on the floor. All over the house. Pillows, wall hangings. He pulled the bedspread down and folded it sort of neatly on the bottom of the bed.

He pulled the blanket up around his neck and closed his eyes. Maybe he could fall asleep for a couple of hours. Maybe she wouldn't get home for a while, and he could have a nice snooze.

The phone rang. Fuck. It was Rosa.

"She *what?* You *did?* I'll be right there." Nick slammed the phone down. He jumped up and went to the closet. He felt all the trousers dangling from their hangers, then the suit jackets, both sides. Shit. He went into the hall and tried the coat closet. Not one fucking cigarette in the house.

He dressed in a frenzy.

□ 2 □

Stephanie got the door open and dropped her pocketbook and tote bag on the floor (must clean it out later). She reached the bedroom, prodded her shoe off with the point of the other, and flopped on the bed. (So tired. I'll close my eyes for a few minutes, then get up and touch my toes ten times.) As she lay back, her head sunk into the pillow, her brain started swimming. (Don't fall asleep now, you'll be up all night. Get up. Blood. Skin. Penises. Must do the laundry.) Stephanie fell asleep, a deep, dreamless death.

She woke up with a jerk and couldn't believe the numbers on the digital clock. Eleven. (Where have I been? Jesus, I have a million things to do, and I wasted the whole night. Gotta pick up my clothes. Wash dishes.)

Gauzy apparitions floated through her head again, and she was suddenly overcome with tiredness. Without getting up at all, she fell back into sleep, and didn't wake up till morning.

□ 3 □

Rosa was waiting in the window for him. He raised his hand in greeting and ran up the steps.

"Now what the hell is this about seeing her?"

"Quick, come in." Rosa pulled him through the doorway. "I'm sorry I wake you up, but something this important, I ain't gonna leave message."

"Okay, tell me exactly what happened."

"Well, after I write letters for Vilma, and she point to

218

them, she spells 'saw Stephanie.' Well—you want some?"
Rosa asked, already pouring. "Well, I not sit there and write
a whole story, by letter, it take a month, so I ask her questions. We have a system—if I ask question and it's 'yes,' she
shake head up and down, if it's 'no,' she do it sideaways. So I
start asking. Lots of questions. 'Is it day of murder? Is it before three? Then I say, 'Is it after?' Then I say, 'Is it four?'
and I go from one to fifty-five and that's when she shake
head up and down and . . ."

"Wait a minute, hold on." Nick Lascano was sitting on the
edge of the chair, cupping a cigarette in his hands. He took a
fast drag. "Are you sure you weren't putting ideas into her
head?"

"No, no. All the time, I tell her what's going on, what you
tell me, what Pete tell me—I gotta talk or I go crazy in there
with her. Every time I talk about it, she get . . . crazy," Rosa
waved her hands above her head to demonstrate Vilma's
distress, "*real* wild, like doctor says she not do. And I always
think she scared of being murdered and I say it's all right,
Vilma, and then I try talk something else. I don't think she
knows 'til last week that she know something. But when I
tell her Pete think maybe he sees Stephanie, she go crazy.
Poor thing, can't talk. So I ask questions. What happens—I
get her out of bathtub, and put on her nightie and bring her
inside and then I go back to bathroom—you know, to get
water out and clean up—she wheels herself to the window
and she sees Stephanie go out, stand on stoop first, look
around. Vilma thinks maybe she wait for someone. But she
see Hector coming and soon as he get inside, Stephanie run
out, real fast. She don't think no more about it 'til other day,
and then when I mention . . ."

"Okay, okay, let me talk to her. Boy, if this is true, it's the
break we need. A witness."

"But, Nicky, she can't go to court, can she, I mean can she
swear, and then shake her head up and down and sideaways
when they ask questions?"

"I'm sure of it. If it comes to that. It might not. What we
need is something to hit Stephanie between the eyes with.
And this is it. It just might do it."

"Do what?"

"Make her break down."

Rosa picked Vilma's key off the hook next to the door. Nick Lascano put his arms around her and gave her a big squeeze. "C'mon, let's go talk to your Mrs. Karlmeier."

□ 4 □

Malcolm Hodges tipped his chair back and began to rock, using his feet as a brace. Why not? It had to be the Hillman girl. No question. She must have done it—God knows what the motive could be. He could see there were some personality differences. She was a real neatness bug, you could tell from looking at her, from talking to her, from the neighbors, her parents. Wechsler was a slob. No question. She even joked about it. Okay. They had conflicts. But, shit, do you kill somebody because she doesn't do the dishes? There had to be something else, but he couldn't figure out what. Rosa Bassetti had come up with something. She saw Wechsler going out that same week with a guy who was not her boyfriend. Nothing unusual about that. She didn't even think about him, it was only the one time, never even mentioned it. Until she sees, what? Hillman going out with the same guy. *After* the murder. Jealousy?

Well, this Spencer was nothing important. They checked him out. For God's sake, he just got to New York, so he couldn't have had time for either of them to fall in love with him. According to Hillman, she didn't even meet him till afterward. Naw, that couldn't be it.

But if she did do it . . . All the evidence pointed that way. Well, circumstantial anyway. The fingerprints on the doorknob, the letter confirming they weren't getting along, opportunity. Well, possibly. But how could a girl do that to another girl? Impossible.

The front legs of the chair pounded on the floor. Malcolm leaned over and put his head in his hands on the desk. His elbows leaned on the picture. That goddamn picture. He couldn't get it out of his mind. The expression. The wounds. The ski pole. God, to die in such agony. He shuddered. What were her last thoughts before she died? Besides the fear. It wasn't so much death, he thought. He wasn't afraid of death. Dying, yes. Death was nothing. Or else, if you believed in Heaven and eternal peace, it was something. So it was either nothing or something pleasant. What was scary about that? Letting go of life scared the shit out of him though.

He imagined himself facing certain death. Tied down, with a knife coming at him. A foot caught in the railroad tracks and the train coming. In a hospital bed, in pain, doctors and nurses shaking their heads to Lydia, "It's too late." That was what he was afraid of. The minutes, maybe only seconds, when you know you're going to die, and try to hold on to life. Or want to anyway.

He could understand how your life *would* flash before you. He'd think of Lydia, of Marcy, of their home, of his mother. Of the world going on, people taking the subway, shopping, sex, walking, music. And it would all continue to go on. *He* was the one who would be leaving it. Going to be separated from it. And he would cry out, he was sure, "Don't let me go" or "No, I don't want to die." It was silly, because it would be over in a second, and for all eternity he'd never think about it again, about missing life, or about his state of death. Or about anything. Some people lived all their lives waiting in fear of those moments. Afraid to cross the street. Afraid to fly.

He looked at Marilyn's closed eyes in the photo, and his stomach twisted. If anybody asked him, he'd have to say honestly that at the very same moment he thought, I'm glad *I'm* still here, and she's the one.

The clothes clinched it. No other answer. The boyfriend definitely remembers it was a pale yellow blouse. Yet at the murder scene there's a striped blouse. Nick can't swear, one way or the other, if Stephanie's wearing yellow or stripes when he first talks to her. A great witness! Didn't matter anyway. Pete's word was good enough. At least to give them something to work on.

Malcolm tilted his chair back again, thinking. She comes

home, minutes, seconds, after Pete left. Marilyn is lying there, maybe sleeping—she just got finished making love—Stephanie comes in, furious. About what? There wasn't time for them to have an argument. No, it was something that happened before. Takes the pole from the corner and, before the girl has a chance to know what's happening, she stands there, lifts it high, and plunges it down into her chest. Doesn't even have a chance to scream. Just opens her mouth, and then it's too late. Then she keeps stabbing her with it. Girl is already dead, but she's in such a fury. She shoves the pole in her, puts the pants in the open mouth, ties the bra around the neck.

They never *could* figure out why the clothes were bloody. If she wasn't wearing them. So Stephanie kills her, and the blood squirts all over her and her clothes. Marilyn's blouse and skirt are just lying there anyway. They take the same size. Probably borrowed stuff from each other. Could even have been hers to begin with. So she's wearing a dark skirt too and she quick changes, puts her bloody clothes on the bed, takes the dead girl's.

Who knows, maybe then she realizes it's okay her fingerprints are on everything—they should be—but there are no stranger's, no indication somebody else has been there. Except Pete. But he's there a lot, and his prints belong too. Maybe she's even rational enough to realize her prints will be the last ones left, on top, and she'll be the logical suspect. So she runs to the door and wipes off the knobs. To make it look like a stranger came in, committed the murder, and got rid of his fingerprints.

Then she goes back and looks around the bedroom. Cleans off the end of the pole. God, it was sticking out of her—she had to look right at her, right at what she'd done. Maybe *that's* when she switched the clothes. She runs out, pulls the door closed carefully so she doesn't make any noise. Forgetting that she wiped it off. Tiptoes downstairs, waits till she sees Hector go into his building, sneaks out. Goes up to Gimbels, calms herself down, buys something, comes back less than an hour later.

Presto.

CHAPTER 27

□ 1 □

Rosa hung up the phone, her heart pounding. She picked up her key and let herself into Vilma's. "Vilma, dear, I'm so nervous, you want some tea, coffee, Nicky just call. He's coming here to meet Detective Hodges and then they gonna go upstairs and get her. Can you believe it? Okay, now don't get excited. Nothing gonna happen. It's not like she's gotta gun and she come down and shoot us for helping to find out. No, I'm just sorry. What she's gonna do? And her poor mama and papa—this might kill them. I meet them once. Nice people. Can you believe? I still don't believe. What coulda happen to such a nice person, sweet girl, she would do anything for anybody, give you shirt off her back? What could happen to make her do something like that? Ah, it's a shame. And in our building too. Now, don't worry, they come in half hour. I come back and tell you all about it. You wanna sit by the window for a while—you can watch them . . . take her away?"

□ 2 □

Two Off Duty's went by before Nick Lascano was able to hail a cab. Twelve thousand cabbies in Manhattan, a little drizzle, and forget it. He shook his head in disgust as he slammed the door. "Eighty-second and First," he said, then leaned back and pulled a cigarette out of the open pack in his pocket. He automatically looked at the driver's name on the hack license, and then thought about Stephanie Hillman. How would she react? Cool? Cry? No, she had to be a kook. Real twisted mind. All the satisfaction in solving a case, finding someone, would be erased. It had happened before. Maybe not with a small-time thief or a gangster type. But the nice person-next-door-he-never-did-anything-wrong kind who cracks up. There was no satisfaction in that. The total degradation and collapse of a human being.

Well, he thought, she's not the one I should be feeling sorry for anyway. Look at what she did. It's the one with the ski pole up her cunt I should be feeling sorry for.

□ 3 □

Malcolm Hodges stood on the subway, shoved against the center pole. The train stopped at Roosevelt Avenue. He was going to change for the Flushing line, change again at Grand Central, and take the express to 86th Street. He was on edge; it would take too long. He'd stay on here and get off at Lex and 53rd and take the bus. Or a taxi. He watched the local stations whiz by the windows, and tried to figure out if that's the way they made animated cartoons. Must take forever.

Ely Avenue. The doors opened, the doors closed. In all the years of going back and forth, he never saw anybody get off at Long Island City. Or on. They should cut it out. Make it go faster.

They had her, that was for sure. Jeez, to think he had tried to get Marcy to move in with someone, get a roommate. Thank God she was by herself, even though it was one step above squalor. Better even she should live with a guy. What terrible thing could Marilyn have done to her to make her go berserk like that?

□ 4 □

Pete opened the door of Friday's. The smoke was so thick that he had to adjust his eyes for a minute before he could even see the bar. Of course you couldn't see it anyway; they were at least eight deep in front of it. He was able to get his arm between two girls and lift his finger. Over their heads, he shouted "Dewar's and soda, please." The bartenders moved quickly, dousing glasses in the sudsy water, shaking cocktails in time to some music in their heads, tipping bottles and pulling them upright after one jigger came out of the measured pourers. Very efficient. But he had no drink. The third time, someone said, "What's yours, bud?"

Relieved, Pete pushed in closer, leaned his elbow on the bar, and looked at the rest of the room. It was packed. The girls were attractive, for the most part. He hated that new frizzy look. But a lot of them had long hair, like Marilyn's, or short, snappy styles. Marilyn was going to cut hers. He would've killed her. Pete was instantly sorry he had even thought the word. Sometimes, when someone died, he was so conscious of it in the presence of the family he always felt on the verge of saying, "How's so-and-so," forgetting that so-and-so was dead. He had done that to his grandmother. He was so panicky that he'd make some mention of his grandfather's death that he just blurted out, "How's Grandpa feel?" And then wanted to crawl into a hole. He was always afraid of doing that. This was just the same.

He loved Marilyn's hair. Everything. Why did he bother to come here? He just really wanted a drink. He should've gone somewhere else. No, he also wanted to be with someone. Very much.

He watched the expressions, the looks, heard pieces of conversation. He finally got his drink. A pretty girl near him was

225

saying to a guy, "Okay, now that the introductions are over, wanna leave?"

Everything out in the open. They must be crazy. Didn't they see *Mr. Goodbar,* or are they just masochists? That's how he had met Marilyn. Well, almost. Except, free as she was, she wasn't crass. Ever. Wouldn't say anything unladylike. But he knew the minute he spoke to her. Knew that she knew he knew. It was all in the conversation between their eyes.

In all those months, the excitement never wore off. Her freshness, her eagerness. But he had learned that she wasn't as simple as she acted. Not by a long shot. It was just that, she kept telling him, "You never know if you're even going to be here tomorrow, so you have to enjoy today." And she enjoyed. Everything. Taking a walk, going barefoot, loving, the movies.

Pete tapped his glass on the bar and nodded. Instant refill. He smiled, glad that her philosophy gave her something. She won't be here any more tomorrows. But she sure enjoyed what she had. That was something. Not much. Cut off so young. All her life ahead of her. Of them. It was sort of understood between them, known, they were going to be together. Permanently. As soon as she had done it all. It wasn't a question of her giving up something. She had admitted that. Pete was what she wanted. She'd be content having him forever. But she didn't ever want to look back and wish she had done something, anything. Just a few more months, she had asked, to get it all out of her system. Shit. If he ever got his hand on the guy, he'd rip him apart. He had no doubt he would.

"Hi," a cheerful voice said, bumping against his chest. "How come you have no one to talk to?"

Pete looked at the petite blond. She was pretty. "Cause, I don't feel like talking."

"Rather ball?" she asked, pressing against him.

"Fuck off," Pete said, turning to face the bar.

CHAPTER 28

□ 1 □

"I'd like to come back to this, but first, we were talking about your anger. You know, you're very clever at starting to open up and talk—when you want to change the subject."

"I wasn't. Okay, maybe I was. But I was just trying to explain. You see, the anger is the same. The same as happiness, as sorrow, as joy, as depression. It's something I can't show."

"Then what do you do with it, the anger?"

"Nothing. It just stays there."

"But it doesn't just stay. It changes, doesn't it? Grows?"

"Yes."

"Tell me about a time when you were really angry. Go on, think of something."

"I can't think of anything."

"You're not trying. What about Marilyn? Think of . . . something that made you really angry."

"A few weeks before . . . she died . . . I washed the kitchen floor. She waited till I was finished, and then she washed a whole bunch of things in the sink and put the little foldup dryer in there, so the clothes would drip all over the floor."

"What did you do?"

"Stormed into the bedroom. Slammed a few drawers. But then, I figured, I was in the shower, and she couldn't very well put the dryer in the tub if I was in there, so I calmed down."

"Stop right there. You see, you're making excuses again why you shouldn't have been angry. I want you to think of a time when you didn't make an excuse for her, or for some-

227

*body. When you were angry and the anger didn't go away.
Now think."*

"There was this day I came home, right after he left. Her
boyfriend. That made me angry to begin with. You know,
being in my bedroom, it is half mine, and I'm coming home
from work and they're screwing. I didn't know he left. I
thought he was still there 'cause the door was closed. That
made me angry to begin with. You know how it is when you
come home . . . you want to change or you just want to lie
down. So I started banging things around in the kitchen. Just
to let her know I was home, and pissed off. Well, when she
was good and ready, she opens the door and gets back into
bed. I went inside and . . . and I almost died I was so mad. I
had gotten this book on . . . on orgasms . . . I wanted to
read it, see if I could learn something about myself, and I hid
it under my scarves. When I walked in, there it was, on her
night table. They had read it, were probably laughing at me."

"Why would they be laughing? Did they know? Did you
ever tell her about it?"

"No. But why else would I have it? They must've. And
talked about it. Saying, 'Poor Steffie, can't do it,' or something
like that. And she—she was lying there. She always smelled
after sex. You know, like a baby is born in a wet cocoon,
that's what Marilyn was like afterward, wet and slimy and
not ashamed or embarrassed and didn't even have the de-
cency to put a blanket over her just lying there naked her
arms under her head probably remembering how terrific it
was how terrific she felt and I was humiliated that she felt
good and I never do and she knew it and besides to think
they had gone into my drawer, touched my things messed
everything up I couldn't stand it. I could've . . ."

"Could've what? Now calm down and tell me what you
were going to say."

"I don't know. But I was furious."

"What did you do?"

"I don't remember."

"What could I say? 'Don't laugh at me, you whore with
your filthy body lying there daydreaming about it feeling all
warm and close and all'? I didn't say anything. I pretended I
didn't see the book."

228

"Go on."

"Then . . . I just, I guess, slammed some drawers. Open and closed. Pulled the blinds up real hard. A few times. Walked around. Threw her skirt and sweater somewhere, they had just left it lying on my bed like I didn't belong there. Kept walking around my ribs felt like they were going to burst from the pressure in my chest. I kicked her underwear, it was on the floor, that awful nude-y stuff she wore that you could see through her nipples and hair and all like a cheap prostitute and I couldn't imagine how he could've been turned on by that, by the cheapness of it and it was just lying there on the floor like they didn't care if I saw it, she didn't care, her eyes were still closed, and they looked in my drawer and how did they know it was there they must've looked through my other drawers too touching everything even my underwear."

"How did you feel? Inside?"

"Nauseous. From the rage exploding in me, getting bigger, my nerves were splattered under my skin."

"And?"

"And I felt it was seeping out of my eyes. Madness. Not angry madness. Crazy madness."

□ 2 □

Rosa was listening behind the crack of the doorway. So she heard them coming back down the stairs. She swung the door open.

"What happen?"

"You sure she didn't go out?"

"Si, I listen. And watch. She's in there."

"Well," Lascano said, "she's not answering. I don't know how she expects to hide. Maybe she's gonna jump out the window."

"Four floors!" Rosa was incredulous. "She kill herself."

"Maybe, that's what she wants to do," Hodges said quietly. "Well you've got a set of keys for all the apartments, haven't you?"

Rosa took the little key out of her stocking drawer, and unlocked the leather jewelry box on the dresser. It had her mother's ring, and a lot of keys. Her skin prickled as she turned over the one with the paper tag saying 4R. They went back up. She couldn't stand the waiting, so she went across the hall and stood in Mrs. Karlmeier's doorway.

"No, they ringing again, I think. Nothing. I hear key, they using. Shh, Vilma, I can't hear."

□ 3 □

"*Sometimes it gets to be too much. I can't tell anymore if I imagined it, like I imagine . . . I don't know, cleaning, when I'm not cleaning. You know, in my mind I say I should straighten up this mess and a part of me gets up and does it and I sit here and watch myself. Step by step, pick up the clothes, put them away, wash them out, whatever. But I'm not really doing it.*

"*Like talking to you all the time in my head. When I do, I really believe you're there. I hear you talking back to me. I force myself to find out things that way. About what I think. And why. Maybe I should come back to you. You seemed . . . I don't know, very gentle. I think you would understand. I think you understood then, even though I couldn't talk to you. Not for real. But I think it's too late now, don't you? And what would my mother say? 'What did we do wrong, only crazy people go, Stephanie.' Maybe I am crazy. Do you think you could help me? I mean if I was able to talk this time?*

"*Maybe I don't know what I really want. I want to belong to somebody, I want to feel close to somebody. But I can't. It gets worse every day, like I'm suffocating more and more, my*
230

breath being cut off. I'm so tired all the time. Like just think-ing about things, or talking to you, makes me tired. I wish I could . . . I don't know, crawl into a hole for a few weeks and maybe when I come out, everything will be gone. Go to sleep forever. Hibernate. Never wake up. Make it all disap-pear.

"So am I pretending I did it and I'm watching myself sort this out in my mind? Or did I do it in one of my dreams, or am I sitting here really having done it and not being sure?

"What will happen to me? Maybe I'll sit here for the rest of my life thinking about it and wondering. Maybe I could call you and ask you. You spoke so softly, so . . . so kindly. I know what you would say. Like I know everything you say in my head you really would say. But no, I don't think I could tell you. I think I really am sick."

□ 4 □

Hodges and Lascano had the door open now. They stood still, listening.

"She's on the phone. Listen. Hear?"

Malcolm strained to hear and then, yes, he heard talking, although neither one of them could make out the words. They tiptoed down the hallway. Malcolm waved his hand at the living room. "Shit," he mouthed, and thought to himself, it's a fucking shambles.

Nick remembered the night he had first come. It was im-maculately clean. Except for the bedroom. Maybe Hillman was the slob. No, he didn't think so. Place hadn't been cleaned up in weeks.

They got to the bedroom doorway. Nick patted his gun un-der his coat, alert. She was still talking. Hadn't noticed them.

They peered in. Stephanie Hillman was sitting on a ball of sheets, surrounded by filth. The phone was hung up. She didn't turn around to look at them, but she must've known they were standing in the doorway.

"Or maybe I'll fade away with my eyes still open. That's what I feel has already happened. Like I'm not really here but I can't close my eyes ever again. I'm a prisoner of my body, and have to watch what's going on."

"Miss Hillman," Malcolm said gently.

"I won't be able to turn away, I'll have to see everything, just like I'm seeing now."

"Stephanie," Nick tried.

"Thing is, it's not going to change. I'm not going to change. Maybe I should stop hoping. Next time I'm with Richard, do you think I ought . . ."

Lascano walked into the bedroom, past the figure sitting on the bed. He picked up the receiver and dialled 911.

"No, I know I won't. Maybe if I tried to talk to him. I don't talk to anybody, you know, except you."

"This is Detective Nicholas Lascano, Second Homicide. Send an ambulance to Five-fifty-eight East Eighty-second Street, Fourth Floor."

ABOUT
THE AUTHOR

Jacqueline Wein works for a New York advertising agency. She has lived and traveled in many parts of the world. This is her first novel.